A
PLATTERING
OF
MURDER

A PLATTERING OF MURDER

A
CHARCUTERIE
SHOP
MYSTERY

J.C. EATON

First published by Level Best Books 2025

First edition

ISBN: 979-8-89820-008-4

Cover art by Dar Albert, Wicked Smart Designs

This book was professionally typeset on Reedsy.
Find out more at reedsy.com

Praise

Booklist Starred Review for *Booked 4 Murder*:

"A thoroughly entertaining series debut, with enjoyable, yet realistic characters and enough plot twists-and dead ends- to appeal form beginning to end."

Suspense Magazine for *Molded 4 Murder*:

"Filled with clues that make you go 'Huh?' and a list of potential subjects that range from the charming to the witty to the intense. Readers root for Phee as she goes up against a killer who may not stop until Phee is taken out well before her time. Enjoy this laugh-out-loud funny mystery that will make you scream for the authors to get busy on the next one."

Recurring Cast of Characters for the Charcuterie Shop Mysteries

- Katie Aubrey – burgeoning charcuterie chef and amateur sleuth, early 30s
- Edith Ellroy – self-centered, overbearing food critic and the ghost who inhabits Katie's house, late 70s
- Ian Monroe – gourmet chef and Katie's boyfriend, late 20s
- Maddie – Katie's best friend and the real estate agent who found her the rental house, 30s
- Lilly-Ann Wentworth- Katie's employee at the Char-Board Sandwich Shop and Charcuterie Catering, 50s
- Matt – Katie's employee at the Char-Board and college student, 20s
- Javie Rivera – Katie's employee, seasoned chef and grad student, late 20s
- Deputy Travis Vincent – Maricopa County Sheriff's Lead Deputy, 50s
- Cora Milbrand – Katie's feisty housecleaner, 60s
- Sterling Moss – Ian's boss and owner of the prestigious Randolph's Escapade restaurant, early 60s
- Imogen Brodeur, restauranteur and owner of The Chanterelle, Edith's earthly nemesis, 70s
- Alberta – Imogen's daughter, 20s
- Colleen Wexby – Katie's nosey neighbor, works at a hospital, 40s
- Mercedes Alvarez – Shopkeeper next door to Katie, 50s
- Marisa Alvarez – Mercedes' daughter-in-law, 30s
- Larken Drimmelspout – Edith's Netherworld Manager

- Rosaline – Edith's acquaintance in the netherworld
- Speedbump – Katie's laidback beagle

Chapter One

Cave Creek, Arizona, Tuesday

"Psst! Katie! Wake up!"

The sickening sweet aroma of honeysuckle hit my nostrils before I had time to process who was speaking to me. And when I did, I sat bolt upright in bed.

"Rosaline?" Even in the dim light, her fuchsia robe was visible, even if her form was slightly transparent. "Why are you here? It's bad enough I have to deal with Edith."

"That's exactly why I'm here. I'm doing you a favor."

"Some favor." I glanced at my alarm clock. "It's three fifteen."

"It's about Edith."

"Are you here to tell me she moved on? She finally moved out of the netherworld into whatever world?"

"We should be so lucky. No. She didn't. And that's why I'm here. To warn you, she's in a snit of a mood. Actually, worse than a snit. Her mood is a foul stench of rotting fish on a pier."

"I've put up with Edith in bad moods. In fact, I can't really think of a time when she was in a good one. Now can I go back to sleep?"

"Don't say I didn't warn you." Rosaline's voice sounded sincere and not snippy.

"Come on, how bad can it be?"

"Bad. Deplorable. Dreadful. Awful. Appalling. Abominable. Frightful."

"Okay, okay. I don't need a litany of synonyms for *bad.* Tell me, what put her in that state?"

"She did. It's her own fault. She got into an argument with one of the midlevel managers and then told everyone that he was her personal colonoscopy."

I opened my mouth, but no words came out. At least not right away.

"Now do you understand?" Rosaline asked.

I nodded. "I take it they altered her wardrobe."

"That's an understatement. No more long gowns or lovely caftans for your roommate."

"She's not my roommate. More like a specter with squatter's rights. So, what do they have her wearing?"

"Mainly burlap. They must have had an abundance of potato sacks."

"Aargh. This is bad. Do you have any idea how long it will last?"

"Until she finds a way to redeem herself."

"She's already working on that, isn't she?"

Please tell me she's working on it.

Rosaline plunked herself on the foot of my bed, inches from Speedbump, who sniffed the air and then went back to sleep.

"Edith's supposed to be working on humility before she can move on. Now, she needs to play nice-nice with the higher-ups. Need I say, she'll be with you for—"

"Don't say it out loud. An eternity. She'll be with me for an eternity."

"I only thought it fair to warn you. Well, ta-ta, I have to get going. It's intake day and I'm checking out the opposite sex. Never too old, they say."

Or too dead.

"Okay, Rosaline. Thanks for dropping by with the news."

"Anytime." And with that, the aroma of honeysuckle disappeared, and the overhead fan stopped running. I glanced at Speedbump, pulled the covers up, and tried to salvage what was left of my night's sleep. It was bad enough that I had to contend with the former owner of the house, who insisted she would move on once I figured out who murdered her. Well, I did! And guess what? Like her fellow spirit, Rosaline, said, "She isn't moving on all that fast." Worse yet, she managed to attract other apparitions to the house, interfering with every aspect of my life.

I'm Katie Aubrey, early thirties and a charcuterie chef. I own The Char-Board sandwich shop and charcuterie catering in Cave Creek, Arizona, having left my former business position in technology. When I said I wanted a change in my life, ghostly spirits were not what I had in mind. Still, having Edith around was helpful every now and then. When she wasn't fussing or complaining.

Edith Ellory was a renowned food critic who managed to send more than a few master chefs over the nearest cliff or into a new profession. Even Gordon Ramsay wasn't left unscathed. I only hoped she'd be too preoccupied to mess with The Char-Board's latest endeavor.

"Come on, Speedbump, let's get some shuteye. I have to be at The Char-Board in less than two hours, and I don't want to look like a cast member from *Young Frankenstein*."

I adjusted the lightweight percale sheet so it rested slightly below my neck, made sure my phone alarm was set, and closed my eyes. Apparently, the extra hour didn't make a difference.

"You look like you could use some coffee, Katie," Lilly-Ann said when I stepped into The Char-Board at five thirty. "Javie and I have the salads made, and I brewed a fresh pot of coffee. Did you have a late date with Ian?"

I shook my head. "No, just a restless sleep."

"Not over that mystery author library event next week? We've handled bigger affairs. Of course, none of them featured famous authors, but still… we're making charcuterie boards, not speaking to audiences."

"Nah, just one of those poor sleep nights." I looked around to make sure Edith hadn't made an appearance. So far, so good. "This is the first time we're doing a dessert charcuterie in addition to the French and Greek-themed ones."

"Petit fours and mini cheesecakes?" Lilly-Ann grinned.

"And then some. We want to dazzle them. It's a full weekend event with Randolph's Escapade providing canapes and The Chanterelle handling the banquet dinner on Saturday. I can't believe the library decided to hold the banquet outdoors by their waterfall. Then again, it's early November, and I was told they rented large heat lamps that are decorative and will warm the coldest of outdoor spaces."

"It should be wonderful. Other than the banquet charcuteries, is there anything else we're supplying?"

"Nope. Saturday's charcuterie boards are challenging enough. Thank goodness we only have one night. Not like the other establishments. Friday evening is the meet and greet with authors and Randolph's is handling that. Imagine Jessica Loundry, Richard Bellmore, and KC Camplin all under one roof! And those are just the thriller authors. Under traditional and cozies, they've got Barbara Beau-Wilton, Arist Arnet, and Lida Singleton. Big names for sure. Also, a surprise guest author. Hold on, I've got the schedule on my phone. Rats! I meant to send it to you."

"No worries. Too bad it's only mystery and thriller. What I wouldn't give for a romance author event. Especially if Deenie Alexandria was there. I've read all her books–*Lavender Love Letters, Beach Sand Under My Toes, Crimson Sunsets, Forbidden Nights*–Oh my gosh—I practically sobbed at the end of that one. Wish I knew what she looked like. I picture a dainty, feminine lady with impeccable manners. You'd think her publisher would print a promo pic or something on the back cover or the jacket."

"Some authors prefer to remain anonymous as far as that goes. Anyway, regarding our event, there's the Friday meet and greet, plus the all-day Saturday author talks and book signings, as well as the Saturday night banquet. Then, a brunch on Sunday. Except for the Saturday daytime events, which are free and open to the public, everything is ticketed since it's a fundraiser for the library."

"Hmm, maybe this is a bigger affair than I had thought." Lilly-Ann bit her lip and then smiled.

"Now, who's worried?" I laughed.

Suddenly, a murky brown color intensified from the kitchen and wafted toward us. Fortunately, I was the only one who saw it. Edith! Making an appearance after all. Worse yet, accompanied by a sewer stench.

"Katie, are you all right?" Lilly-Ann asked.

Before I could answer, Edith spoke. "Did you say The Chanterelle? Is that she-witch Imogen going to be there? Good! I'll make sure it's the last event she caters."

"Don't you dare!" The words slipped out of my mouth before I knew it.

"Don't I dare what?" Lilly-Ann crinkled her nose and tilted her head.

"Um, worry about the event. It'll be spectacular."

"Not if I have anything to do about it!"

"Shh!"

"Maybe you need that coffee, after all. Hold on, I'll go in the kitchen and pour you a cup."

I gave Edith the stink-eye. "Control yourself. And by the way, you look horrible. Brown is definitely not your color." *And potato sacks are only for races at picnics.*

"Don't remind me. And this material itches too!"

"You can feel itching?"

"You'd be surprised the torture those picky middle managers up there put us through."

"Well, don't put me through any trouble. This business has a reputation to keep, and we're just getting known. You need to end that fixation of yours with Imogen."

"Imogen Brodeur is a snotty, self-centered diva who would step over bodies to get what she wants."

This, coming out of the horse's mouth...

"I understand she plagiarized your work in culinary school, but still, it's time to move on."

"Never! And by the way, petit fours and mini cheesecakes are so overdone."

"You had something else in mind?"

"Ah-hah! You need my culinary expertise after all!" Edith crossed her arms and puffed out her chest, exaggerating the size of the burlap bag.

"I don't need anything."

"Are you sure? The coffee's nice and hot."

I turned as Lilly-Ann handed me a cup. "Uh, just thinking out loud. Sorry."

"Oh my gosh, Katie. We open in ten minutes. I'd better get a move on.

Good thing Javie's ahead of the game. And Matt won't be in until the lunch rush. He's got classes this morning. Funny, but usually he's the one in need of coffee. Those college kids keep all kinds of late hours. Except for Javie. He's like an Eagle Scout."

I took a quick sip of the robust coffee. "He's also older and will be headed to grad school. He said adios to fun and parties a few years ago." Just then, my cell phone buzzed, and I looked at the ID. My mother. "I've got to take this. I'll join you in a minute."

Lilly-Ann scurried to the kitchen just as I heard my mother say, "Katie! I'm glad I caught you. I'm in a situation with your aunt Regina. She decided to visit us next week from Hoboken, and the house will be all torn up. We're getting new flooring. Non-slip tile. She'll need to stay with you."

"That's not a great idea, Mom. I mean, not that I don't want to help, but I don't have time to contend with—I mean, *visit with,* her. I've got a huge event coming up, and we started a new menu, and well, I'm at work all the time."

"You don't have to show her around or entertain her. Not like the last time when she insisted we drive her to the Grand Canyon in the dead of winter. Good thing it was closed to visitors. All she needs this time is a place to stay. She's even renting a car so you won't have to drive her around."

"Can't she stay in a hotel?"

"No. She's family. Your father's only sister."

"What about my father's only son? Can't she stay with him? It's closer." My voice rose an octave.

"It would be awkward."

Not as awkward as sharing a house with a persnickety spirit who refuses to move on.

"And your brother has to be available for dental emergencies," she added.

"I have to be available for restaurant and catering emergencies," I whined back.

"I'm sorry, honey, but your father already assured her it would be fine."

"Then have him un-assure her. Tell her I had a sewage backup. Tell her I have a bedbug infestation. Tell her anything."

"Stop being so dramatic. It's only a week. And during the day, she'll be with me. Well, mostly. What could possibly go wrong? I'll talk to you later. I have an appointment in forty minutes."

And with that, my home-staging mother managed to set the stage for a catastrophe. Mine! Complete with more trimmings than a Thanksgiving turkey.

Chapter Two

Thursday

I spent the next day and a half reviewing dessert charcuteries and coming up with more excuses for Aunt Regina not to stay with me. Unfortunately, they fell on deaf ears, compelling me to have "a discussion" with Edith. Well, not so much a discussion as a negotiation.

We were in the living room where Edith sprawled out on the couch, her bland burlap bag-dress blending into the cushions. I was a few feet away, seated in the only free chair since Speedbump decided to commandeer the other one. It was a quiet Thursday evening until the doorbell rang and Colleen Wexby stood on the front porch, a flyer in her hand.

"Hi Katie! Sorry to bother you at night, but I'm handing out flyers to the people on this block to let them know we've had a number of break-ins and minor thefts. And Drue O'Neal was positive she saw someone poking around her back window while she did the dishes. You'd think the sheriff's office and the marshal's office would be the ones doing that, but apparently not. I feel it's my responsibility as a steward of our little historical neighborhood to keep everyone informed."

"Is Drue the lady with the glasses that look like Coke bottles where the lenses should be?"

"She's slightly visually challenged, but she insisted there was a peeping-Tom."

"Um, good to know." I took a flyer and watched as she crossed my name off in a small notebook. I mumbled to myself, but she heard me. "Break-ins, huh? That's perfect. Hadn't thought of that excuse." *It better work on my mother.*

"Perfect? What do you mean?" Colleen furrowed her brow.

"It's perfect that you're doing this. Our neighborhood is fortunate to have you keep watch."

"I appreciate that. Not many people do."

"Ask her if she'll spy on Imogen." Edith hovered next to me and scratched her neck and arms.

"I'm not doing that."

"Huh?"

I flashed Edith a look and faced Colleen. "What I meant *was,* 'I'm not as dedicated as you are.' Thanks Colleen. Got to get ready for tomorrow."

Colleen brushed the hair away from her face, nodded, and took off as I closed the door behind her.

"Quit doing that, Edith! You interrupt my thought process, and I wind up answering you when someone else is right there."

"It's not my fault you're impulsive."

"And you're impossible. Listen, my aunt will be here for a week. I doubt I can get out of it, although the break-ins are a new angle, and I'll try that on my mother. What I need from you is your word that you won't pull your usual stunts. You need to remain quiet and passive."

Like telling a flea-bitten dog to stop scratching.

"I will, but only if you let me have my way with Imogen during that library event."

"You'll create a disaster!"

"Only as far as Imogen is concerned."

I gritted my teeth and created a sharp, snapping sound. "People paid beaucoup bucks for tickets to the banquet. You'll wind up ruining their meal."

"I don't intend to mess with the food. Only the Queen Bee herself. Besides, those events are always snooze fests."

"Bad idea. Can't allow it."

"Then I suppose your aunt will just have to contend with whatever I drum up around here."

"Lights flickering? Ice cubes? Cold drafts? All perfectly explainable."

"Ah-hah! But not the sensation of bedbugs biting or no-see-ums buzzing around. The only way you'll be able to explain that is by poor housekeeping."

"You wouldn't dare." I narrowed my eyes and looked directly into her translucent face. Unlike other times, when Edith was more visible, she was filmy. Most likely to minimize her awful attire.

"Tell you what. I'm a reasonable person. I won't go to extremes with Aunt Regina if you agree I can pester Imogen."

"Pester. P E S T E R. Not provoke, perturb, or push-over-the-edge. Fair enough?"

"You've got a deal, Missy!"

Somehow, it didn't feel like much of a deal, but then again, it never does with Edith. The library author event was the first of its kind for Desert Foothills, and the last thing I wanted to see was its demise due to a decades-old feud between a departed spirit and her living nemesis. Worse yet, I feared my aunt Regina would be thrown into the mix, culminating in nothing less than a full-blown calamity.

"I'm not going to win this one, Edith, and the timing couldn't be worse. My aunt will most likely arrive the same time I have that author event. And no matter what my mother says, I'll be expected to entertain her."

"I can entertain her."

"Nice try, but no. An emphatic NO! Oh my gosh! I'd better clue Ian in. He usually spends a night or two here."

"You don't have to tell me. His snoring is worse than a bear's."

"You watch us while we sleep?"

"It's not as if you do anything else. Honestly, it's like watching *'Pollyanna Meets One of the Hardy Boys.'*"

"Boundaries, Edith. Remember?"

I grabbed my cell phone and tapped Ian's number. We'd spoken earlier, but that was before my mother dropped the Aunt Regina bombshell.

"Hey there," I said. "I may have some bad news."

"You can't go out for dinner tomorrow night?"

"Not *bad* as in eating out, but *bad* as in not being able to do much else next week. My aunt Regina from New Jersey is being foisted on me. She's my father's sister and was supposed to stay with them for a visit, but their house will be torn up since they're putting in new tile. I'm still trying to find a way out of this."

"I take it you and your aunt aren't that close."

"Um, not really. I've only seen her for family engagements over the years and the occasional visits she had with us while I was growing up. Each time with a different husband. I think she just ditched number three in the divorce lineup. Anyway, she's a copy editor for a high-profile publisher in Hoboken, New Jersey. In fact, she's the head of their mystery division."

"Sounds interesting."

"From what I remember, it wasn't. Anyway, I'll fill you in on the gory details tomorrow. Really sorry about the following week."

"Don't be. We'll be so busy prepping for that library shindig that neither of us will have breathing room. Sterling's been a basket case over that library deal. He's a huge fan of Richard Bellmore. Has all of his books, including a first edition of *The Capstone Caper*."

"I wouldn't have thought your boss would be a fan of thrillers. He seems so…so…well, nervous all the time."

"That's Sterling Moss for you. If he wasn't rubbing his hands together or tugging at his ears, we'd think something was wrong. This past week alone, he had us make a dozen different canapes and scrutinized each one to determine if it would be a good match for Mr. Bellmore's illustrious palate."

"How would Sterling know that?"

"Facebook, apparently. On the guy's fan page."

"Oh brother. By the way, did we ever decide where we're eating tomorrow?"

"Anywhere you want, as long as they don't serve canapes! Nite-nite, babe. Hate to make this a short call, but I'm absolutely exhausted. Miss you."

"Not for long. And I love the way Friday nights morph into Saturday mornings."

"Me too!"

We ended the call, and I was about to set the phone down when a text came in from Allison Albright, the director/librarian at Desert Foothills. Its one sentence made my throat tighten: *We need you to provide small charcuterie trays for each of the book talks on Saturday.*

My mental math kicked in with "lucky seven," and I remained frozen in place until I heard Edith's raspy voice. "Make dessert ones. I want mini chocolate mousse."

Chapter Three

Saturday

Ian was up at daybreak Saturday morning and pleased that his pumpkin-spiced pancakes with mini chocolate chips were every bit as delicious as they looked. Had it been me in the kitchen, we would have eaten Raisin Bran. Surprising that both of us were ravenous, considering we stuffed ourselves on deep-dish pizza the night before.

"Doubt we'll be eating a full breakfast next weekend." He laughed as he finished the last pancake crumb. "I'll be lucky if I have time to eat a fiber bar."

"I know. And now, of all things, I have to come up with seven mini charcuterie trays. The library committee thought it would be a nice touch to have one at each author talk. Yikes! That's only six days away."

"Did she specify what kind?"

"I did! I did! I said to make dessert ones!" Edith's annoying voice echoed throughout the kitchen, and for a brief second, I winced.

"You okay?" Ian crinkled his nose.

"Um, not really. I'm leaning toward the standard cured meats and cheeses for the morning book talks, and maybe some egg salad variations, with dessert charcuteries for the after-lunch talks."

"Sounds like a lot of work."

"Javie and Lilly-Ann can handle it with me while Matt focuses on the sandwich crowd. By offering a variety, it'll be sure to satisfy everyone, and maybe we'll pick up a number of new customers." I raised my voice slightly, and it didn't go unnoticed. Edith allowed one ice cube to pop out of the refrigerator dispenser and roll under the kitchen table before calling out, "I'm off!"

"You might want to get that fixed." Ian picked up the cube and tossed it into the sink.

"It only happens once in a while. Most likely a small glitch." *Or in this case, something that rhymes with it.*

"Wish we could linger for the day," he said, "but I've got to hightail it over to Randolph's to make sure we've got everything we need for that event. Then, before I know it, the lunch patrons will arrive."

"Yeah, same here. Only I don't have to worry about a nervous boss. I *am* the nervous boss."

Ian stood, walked behind me, and wrapped his arms around my shoulders before planting a few soft kisses on my neck.

"Finally! Some action!"

I jumped at the sound of Edith's voice.

"Wow." Ian leaned forward and flashed a smile. "Didn't think I had that effect."

Before I could respond, his cell phone rang. "Better take that call. Probably Sterling."

As Ian walked to the counter where he'd placed his phone, I glared at Edith and mouthed, "Enough!" Then, I moved the dishes to the sink while Ian took the call.

"Yep, Sterling, all right. I need to take over for Trenton, our chef. He's still in Cabo San Lucas for his sister's destination wedding. He was supposed to fly back last night but the plane had engine trouble. He won't get a flight back until tonight if he's lucky." Then, he grinned like the Cheshire Cat. "You know what they say about understudies. Granted, it's not Broadway, but this could be my big culinary break. Then again, it's only for a day."

I turned and gave him a hug. "You're an incredible chef, and your turn will come soon."

A nauseating brown haze filled the kitchen. "I've heard better lines on the romance channel. Maybe later, I'll teach you some of mine."

"Not interested."

"Huh?"

"I'm not interested in any other chef but you."

"Good. Because I don't need all the competition."

I hugged Ian even tighter and then loosened one hand to usher Edith away. If she couldn't be still for one of Ian's stays, I dreaded what would happen with a full week of Aunt Regina.

Ian and I tidied up the kitchen in record time, got Speedbump fed, and exited the house with a full five minutes to spare.

"I'll text you later," Ian said. "Don't forget—Tandoori Murgh Chicken at my place on Tuesday. I'll make a mild version for Speedbump. Beginning Wednesday, I'll be working nights and then the big shindig."

"And then Aunt Regina. At least her sojourn is only a week, and my mom said she'll be the one entertaining her."

"If only we could find someone to entertain Sterling." A quick kiss, and Ian raced to his car while I used the remote to open the garage door and start the KIA. Minutes later, I cruised down Cave Creek Road. Early-hour light traffic made for a quick trip and a decent parking spot near The Char-Board.

I was about to turn off the engine when a phone call came in over the speaker.

"Katie, there's been a change in plans."

"Uh, Hi Mom! Aunt Regina's not coming after all?" I tried to hide the enthusiasm in my voice.

"Oh, she's coming all right. Only sooner. She was able to get more time off from work, so she booked an earlier flight."

"How much earlier?" *And it better be hours, not days.*

"She's taking the red-eye from Newark and should be at Sky Harbor at five thirty-eight Wednesday morning. Like I told you, she reserved a rental car. I told her to drive straight to Cave Creek, but I wasn't sure if she should go to your house or go directly to your sandwich shop."

"Wednesday. This Wednesday."

"Yes, that's what I said."

My mind did flip-flops as I thought of Tuesday night's dinner and tried to figure out how fast Speedbump and I could race home from Ian's place in Carefree the next morning. No way could I drop off the dog and then greet my aunt at The Char-Board.

"Uh, tell her to drive to my house. And text me first."

"I'll have her give you the information, and you can put it on Flight Aware. That way you'll know if there was a delay."

Oh, trust me, I'll be praying for one.

"Just a week, right?"

"More or less. I have to go, honey, I'm already late for an early massage I booked."

And with that, the call ended, and my morning aggravation began.

"Katie," Javie said as soon as I walked into The Char-Board, "Matt got a flat tire so he won't be in until later."

"Guess that'll just be the three of us. Lilly-Ann should be here any second."

"Not exactly. Animal control and the sheriff's office are in front of her house, trying to corner a huge diamondback. She called a few minutes ago. Said as soon as they get the snake out of there, she'll be in. Apparently, the deputies told her and her neighbors to stay inside. Said they've had a few reports of rattlesnakes in the area, even though it's November. Must be the warm sunshine."

I glanced at the wall clock and followed Javie into the kitchen. "I'll get the coffee going and make sure we've got the breakfast items lined up and ready to go. Glad we ordered extra brioche and sourdough bread. They go fast on Saturdays for some reason."

Javie nodded. "I'll get a handle on the salads in between cranking out breakfasts."

"Hopefully Matt and Lilly-Ann will get those going as soon as they arrive. That is, if there are no more rattlesnakes and Matt's able to get that tire repaired or replaced. Used to be cars came with a spare or one of those little donut tires. Now, they need to be towed to the shop."

Javie immediately started cracking eggs and placing them in small bowls, ready for the frying pan. He lined up the bacon, chorizo, and sausage in time for our first customers. And not a second too soon. A table of four announced themselves, and I raced out of the kitchen. They were immediately followed by two more regulars. Thankfully, our tables had been set with utensils and napkins yesterday, so all I needed to do was grab the coffees and pray for the best.

"Good thing you splurged on those state-of-the-art coffeemakers," Javie said. "They're already brewing regular and decaf."

"Want to know what's brewing? I'll tell you."

Edith's question and answer jolted me momentarily.

"No way." I crinkled my nose at her flickering form. With any luck, she wouldn't materialize right away.

"Yeah, really! The coffee's ready."

"Thanks, Javie."

I grabbed two cups, got them to the regulars, and then asked the table of four what they'd like to drink. *Please make it coffee.*

At least the drinks were in my favor as three more people trickled in, followed by a few more.

"You'll want to hear this," Edith announced. She plopped herself on a stool in the kitchen as I handed Javie the orders.

"What? Just tell me what and get it over with."

Javie tilted his head and laughed. "Relax. I've got it covered. Four breakfast sandwiches with bacon, one with ham, and one with only egg and cheese. A few orders of cinnamon toast and two chocolate-filled croissants."

"Um, great. Terrific. I'll get them out there as soon as they're ready." I turned to Edith and glared. Not that it made a difference.

She puffed her chest, making the burlap sack of a dress look even worse. "I know who the guest author will be next weekend. I overheard Rosaline telling someone. Honestly, that woman has her eyes and ears in everything. This world…that world…she's the gossip queen of the Great Beyond."

"Okay, fine," I whispered. "Who?"

"Dame Judith Smyth."

"The most famous mystery author of the century? *That* Judith Smyth?

Are you sure?"

"Rosaline is. For a gadfly, she's a pretty decent fact-checker."

"On my gosh. Judith Smyth must be at least ninety years old. Maybe older."

"Ninety-four. And still sharp as a tack. Just released a new novel."

"Ninety what?" Javie called out. "Did you say something about ninety?"

"Hoping we can make it through the next ninety minutes."

Javie shrugged. "We will. Three more orders up!"

I was one inch away from becoming frazzled as I raced orders to customers, cleared tables, took orders, and re-filled coffees. Oddly enough, no one seemed to notice we were short-staffed. Then, just as I was about to find a white dishcloth and wave it in the air, Matt and Lilly-Ann walked in.

"Kitchen!" I said, and they both nodded. Ten minutes later, it was as if they'd been here all along, and Javie was able to catch a breath. But just as my pulse slowed to what I figured was normal, a text came in from Aunt Regina: *I will be attending a major book event at the Cave Creek Library next weekend. Shall I get you tickets?*

Chapter Four

Saturday, Wednesday

I stared at the text as if it was a death threat. And in many respects, it was. Aunt Regina had no idea I was catering the event, and I knew her penchant for detail would rear its ugly head in my business if she got a foothold. Yep. A death threat, all right. The death of the weekend. Forget the lost time with Ian. Now I'd be losing my mind.

"Everything okay, Katie?" Lilly-Ann asked as she prepared the chicken salad. "You haven't stopped staring at your phone with your mouth open."

"It's a text from my aunt. She's coming to the library event."

Lilly-Ann shrugged. "That should be nice."

"No. No, it won't. Heaven help us if she sticks her nose into our catering business." *Bad enough I have Edith doing that.*

"Didn't you tell me she's a bigwig copy editor from back east?"

"Uh-huh. And if it turns out she was the copy editor for any of those authors, I dread what will happen. You have no idea how picky and demanding she is. I imagine they'll all be lined up to do her in. Just like *Murder on the Orient Express.*"

"Come on, it can't be *that* bad."

"Oh yes, it can. The last time she visited, she rearranged my mother's pantry so that the foods were stored alphabetically. If that wasn't OCD enough, she did the same with my father's tools in the garage. Only she didn't know the name for some of them, so she lumped those all together."

"I take it she doesn't visit often."

"Once a year. It takes my family eleven months to recuperate."

Lilly-Ann winced. "Will she be spending time in here?"

"Not if I can help it!"

The next four days vaporized before I knew it, and Ian's mouthwatering Tandoori Murgh from last night was now a pleasant memory. The sun hadn't reached the horizon as Speedbump and I drove home to get there before Aunt Regina arrived.

The Flight Aware notification on my app said her plane was scheduled to land at 5:38, or in driving terms—fifteen minutes from now. My brain struggled to work overtime as it calculated how long it would take her to disembark, get luggage, and pick up her rental car.

"The way I look at it," I said to Speedbump, "we'll be home in plenty of time for me to change clothes, grab a donut, and drink another cup of coffee. Thank goodness I have a Keurig. At least you got to eat some kibble at Ian's."

The dog looked up briefly from his curled-up position in the passenger seat and then shut his eyes.

"Yeah, it's early for me, too." I reached over and patted his head.

"What about me? It's early for me as well. But does anyone care? Does anyone ask? Does anyone say, 'How was your night, Edith?'"

I looked at the rearview mirror, and sure enough, Edith was sprawled across the back seat, looking more like a full laundry bag. I spun my head. "If by *anyone,* you mean me, then I suppose not. I didn't even know you slept."

"More or less. In a manner of speaking. But I don't think either of us will be getting much sleep with your aunt looming about."

"What makes you say that?"

"I heard your conversation with Lilly-Ann. OCD people never stop. She'll be arranging and re-arranging things at all hours. And where am I supposed to plant myself? It's bad enough I've been relegated to the guest room since you took over my bedroom."

"Try the couch. Oh, what am I saying? You can float or drift anywhere.

And maybe it would be a good time to do so in your realm. Maybe even apologize to that middle-manager."

"Larken? Not on your life! Oh look!" Edith pointed to a sheriff's car in front of Colleen's house. "Isn't that your nosy neighbor with her hands on her hips? It looks like she's got the poor deputy trapped in his car. Swing over and let's see what the fun's about."

"I don't have time. Chances are, it's about a peeping-Tom she heard about. I've got to get inside and get ready for Aunt Regina." I clicked the garage door opener, drove inside, and darted out of the car. Speedbump sauntered his way inside, stopping to sniff at the mat by the door.

No sooner did I plunk a K-Cup into the Keurig and change into my restaurant garb when the doorbell rang.

"Might as well get this over with," I said to Speedbump. He yawned and then exited out the doggie door, displaying absolutely no interest in who was out front.

I opened the door, and my aunt thrust a cumbersome carry-on at me. "Thanks, Katie. I'll just wheel in the rest of my luggage."

The rest of her luggage? How long does she plan on being here?

"I parked in your driveway. By the way, do you know why there's a sheriff's car a few houses down?"

"One of the neighbors thinks there's a peeping-Tom. No big deal. It's always something."

My aunt glanced at the street. "Until the peeping-Tom turns out to be a serial killer. You have no idea how many of those cases we hear about in New Jersey." Then, my aunt stepped inside, closed the door behind her, and let out a gasp that most likely took the air out of her lungs.

"What? What's wrong?" I looked around and everything was as normal as could be.

"Your house! It's like a paint explosion for the eyes! Goodness! All those dizzying colors! And the Day of the Dead pottery. Very unsettling. And right next to Russian nesting dolls." She took a few more steps inside. "Turkish Ottomans? Did Pier 1 have a going-out-of-business sale?"

"Um, actually, these belonged to the former resident, and I've grown quite fond of them."

"Has your mother been here?"

More times than I want to count.

Then she continued. "I'll have plenty of time this week, and I can help you redecorate the place and rid yourself of those eyesores."

At that instant, a cascade of ice cubes hit the kitchen floor, and my aunt jumped. "What was that?"

"My refrigerator. It's a bit wonky at times and spews out ice cubes. The dog actually looks forward to it."

"The dog? Your mother didn't mention a dog."

"He came with the house. In fact, he'll probably come in any second. He's in the yard."

As if on cue, Speedbump meandered in and walked over to my aunt. He sniffed at her skirt and then proceeded to curl up on the kitchen rug. At least he didn't pee on her leg.

"Not much of a watchdog," my aunt said.

"You'd be surprised. Come on, I'll show you the guest room." I grabbed one of her suitcases along with the carry-on and walked down the hallway to the small guest room where I had put fresh linen on the bed and left a few decent towels.

"At least this room isn't as jarring," my aunt said. "Although that Dali print of the face eating another face is quite disturbing. Maybe you can remove it so I don't have nightmares."

The now familiar brown haze appeared in the room. "Disturbing? It's one of my personal favorites. *Hell 30—The Men Who Eat Each Other.* The original was a woodcut. And if you don't watch it, I'll give you nightmares!"

I shot Edith a look and tapped my aunt on the arm. "It's above the bed. You won't be looking at it."

"Oh, I suppose."

I offered my aunt a cup of coffee and showed her where everything was in the house. "I've got to head out to work," I said. "Speedbump's been fed and he'll be fine."

She looked at the dog, who had now moved to another rug. "I'll get settled in and then drive over to your parents' place. Your mother's got the day already planned."

Thank Heaven!

"Um, you mentioned that you were getting tickets for the Desert Foothills Library Event this weekend. I won't need one. I'm one of the caterers."

"Splendid! Since one of the authors is with our publishing company, and I happen to be his copy editor, this entire vacation of mine is tax-deductible. Isn't that wonderful?"

Not for the author.

"Yeah, wonderful. Oh, please help yourself to the snacks in the pantry and whatever looks edible in the fridge. I don't really do a lot of cooking."

"Thanks. I'll text you my plans, and I'll see you later. Can't wait to visit your business. The Char-Board, right?"

"Uh-huh. Um, can you tell me which author you edit?"

"Richard Bellmore, and his ego is bigger than the thriller tomes he writes. True, he's a number one bestseller and a household name, but when it comes to the nuances of the written word, he's a shallow water swimmer. Without me, he'd drown."

"I see." *And I also see where this may be going.*

"Straight down the drain!" Edith announced. "Don't look now, Missy, but you've got a bumpy ride in store."

Chapter Five

Edith wasn't kidding when she said it would be a bumpy ride. But bumpy didn't come close to the white-knuckle experience that awaited me that weekend. By Friday, my aunt had rearranged all of my closets and the pantry, stopping short of getting into my desk drawers.

Thankfully, my parents kept her busy with shopping, dinners out, and sightseeing, but come Friday, I was on my own as far as Aunt Regina was concerned. And while Ian and I spoke and texted, both of us were anxious to be together. Unfortunately, the library event wasn't the perfect venue for that.

"I've got to get to The Char-Board in a few minutes," I told my aunt. It was a little past five am, and she was an early riser.

"I'll be more than happy to stop in and help, once I finish my coffee and Danish. I really don't have anything else to do. Then again, your entire kitchen could use a reorganization."

The expression "Six of one, half a dozen of the other" sprang to mind as I considered the lesser of the two evils.

"Uh, sure. You can greet the customers and get them coffee. That way, the rest of us could work on the charcuterie boards for tomorrow's book talks. That's seven detailed mini-boards. We'll have our work cut out for us."

"Consider it done! I'll be there ASAP."

I felt a burning sensation in my throat, and it wasn't from the coffee I drank. I kept reminding myself it was only for a few more days, but so was the chickenpox. I said thanks and headed to my car. The second I opened The Char-Board, I heard Javie's voice. He was a few feet behind me, and I could feel the energy he had.

"Good Morning! Are you all set for tonight?"

"Tonight? You mean tomorrow. The charcuteries for the book talks. Don't tell me I forgot something for tonight."

Javie laughed. "Naw, I just thought you'd want to go there and mingle."

"I want to go there and see Ian, but I don't want to get in his way." Then I stopped short. "Oh my gosh. My aunt will be going. I'll *have* to go after all. If I don't do damage control, it may get ugly."

"What do you mean?"

"My aunt's the copy editor for Richard Bellmore. And she's as nitpicky as they come. Worse yet, she has no filters whatsoever."

"Aargh. Glad I'm not in your shoes."

Just then, Lilly-Ann appeared. "Morning, guys! Matt's right behind me. How's it going?"

"I'm fine!" Javie grinned. "But Katie may need to replenish her Tums."

"Aunt Regina?" Lilly-Ann laughed.

"And then some. But don't worry. All of you will get a taste of her in a matter of minutes."

"A taste of what? Something new?" Matt walked in and looked at us.

"That's what happens when you get in late," Lilly-Ann said. "You miss the whole conversation. Not food. Katie's aunt!"

"Huh?"

I looked at Matt. "My aunt's coming in to help today. And I use the term *help* lightly. It was that or she'd rearrange my kitchen."

"She can rearrange my dorm room if she wants. It's a pit. Between school and work, who has time to clean and do laundry?"

Just then, a text came in from Maddie. "Got to take this. It's my girlfriend, Maddie. You guys remember her, right? The real estate agent who found me the rental house."

Matt perked up. "And how. Talk about hot!"

Lilly-Ann grabbed his elbow and ushered him into the kitchen. "Come on, Lothario, we've got work to do."

"Who's Lothario?" I heard him ask as I read Maddie's text: *Are you available next week? After that author event. Need you to see a property I'm representing.*

I texted back: *Why?* and attached an emoji with a puzzled look.

Maddie wasted no time texting back: *Three offers fizzled. The clients think the house is haunted. Need your take on it.*

Wonderful. Just because I live with a ghost doesn't make me an expert on them.

I quickly added: *I'm not a psychic,* to which Maddie replied: *Even better.* She followed it with a crazy emoji.

The tip of my index finger tapped the thumbs-up sign, and I sent it. I figured I could always get Edith to accompany me and let me know if the place should come with a "hands-off" warning. It was the least I could do for my best friend.

A minute or so later, I helped Javie get the breakfast items in order while Lilly-Ann started on the salads and Matt made the coffees. At the sound of the door opening, he stepped into the dining area and returned in a flash.

"Is your aunt a tall brunette woman with dark-rimmed glasses and chin-length hair? Kinda looks like a news anchor in her forties."

My stomach flipped. "That's her." I raced past Matt and muttered something about flipping the Closed sign to Open.

"Aunt Regina! Welcome to The Char-Board."

"This is lovely," she said, darting her head in every which direction. "I see you have the tables all set. I can make sure the utensils are properly distanced."

"Uh, that won't be necessary. This is a really casual place. *Really* casual. Come on, I'll introduce you to the employees, and you can stash your bag in the drawer under the cutting board."

My aunt followed me into the kitchen and met the crew in one of the fastest introductions on record.

"The customers are coming in already," Matt announced. "I didn't even fully flip the sign."

I looked at my aunt. "I'll seat them and you can start to bring out coffees.

Most will want regular, so I'd offer those. If they want decaf, just grab a cup. We keep it brewed all day."

"No worries. I can handle it."

And for the first fifteen minutes, she did. Until a group of four women came in and began to discuss "the poor editing that publishers allow." That cinched it for my aunt, who, like Edith, seemed to have no boundaries. She immediately thrust herself into the conversation so that everyone within a thirty-yard radius overheard.

"Do not blame the editors," she said. "Sadly, the authors have the final say. And some of them do not scrutinize their proofs, so all sorts of errors occur. Some of them quite noticeable. Like Alicia Venstrum's senior sleuth novel, where the protagonist said, "Bring me a Boost, but it was written, 'Bring me a poop.' Can you imagine? And who gets blamed? You guessed it -the editors!"

The women were speechless. Good thing Lilly-Ann was only a few feet away. She tapped my aunt on the shoulder and told her that she was needed in the kitchen. And that's where Aunt Regina remained for the day. Thankfully, she knew how to make salads, prepare the cured meats, and slice the cheeses for the charcuterie trays. All the while, Edith took it in, languishing on the counter and laughing every few minutes. The day couldn't have ended fast enough.

I was mentally and physically exhausted, but determined to get through the author "meet and greet" at the library. It was a ticketed event for sixty or so patrons with a "speed-dating" format that, according to the librarian, was quite popular at author conventions.

One thing for sure, Ian would be on "full alert" the entire time as Sterling was one of those patrons and would be studying each and every canapé that wafted his way when he wasn't fawning over Richard Bellmore.

As my aunt and I got into the KIA, I took a breath and said, "I know you have issues with Richard and maybe even other authors, but please, try to let it slide by and enjoy the event."

"Some things don't slide. They stick in your throat until you cough them up."

And if that wasn't enough, Edith just *had* to add, "That's exactly how I feel about Imogen. She sticks in my throat like a horse-pill."

"Suck it up and swallow that horse-pill!" The words spewed out of my mouth before I realized it.

"Katie! I've never seen you so adamant. Fine, I'll try to keep my comments to myself."

"Thanks. I appreciate it." I spun around to the backseat and eyeballed Edith. Then I mouthed, "I wish everyone would keep their comments to themselves."

The parking lot in front of the library was full, so I had to find a spot a few yards up on the hill. I'd spoken with Allison earlier in the day, and she told me I could watch the event with her from a corner in the room since all the seats at the tables had been spoken for.

The attendees were assigned a specific table and would remain there, while the authors would move from table to table at an announced time, giving everyone equal access to them. Servers from Randolph's Escapade would be bringing out an assortment of fancy canapes with a full wine bar set up in the rear of the room.

I spotted Sterling the minute I walked into the large conference room, and couldn't believe it when my aunt's seat was at his table. Fortunately, she hadn't met Ian, so I didn't have to worry about what might have come out of her mouth. Especially since Sterling had no idea his up-and-coming chef was seeing a charcuterie caterer who was seven years older than him.

In fact, Sterling still insisted I meet his nephew, a molecular chemist, who had recently relocated from Colorado and was in charge of some lab at Arizona State University. So far, I'd be able to dodge Sterling's overtures, but I wasn't so sure I could dodge his efforts much longer without giving him a full confession. One thing is for sure—it wouldn't be tonight.

With a quick wave of the hand, my aunt darted off to the festively decorated tables featuring a fall décor of pumpkins, cornucopia, and pinecones. The authors hadn't yet made an appearance, but it was only a matter of minutes. The servers had already arrived, and I glimpsed trays of bacon-wrapped scallops and mini-quiches.

Suddenly, another text appeared from Maddie. It read: *Make it four offers that bit the dust. The house inspector told the buyer the place is seriously haunted.*

Chapter Six

Friday

My aunt commandeered the seat next to Richard's, and I shuddered. *Please don't elbow him with snide remarks about his writing.* He hadn't gotten to the table yet, and I held my breath that he wouldn't skirt out the rear door upon seeing Aunt Regina.

As it turned out, that was the least of my problems. Edith planted herself behind Richard's chair, casting a horrible brownish haze in the air. Then, a new haze arrived. Turquoise blue. It drifted across the table, turning the brown haze into beige.

"Rosaline!" Edith shouted. "What are you doing here, and more importantly, how did you get your hands on Princess Margaret's iconic caped blue gown that she wore to the Queen's 90th birthday?"

Rosaline glided closer to Edith. "I fancy Richard Bellmore. We can drift around for eternity together once he gets here."

He'll be drifting around eternity all right. An eternity with my aunt at his throat.

With a brush of her hair, Rosaline continued. "As for the gown, I just cozied up to Larken and played nice-nice. Something you should consider if you ever expect your wardrobe to change."

Just then, Allison walked to the front of the room and announced, "Good Evening Everyone! Please welcome our esteemed authors!"

A round of applause followed as the seven authors lined up and acknowledged their audience. Allison went on to explain how the event would work as the authors seated themselves at their designated starting table.

I took a breath, bit my lip, and prayed my aunt would refrain from going "Full Yellowstone Beth" on Richard. So far, so good. Except for Edith and Rosaline, who jockeyed positions to get closer to the poor author.

Meanwhile, more servers appeared and seamlessly brought canapes to the tables. I saw large prawns, stuffed mushrooms, and mini shish kabobs as one server passed by. Then another appeared with persimmon bruschetta and Swedish meatballs. If my stomach wasn't in such a knot from keeping an eye on my aunt and watching the juvenile display from the great beyond, I would have reached out and grabbed something. Instead, I tiptoed out and walked to the library kitchen to catch Ian for a few seconds.

He caught my eye as he gave the nod to a server with full trays of wasabi shrimp and smoked salmon. "Hey there! I was hoping you'd stop in. Wish I had more time, but we're churning these out in record speed. Any idea how the event started out?"

"It seems to be running smoothly. And your canapes look fantastic."

"I can get you a plate."

"Maybe later. I've got to keep an eye on my aunt. Unpredictability is one of her character traits." *Along with a penchant to always be right.* "Your boss is seated at her table. If they get to talking, I'm positive Sterling's nephew will come up in conversation along with her 'single niece.'"

"We're going to have to come clean, you know." He winked and flashed that adorable smile of his.

I winked back. "Better get going. Great job, by the way!"

A minute or so later, I was back in the conference room, just in time to hear my aunt and Richard trading snide comments as Richard headed to his next table. Unfortunately, Aunt Regina headed there as well.

"Before you send me your corrected edits, you need to read your work out loud. Obviously, an eye exam would be in order." She leaned over his shoulder as he pulled the chair out and seated himself.

"Constructive edits are one thing," he hissed, "Insane edits are another."

"Insane? What's insane are your ill-conceived manuscripts that require a good dose of revision."

Richard turned and glared at her. "This is a conversation for another time, Regina."

"Oh, don't worry. I'm here for the entire weekend." With that, my aunt stormed back to her table, in time to chat with KC Camplin, who, thankfully, worked with a different publisher. I recognized the ruddy barrel-chested cowboy-turned-author from his photo in our local newspaper. Up close, his muted freckles made him appear younger than his fifty-nine years, according to the article.

"I think things are going well," Allison said as she walked toward me. "Although it looked like a bit of a scuffle over there. Then again, it was probably nothing. Fans can get overly exuberant."

I nodded. "I imagine it will be more exuberant tomorrow when the general public arrives for the book talks and signings."

"Yes, speaking of which, I can't wait to see the charcuterie trays, especially the fall desserts."

And I can't wait for this event to be over, especially with my aunt one step away from causing a riot.

I began to relax in the half hour that followed, and even indulged on a few of Randolph's Escapades' canapes. And just as I began to feel somewhat tranquil, I heard my aunt's voice. She was loud, brazen, and impossible to ignore. "And another thing…"

Expecting her row with Richard to continue, I tried to spot him. And when I did, he was chatting quietly at a table in the far left. My aunt, however, was back at her table, engaging in a less-than-pleasant conversation with cozy mystery author Dame Judith Smyth. *The* cozy mystery author of the century.

Shoot me now! Make it quick!

With the fastest speed I could muster, I charged to the table with absolutely no plan in sight. Until I spotted a server and grabbed the tray out from under him. "It's okay. I know the chef." The poor kid widened his eyes and raced to the library kitchen.

"Mascarpone canapes with sprouts and red onions, anyone?" I thrust the tray in front of my aunt and gave her the evil eye. "Behave," I whispered. Then, for some unknown reason, Edith decided to assist me.

She summoned a few of her infamous no-see-ums to hover around my aunt's neck and ears, causing her to swat at them while trying to act nonchalant. It didn't work. In a matter of seconds, the people seated on either side of her started to rub their necks, even though Edith hadn't disturbed them.

"Could this be a food reaction?" one of them asked.

I froze. It was the last thing Ian, or the library for that matter, needed. With a slow breath, I answered, "Food allergies usually cause choking sensations or full-body itching and rashes. I think this is a reaction from nerves. You know, the excitement of being around the most famous authors in the country. And, in this instance, the world. I smiled at Dame Judith, and she blushed.

Edith took the hint, and the no-see-ums vanished. Then, I tapped my aunt's arm and whispered, "No drama."

At that moment, Allison announced for the authors to move to another table, and I couldn't have been more relieved. I ushered my aunt to the side of the room and spoke softly. "You've upset two authors. Please don't make it three."

"I find it very difficult to contain myself when I'm in the right."

"Give it a try. It might surprise you."

My aunt rolled her eyes and mumbled something about using the restroom. Then, as if the night couldn't be worse, Sterling approached me.

He was as upbeat as ever. "Katie, how wonderful to see you here. I always enjoy sharing events with The Char-Board, and this one is off to a marvelous start."

"For sure. Your canapes are amazing. Absolutely amazing."

"Speaking of amazing, my nephew Warren is now in charge of the molecular chemistry laboratory at Arizona State University. I really wish he'd meet a lovely lady like you. He's in his forties, never married, and extremely hardworking. Collects fossils and Star Wars memorabilia. You should see his Jedi Warrior figurines. Quite the assortment. I think both of you would hit it off."

Not in this lifetime.

"He sounds intriguing, but—"

"Wonderful! I'll have him call you at The Char-Board."

I opened my mouth to reply, but a barely audible whimper came out. Sterling patted me on the shoulder and darted back to his table while I stood there, dazed and voiceless.

Chapter Seven

Friday, Saturday

"Jedi Warriors, huh?" Ian couldn't stop laughing when I ducked into the kitchen at the close of the event. His crew was too occupied wrapping leftovers and cleaning up to bother listening to us. The library went with the paper plate and faux silverware in lieu of running their small dishwasher. A smart move in my book, making it easy for all of us.

"One food presentation down, three to go," I said. "And all of them with my aunt. She was insufferable tonight. I've been terrified of leaving her alone for more than five minutes."

"Where is she now?"

"The ladies' room. Pray she doesn't alienate any of the female authors who might have gone in there."

Ian looked around and then squeezed my hand. "You'll get through this. We all will. I'll text you tomorrow. We don't come on board again until the banquet at seven. By then, you'll be exhausted from preparing and refreshing all those charcuterie trays."

"Javie will be joining me, and Lilly-Ann will come after the lunch rush. Matt will lock up The Char-Board once he's done with the clean-up. Said the extra hours will come in handy with Christmas right around the corner."

"Good thinking on his part." From the kitchen window, Ian looked out at the front parking lot, clearly visible under the bright outdoor lighting. "Looks like Richard Bellmore has got quite the crowd of fans surrounding him. Oh my gosh! That's Sterling. Once he starts talking, Richard's eyes are going to glaze over."

I turned and looked as well. "Yep, quite the fan club. Oh no! Did you see that? Some woman just elbowed your boss aside and swooped in on Richard. Now she's latched on to his arm. At least we know one thing—it's not my aunt. She wouldn't have latched on; she would have bitten it!"

"That's the price you pay for fame. I'm sure the guy is used to overly zealous fans."

"She's overly zealous, all right. More like obsessed. If she were any closer, their lips would be touching."

Just then, a car backed up, and the impromptu ensemble broke apart as the driver made his or her way past them.

"Look now! Richard took off like a marathon sprinter."

"Yeah, I'd better do the same before my aunt makes this night even worse." I gave his wrist a squeeze and hightailed it to the main doors where she was waiting.

"That was a splendid evening, don't you think?" From the cool, calm smile on her face, it was obvious Aunt Regina hadn't a clue about her interactions tonight.

"I need to get to The Char-Board early tomorrow to make sure we'll be all set for the book talks. Lots of charcuteries that will need replenishing. Can you drive yourself to the library?" *And not cause dissension?*

"Absolutely. The library will have coffee and donuts prior to the event, so I'll grab something there."

"Great! By the way, other than Richard Bellmore, are there any authors you've worked with?"

"No. But when I started out as the acquisitions editor, I rejected Lida Singleton's first novel and, come to think of it, Arist Arnet's as well."

A now-familiar brown haze accompanied us as we walked to my car. "I'd keep an eye on her if I were you, Missy. They may all come gunning for her if she's not careful."

"No kidding!" I rolled my eyes at Edith when my aunt turned her head toward me. "It's not that earth-shattering."

"Uh, I guess not. Considering it's part of the industry."

"Indeed. And as an esteemed editor, I intend to keep that industry to the highest of standards."

"Like I said," Edith's brown haze grew in intensity, "I'd watch it if I were you."

It wasn't as if I put much credence into the spirits of the afterlife. If Edith was a prime example, then she could only see the past and the present. She was a ghost, not a soothsayer. Still, she could size things up pretty well, and it didn't take a full-blown psychic to figure out Aunt Regina's propensity for stirring the pot.

I set my alarm for 3:45, so I could get the charcuterie process underway. Matt and Lilly-Ann would be able to manage breakfast and lunch, and between Javie and me, we'd be able to transport the items to the library and complete the setups in their kitchen. A lofty task, but one we were used to.

As it turned out, that was the easy part. It involved food, not personalities. And while Javie and I prepared the breakfast charcuteries for the first group of book talks and signings, my aunt continued her personal onslaught on the authors. At a little past nine, Allison walked into the library's kitchen and pulled me aside.

"I'm really sorry to bother you, Katie," she said as she rubbed her palms together, "but there seems to be a bit of tension between Lida Singleton and your aunt. During the break, they had words, and now Lida is missing. I imagine she took a walk to compose herself before the next session, but if she doesn't come back in the next fifteen minutes, I'll need to juggle things around."

"Did you want my help locating her?"

"Oh no. We'll find her. What I need, what I hope…would be if you could have a word with your aunt to not engage in the kind of conversations that rile our guests. This is the first event of its kind, and we want it to be a success. I'm so sorry to bother you with this, but I don't know what else to do."

"Don't feel bad. I understand." *More than you think.*

"Thanks. I'll let you get back to your charcuteries. Judging from the two trays over there, they'll be a big hit."

I smiled. "Let's hope so."

The second Allison left the kitchen, I told Javie what was going on.

"I'll take it from here," he said. "You better find your aunt before she turns this author event into an episode of *Survivor*."

"On my way!"

I wasn't sure which book talk my aunt had next on her schedule, but the small conference rooms were all in the same area, so I figured I'd start with the first and keep on going. It was Arist Arnet, but my aunt wasn't in the audience. Lucky him, for now. Next was Jessica Loundry's room, and Aunt Regina wasn't there either. I continued on until I had exhausted all of the rooms, and still no sign of my aunt. Maybe she took a walk, too.

Ha! I should have been so lucky. When I returned to the kitchen, my aunt had seated herself adjacent to the counter, offering advice to Javie. She was worse than Edith. At least when Edith offered advice, or in her case, *directives,* no one heard her.

"What a nuisance!" Edith exclaimed, hovering between Javie and my aunt. "I'd stay and watch the fun, but I have some business to attend to."

"Not Rosaline and those gowns," I whispered.

"If I don't get this burlap off of me, I'll break out in hives." And with that, a brown swirl of dust appeared and vanished in an instant, along with Edith. Unfortunately, no swirl, brown or otherwise, was going to vanish with my aunt.

I walked over to her and Javie and cleared my throat. "Aunt Regina, shouldn't you be attending those book talks?"

"Lida's was enough to put me to sleep. I thought I'd take a little break."

"Maybe you can take it during one of the other talks. Lots of people zone out during them."

"Oh, I suppose you're right. KC Camplin is usually quite interesting. And he's got that super macho cowboy thing going." She looked at her Smart Watch and stood. "The talk begins in six minutes. I'll catch up later."

"Great."

I stood still until I was certain she was a good way down the corridor before I spoke. Even with the door closed, I worried my voice might carry.

"I don't think I'll last the weekend. Let alone the rest of the week. Remind me to buy a white scarf and wave it from my roof!"

Javie laughed. "You haven't seen anything. My uncle Ernesto fills the house with cigar smoke and tells the same stories over and over again. And my aunt Eufemia drives my mother crazy in the kitchen. When she comes, we refer to the visit as "The Enchilada Wars.""

I laughed. "I guess I can survive."

Wishful thinking. I had no idea that things would go from barely tolerable to "get-me-the-heck-out-of-here" in a matter of hours.

Chapter Eight

Javie and I hustled with the breakfast charcuteries and seamlessly shifted into the lunch ones without blinking an eye. Lilly-Ann arrived in time to handle the more complex designs that required lots of attention to detail and a certain finesse with the edible flowers and herbs.

Then, of all things, Richard Bellmore ducked into the kitchen. He closed the door and leaned against it, catching his breath. "Sorry, folks. I just had to get away for a few minutes and thought this was the safest place."

I gulped. "It didn't happen to involve Regina Louisa Aubrey, would it?" *Unless she's using one of her married names.*

"You know her?"

"In a manner of speaking. Yes. She's my aunt."

"Good grief. You poor girl. But no, I'm trying to get away from a crazed reader. Totally obsessed. She's been in all of my book talks and literally threw herself on top of me last night. Muscular woman in a peacock print dress. Curly brown hair and tortoise frames."

"You really should let the librarian know. She'll handle it discreetly."

"I suppose you're right. Hiding in the kitchen is the coward's way out. Still, everyone needs a respite from lunacy once in a while."

"Do you think that was the case when Lida went missing yesterday? True, it was only for a little while before she reappeared as if nothing happened, but still, it does raise the question as to why."

Richard squinted and kept his voice low. "Lida's not the most stable person if truth be told. I was on a panel with her once, and she fell to pieces when a reader questioned her use of foreshadowing."

"Ouch."

"True that! You can't be in this business if you're going to have thin skin. The vipers are everywhere. Whoa. Look at the time. I better get going."

"Darn it," Lilly-Ann said. "I should have asked for an autograph. Then again, he didn't need another starstruck fan."

"Time to move the next charcuteries in," Javie announced. "We're right on schedule."

We loaded a few trays onto the serving cart, and I followed Javie to the first room. Like yesterday's meet and greet, today's book talks were filled with readers who were lined up waiting to be let inside the rooms. One of the interesting things was that once one book talk ended, the rooms were to remain vacant for ten to fifteen minutes for clean-up. That allowed us to remove the prior trays and set up the new ones.

When we reached the one that listed Jessica Loundry, we spied her and Richard having words off to the side. Her book talk hadn't started, and none of the people had entered the room yet. I reached out my hand and held Javie back. "Shh! Stay behind the door where they can't see us. Might as well listen."

Their voices, although low, were clearly audible. Jessica's arms were crossed, and she locked eyes with Richard. "Don't tell me you didn't bribe those judges, Richard. My book was a shoo-in for the Claremont Award. It's been on the New York Times Bestseller List since last March, and where has your book been? Other than gathering dust on bookshelves."

I poked Javie. "This can't be good."

"I can't help it if readers prefer my style of writing to the endless drone and description you provide. By the time the detective solves the murder, ten other bodies will have cropped up. That's how slow your books move."

"That Claremont Award didn't mean a whole lot to you, but I needed the monetary award that went with it. You didn't. For me, it meant financial survival for a while. For you, it was just another shiny thing with perks."

"Hey," someone from the line behind us shouted, "when will the door be opened?"

Wasting no time, I replied, "Give us a minute. Change of charcuterie boards." With that, I let the door bang open as Javie and I wheeled the cart into the room.

"We've got to get set up," I said.

"No problem." Jessica looked at Richard and eyeballed the door. Then she turned to us. "Love your presentation. Mouthwatering and eye-catching. I'll be back in five minutes."

"Thanks."

"And I'd best get into my room. Maybe with any luck, that woman in the peacock dress will be elsewhere."

The only person I wanted to be elsewhere was my aunt, but that wasn't about to happen any time soon. I kept my fingers crossed she'd be absorbing every one of KC Camplin's words or falling into a deep food coma from indulging. Either way would have been fine.

"Boy, talk about conceited," Javie said. "I never figured authors to have the egos of actors."

"These are bestselling authors. Their names are household words. I suppose it goes with the territory."

At that instant, I spied Edith and Rosaline having what appeared to be a relatively normal conversation. *Relatively* being the key word. They were seated on the windowsill with a view of the waterfall behind them. Had they not been apparitions, their tableau would have resembled a late 17th-century painting that I would have titled—*Baroness and her Maid*.

"If you'd just show me how you conjure those no-see-ums," Rosaline said, "I'll speak to Larken myself about your wardrobe."

"Why do you want to summon no-see-ums?"

"I want to get that obnoxious fan away from Richard. She can't have him."

"*You* can't have him, either. You're dead."

"A minor inconvenience. Everything works out in the end. So, yes or no?"

"Fine. I'll show you, but if you don't keep your word with Larken, there's no telling what I'll do. I don't even know myself half the time."

"What do you mean?" Rosaline asked.

"My skill set. One minute I can barely manage wafting in and out of this realm, and the next minute, I can catapult myself into an entirely different one. At first I thought it involved practice, but now I'm not too sure."

"Hold on. Last time we spoke, and need I remind you that you held it over my head, you told me your abilities *were* a result of practice and focus."

"Most are, like the snapping in and out of places. But others…well, let's just say…they happen."

Rosaline flinched back and nearly bumped into Javie. "Aargh! Please don't tell me you're 'one of those.'"

"'One of those *whats?*'"

"Ghosts whose talents evolve faster than the usual timeline in the spirit world. And don't beguile yourself into thinking it's a good thing. You'll get a reputation for being unpredictable and unreliable."

With no one nearby, I couldn't help but put in my two cents. "Forget it, Rosaline. Edith is already unpredictable and unreliable."

"Why do you keep looking out the window?" Javie gave me a poke. "Is there something I'm missing?"

"Uh, sorry. Just wondering how tonight's banquet will go. They start setting up in an hour or so."

Edith whirled over to me in a cloud of dark dust. "For your information, Missy, the word is *free-spirited.* And by the way, tonight I expect to be wearing the 2003 mint green dress Jennifer Lopez wore to the 75th Academy Awards."

"What do you do, keep a diary of famous gowns?"

"What?" Javie asked. "I think I misunderstood what you asked."

Ugh. Not again.

"Um, I said we should keep a diary of our famous gourmet foods."

"Oh. Good idea."

When we finished placing all of the charcuteries, I moseyed over to the book room where the signings were to take place. It was the only break I'd have until Javie, Lilly-Ann, and I would have to clean up.

Poisoned Pen Bookstore in Scottsdale was handling the sales, and they were already inundated. I couldn't imagine what a frenzy it would be when the authors arrived at their separate tables to sign books for the buyers.

As I walked inside, a woman poked the man next to her and said, "Did you know that Richard Bellmore and Barbara Beau-Wilton used to date each other? I read it on a celebrity gossip site a few days ago."

"It was a gossip site, Patricia, not bona fide news. Come on, the line's moving."

I chuckled and perused the selection of novels from all seven authors. A sudden tap on my shoulder, and I spun around. "Aunt Regina."

"We're in between book talks. Thought I'd see which books are going fast. Not that I'm in acquisitions anymore, but old habits die slowly. By the way, I thought I'd do a bit of shopping after the event. I hope you don't mind."

Don't mind? I'm doing cartwheels!

"Great idea! My crew and I need to clean up, return trays to The Char-Board, and handle any odds and ends that Matt didn't do."

"The banquet begins at seven with cocktails. I'll drive myself since you'll most likely be relaxing at home until the brunch tomorrow."

"Splendid!"

Just then, that "oh-so-annoyingly familiar voice" murmured in my ear. "Don't you dare stay home! We are going to that banquet! Imogen is catering it, and there's no way I'm going to miss out on pestering her. That was your own word—pester. We agreed I could pester her. Not provoke, perturb, or 'push-over-the-edge.' Your words. Remember?"

"Um, come to think of it," I said to my aunt, "I may drive over to the banquet, just to get a sense of how the event is progressing. I can always say I forgot something of ours in the kitchen that we needed for tomorrow's brunch."

"Very well. We'll cross paths then, if not sooner. Oops. I'd better get into Arist's talk. At least his books are witty and humorous. Too bad he's with a cozy publisher and not my publishing company."

Fortunate man.

"Sounds good." I waited a minute or so and then headed back to the kitchen.

"You just missed Sterling Moss," Lilly-Ann said. "He was between book talks and wanted to show you a photo of his nephew. Didn't you tell him you were dating Ian?"

"Not yet."

"I'd tell him sooner than later," Javie chuckled.

"Why? What did Warren look like? Oh gee. I don't want to be one of those superficial people who judge others by their looks. Forget I asked."

"He looked fine." Then Javie faced Lilly-Ann, and the two of them broke up laughing so hard that they couldn't catch their breath.

"Really awful? Absolutely scary?" I widened my eyes as Javie described the details.

"Not Warren. His figurine collection. The photo was taken with him standing in front of a hoarder's nest of Star Wars memorabilia, assorted fossils, and one giant stuffed squid on the wall."

"It must take him hours to dust," Lilly-Ann said, trying to keep a straight face.

"I'll make it a point to say something to Sterling as soon as possible."

As soon as the last book talk session ended, we packed up, tidied up, and headed to The Char-Board. Thankfully, all went well, and I was home with the entire house to myself for at least an hour. Ian texted and asked how it went. Said he'd call late in the evening since he was working non-stop at the restaurant.

I texted back: *Lots of drama but no Oscars.* Then I bit my tongue. The weekend was only half over, and I didn't want to jinx it. Dealing with Edith and now Rosaline was bad enough. Toss in my aunt, and the three-ring circus was complete.

"Come on, Speedbump," I said. "Might as well take our evening walk while there's time. If I sit down, I may never have the energy to get up later."

Wrong choice. Or wrong direction. Either way, I walked straight into Colleen as I headed down the block. She had just placed the outgoing mail flag on her box when she spied me a few yards away.

"Katie! You missed all the excitement last Wednesday. Remember that peeping Tom I mentioned? Well, someone did a little peeping at my house and I immediately phoned the sheriff's office to make a report."

"Did you see them?"

"Not exactly. But I saw what he or she, probably a HE, left on the windowsill to my bedroom. It was one of those tiny screwdrivers. Like the kind you get in a traveler's kit. I think whoever it was thought they could jimmy open the window. Something must have frightened them, and they took off and left it."

"Hmm, that *is* odd, but there might be another explanation."

"That's what Deputy Vincent said, but he took the screwdriver and completed a report. From now on, my alarm system stays on ARMED. You might want to do the same."

I nodded. "Thanks for the update."

"How's that library affair going? I really wanted to attend, but it was way too costly for the banquet and all that. Plus, I had a prior commitment for today that I couldn't reschedule. Richard Bellmore is one of my favorite authors. Oh well. Maybe another time. Say, The Char-Board must be pretty busy providing all those charcuterie boards."

"Great turnout and fantastic authors."

"So I heard. Frankly, I was surprised to read Richard and Arist were under the same roof."

"Why? What's going on with them?"

"Richard is engaged to Arist's ex-wife. I read Arist wasn't taking it well."

My stomach crash-landed to my knees. *This is worse than a gothic romance.*

Colleen tilted her head and kept talking. "It was quite the scuttlebutt in the tabloids. Threats. Accusations. Frankly, I'm surprised one of them didn't wind up six feet under."

Speedbump yawned and plopped himself at my feet. "Uh, I guess that's my cue. Interesting chatting with you, Colleen. Have a nice night."

"You as well. And use your alarm system."

Forget the peeping Tom and the alarm system. I needed a full-blown warning system if what Colleen said was true. Bad enough witnessing the tension between Richard and Jessica. And that was only business. In Arist's case, it was personal, and I kept my fingers crossed it would remain so.

Chapter Nine

Saturday

"Hurry up, Hurry up," Edith huffed. "I want to get there while Imogen and her crew are setting up."

Thankfully, my aunt hadn't returned from her shopping venture, so I was free to talk. "You are *not* to mess with the food or the serving of food. Understood?"

Another huff. "I suppose."

I put on a dark pair of slacks with a modest blouse, intending to remain out of the limelight. "Okay, let's get it over with."

Seconds later, having fed Speedbump and left a note for my aunt, I headed to North School House Road and the library. This time, with Edith in the passenger seat, admiring her mint green gown.

"At last! The feel of soft fabric again."

"I don't understand how you can feel anything."

Edith shrugged. "Neither do I. At least Rosaline kept her word. Got to admit, she was a quick study when it came to summoning the no-see-ums. One of these days, we'll have to exchange skill sets. It's a changing netherworld, you know."

I did a mental eyeroll. "So I've been told."

Sixty ticketed guests were about to enjoy a culinary masterpiece from The Chanterelle, and I was curious as to what it would be. When we arrived, two of Imogen's vans were parked out front, and four employees unloaded carts with what I imagined were some of the pre-prepared dishes, like the salads and such. The main course was most likely pre-prepared as well, needing only oven or stove warm-up. Not the best scenario, but one that caterers were used to.

"At least we're early enough to get a decent parking spot," I said, but Edith had already exited the car and was probably in the kitchen by now. I hurried inside, keeping a low profile in the kitchen. On a small table near the door were the fancy menus that would soon be placed on the outdoor tables.

One glance and I was positive my aunt would be in a food coma by the end of the night. Salmon timbales, pumpkin quiche, and caramelized goat cheese tarts were the appetizers, followed by French chestnut soup and a simple green salad. Next were the main dishes, and I imagined the attendees selected those ahead of time. Tarragon and lemon chicken, seared scallops on pea puree, monkfish with thermidor sauce, and mushroom bourguignon as the vegetarian selection.

The crusty baguettes and homemade butter were also on the menu. In spite of snacking on the leftover tidbits from our charcuteries, I salivated as I read the menu.

"Can I help you?" I looked at the thin, twenty-something girl with spiked purple and orange hair and recognized her instantly. It was Alberta, Imogen's daughter. The last time I saw her, she was lip-locking with a boyfriend in his car.

"Uh, yes. Thanks. I'm Katie Aubrey, from The Char-Board. We're doing the charcuteries for the event tomorrow, and I think I may have left my folder in here. Hope you don't mind if I look around."

Alberta shrugged. "I don't mind, but watch out for my mother. See that woman over there with the silver hair and glasses? Looks like she's already having an issue with someone."

I widened my eyes in horror as Imogen shook her head, swatted at her shoulders, and proceeded to bend down and shake her hair. "Wow."

"Yeah," Alberta said, "She must be really ticked. Just keep a wide berth."

I wanted to tell her that her mother was combating no-see-ums from her college nemesis, but instead I nodded and muttered that I understood. "By the way, would you mind if I hung out and watched you? I'm always eager to learn new things in the industry."

"I'm cool with that. But I don't know what you'll learn. Most of the meal was pre-prepared. But go ahead, knock yourself out." Alberta grabbed a large baguette and proceeded to slice it when Imogen's voice rattled the kitchen.

"Alberta! Get over here. Keep an eye on the thermidor sauce. One degree off and it will taste like canned chowder. Get yourself over here!"

Alberta turned to me. "See what I mean?"

I nodded and muttered, "Good luck." Then, under my breath, I mumbled, "Take it easy, Edith. The night is young."

Then, out of nowhere, Rosaline wafted in. "I looked at the seating chart. Richard is near the waterfall, and I'll be right next to him on one of those boulders. The spray should be delightful. Good thing I don't have to worry about the extension cords from those LED fairy lights. Their maintenance crew has been at it all day."

"Think I'll have a look," Edith said.

I moved next to the rear door by the patio in order to be out of earshot. "Don't you dare make Imogen trip and fall."

"You are *such* a goody-two-shoes!"

Glancing at the waterfall, I saw what Rosaline mentioned. The dancing fairy lights in shades of amber, yellow, burnt orange, and white were absolutely dazzling. And true, there were cords on the ground, but not near where anyone would walk.

"I'm stepping outside," I said to no one in particular. Behind me, Edith and Rosaline chatted, but I paid no attention and instead, focused on the banquet set up. It was magnificent. Absolutely magnificent. I suppose it would have to be, considering the price tag for the event.

There were eight tables with six to eight chairs, each chair with an autumn wreath on the back. Stunning fall centerpieces and matching linen napkins completed the look. Not to mention the silver plastic cutlery and elegant disposable wine and water glasses.

Place cards with the guests' names on them were embellished with gold leaf designs. I walked to the tables closest to the waterfall to see where Richard was seated. To his left, Sterling had one of the coveted places of honor, and to his right was someone named Wilsetta Frum. I pictured a sweet silver-haired woman from the Midwest, but as I later found out, Wilsetta was middle-aged with slightly unkempt brownish red hair and terrible taste in lipstick and blush. As I moved around the table, I held my breath that my aunt would be seated elsewhere. Lamentably, she wasn't. Her chair was directly across from Richard's, and within seconds, my throat tightened.

"If one of those womanizers makes a move toward Richard, I'm going to unleash my new skill," Rosaline announced. She flitted around his table, reading the place cards. Then she looked at Edith. "How do you intend to amuse yourself?"

"By watching Imogen Brodeur have a panic attack. I'm on a tight leash, though. Can't mess with the food, but Imogen herself isn't off limits."

And that was the moment every hair on my body stood at attention.

Chapter Ten

Saturday

Assuming an out-of-the-way spot between the kitchen and the outdoor patio, I watched as the guests entered and took their seats at the tables. My aunt was one of the first to arrive and immediately swamped her place card with Sterling's. I marched over and held out my hand. "The seating was carefully arranged for a reason. Please don't mess this up. Sterling Moss is a big fan of Richard Bellmore. You wouldn't want him to miss out, would you?"

My aunt returned the place cards to their original spots. "I suppose anything I have to say can be said from across the table."

"Or not at all. Try 'not at all.'"

My aunt seated herself, and I returned to the kitchen with a soft mint green haze accompanying me. The appetizers were served without incident, but I knew better than to think all would be right with the world.

The next dish was the chestnut soup, and the aroma was enticing. Three jumbo pots simmered on the stove as the servers approached with bowls that they filled before placing them on serving carts. *Please let this end well.*

Imogen barked directions at everyone, including Alberta, who gave her mother hand gestures behind her back that would get most people thrown out of an establishment. I tried not to laugh, but it was impossible. Grabbing a napkin, I feigned a coughing fit until I regained my composure. Then the worst. When all of the servers had left the kitchen with the soup, Imogen peered into the pots, and Edith seized the opportunity to lean over her and produce an ear-splitting sound.

Imogen jumped back, stumbled, and crashed into the counter, knocking over a large tray of iceberg lettuce that rolled across the floor. Worse yet, she managed to trip over one and skid unceremoniously on her rump.

With that, Edith announced, "Let the festivities begin!"

"Not on my watch!" I shouted, to which everyone in the kitchen stopped what they were doing and looked at me. "Not that I'm watching," I repeated louder. "But we should help that woman."

Imogen looked up from the floor. "Do I know you? You look familiar."

"Katie Aubrey. Owner of The Char-Board. I'm catering this event as well and wanted to watch your mastery in progress." *Whew!* "Are you all right?" I reached a hand and she stood.

"A bout of tinnitus, that's all. It came on suddenly. It's horrible."

"Yes, it is." I furrowed my brow at Edith and gave her a dirty look.

Needless to say, the servers were able to deliver the salads and the main course without interference. But that didn't mean the guests didn't make up for it. A quick glimpse at Richard's table from the open kitchen door, and I watched Wilsetta Frum thrust a spoon at his mouth, coaxing him to try her dish.

When he held up his hands and tried to back away, she grabbed both of them and moved toward him. That's when Rosaline unleashed a swarm of no-see-ums at Wilsetta's face. Suffice it to say, Rosaline hadn't much practice, so the no-see-ums were larger than usual and swarmed the entire table. They weren't visible, but they sure were noticeable.

"Do something, Edith!" I mouthed.

"I am! I'm watching this. It's hilarious."

Suddenly, someone from the table next to them yelled, "I think table 4 is having a reaction to the food. Someone should call 911."

"Now, Edith! Do something now!" I rushed to the patio, hoping Edith wouldn't stall. A few of the guests left their tables and charged over to Wilsetta's.

Following a long sigh, Edith hovered over the table and within seconds, the no-see-ums were gone. And so was Richard. In all the commotion, I hadn't noticed him leave. And who could blame him? I figured he took a breather in the men's room or maybe even out front. But Richard wasn't my concern. Imogen was. And Edith wouldn't leave the party without a final shot at her nemesis.

Then, I had an awful thought. What if Richard left the affair altogether? I had to stop him. It was the least I could do, considering this mess originated in my camp. I spun around, motioned for Edith to follow, and headed towards the men's room. That's where I saw Richard and Arist face-to-face. I wedged myself into the alcove between the restrooms and listened.

"All she's interested in is your money," Arist said. "If it dries up, she'll move to the next Daddy Warbucks."

Richard chucked. "Don't worry about that. I'm not a cozy mystery writer who's lucky to pull in four to five grand a year. Multiply that by a hundred and you'd be getting close."

"Don't say I didn't warn you." Arist stormed past the alcove, unaware I was huddled in there. He pounded a fist into an open hand but closed his eyes in the process. Maybe it wasn't bravado after all.

The mint green haze intensified, and Edith appeared with her hands crossed. "Snarly bunch of authors, I'd say. Come on, I'm not done with Imogen."

"Well, I am. I'm tired and I want to get some sleep. We've got to cater the breakfast brunch in the morning."

As Edith and I made our way toward the exit, Aunt Regina appeared on her way to the ladies' room. She didn't see me in the alcove, but there was no way Richard could escape her. Lucky for Arist, he had already vacated the area.

"Richard," my aunt called out. "I was thinking of assigning a ghostwriter to assist you."

"What? Have you lost your mind?"

In the next few minutes, their conversation escalated into a full-blown argument that carried all the way down the corridor. A few servers left the kitchen to listen, as well as some of the event attendees who made the mistake of heading to the restrooms between courses.

I wasted no time leaving the alcove and racing toward the combatants. "Aunt Regina! You'll miss the dessert. And I need to head home. Come on, I'll escort you back to the table."

My aunt fixed a death stare at Richard and then, in a loud voice, announced, "Too bad I wasn't seated next to him. I would have shoved him into that waterfall!"

"And you think *I* gave Imogen a hard time?" Edith wafted past me, and in a flash, the greenish haze vanished. I turned to Richard and mouthed, "So sorry. Please don't leave the event."

He mouthed back. "I won't."

My nerves were all but shot by the time I walked my aunt back to the table and had thanked Alberta for letting me observe The Chanterelle at work. I was aghast when my aunt leaned her arm across the table to attract KC Camplin's attention as he walked by. He then paused to say something to Richard before moving on. At least there were no fireworks. Not then, anyway.

I took one last look at the patio area with its blinking fairy lights, cozy heat lamps, and delightful floral displays. I wanted that image to remain in my head for a long time, but daylight had a way of changing everything.

Chapter Eleven

Sunday

With The Char-Board closed on Sunday, I didn't have to worry about being in two places at once. Ian texted me at sunrise, even though we chatted into the night about the tension-filled banquet.

Randolph's Escapade was providing cold canapes in addition to the charcuterie breakfast boards we were bringing. That meant Ian and I could commiserate in between runs to and from the conference room. Allison had told me that library volunteers would be the ones tidying up the patio once the banquet was over that night, and that the rental company would be removing the heat lamps on Monday. Even though we weren't going to serve breakfast there, she wanted it open at eleven for its ambience and photo ops. Until then, it would remain closed with the curtains drawn due to the colder morning temperature.

Lilly-Ann and I arrived at a little past six to prepare the charcuteries. Javie showed up at seven as planned and moved the trays onto the credenza in the large conference room. At the same time, Ian and his crew brought out platters of breakfast crudites and assorted pastries.

"Sterling had the time of his life," he told me as we looked at the serving table. "Said he and Richard were able to have a quiet talk in the library's reading area after the event. He asked if Sterling could keep an eye out for Wilsetta since she scared the daylights out of him."

"Wilsetta? I'm surprised he didn't mention my aunt to your boss."

"Oh, he did. But I didn't think you'd want to hear it."

"It's almost nine," Lilly-Ann called out as we returned to the kitchen. "The attendees will start arriving. The brunch begins at nine-thirty."

"At least it's a ticketed event, so that's only sixty or so people," I said. "And one high-maintenance relative."

Ian laughed, and we both moved to our respective areas to get things going. Thankfully, there was no sign of Edith, but I wondered if Rosaline still attached herself to Richard.

Unlike the banquet, the attendees were free to seat themselves at any of the tables in the room. Small butter rolls and assorted jams and jellies graced the tables in addition to cups of whipped butter, compliments of Randolph's Escapade.

Twenty or so minutes later, Allison welcomed the readers and told them to enjoy the wonderful breakfast charcuteries and brunch canapes. It was the first time I let myself relax during the event. With any luck, we'd be packed up and out of the library before two.

Judging from the oohs and aahs, the charcuteries and canapes were a big hit, and that meant more engagements for The Char-Board. Ian and I stood off to the side of the credenza and watched as people loaded and reloaded their plates.

Just then, we heard an ear-piercing shriek, so we bolted for the kitchen. With Imogen absent, I doubted it was Edith, but then again, she was as unpredictable as the weather.

The shriek turned into a scream, and it didn't emanate from the kitchen.

"Where's that coming from?" I grabbed Ian's arm.

"The patio."

He pulled the curtain open, and we fixed our eyes on a library volunteer who stood over the waterfall. I could see that one of the heat lamps had fallen into the water, but I couldn't imagine why that deserved a blood-curdling howl.

Then I left the kitchen and stepped closer to the waterfall. As I did, Ian pulled me back. "Don't look!" But it was too late. A man's body, face down, was floating on the water below the falls. Black trousers, white shirt. The attire most of the men wore to the banquet.

I could see the cord to the lamp was still plugged into the outlet a few yards away. Either it got knocked into the water and took the victim along with it, or, more than likely, it had help.

"Can you find Allison?" Ian asked. "I'm calling 911. Don't touch anything."

Luckily, only the two of us, along with Lilly-Ann, Javie, and a few of Ian's crew, heard the scream and had now made their way to the patio. I imagined that in a matter of minutes, it would be worse than Grand Central Station in New York.

"On my way," I said, barely audible.

Allison had the good sense to inform her staff to keep everyone in the conference room. Then she stepped out to the patio and gasped. "I hope the sheriff's office hurries up. This is incomprehensible. One of the attendees must have gotten too close to the waterfall and tripped over the heat lamp. Oh my gosh. That person was electrocuted." She took a few deep breaths and continued. "We've never had anything like this happen."

Then she walked closer to the waterfall.

"Don't!" Ian said. "Wait until the sheriff's deputies get here. And the fire department. There's nothing we can do for the victim now."

Lilly-Ann stood with a hand over her mouth while Javie moved closer to Allison.

"The brunch!" she gasped. "I've got to get back in there. I'm supposed to run this event, and I can't think straight."

"I'll go with you," he said. "Whatever you do, don't say anything. Let the sheriff's office deal with it."

"I thought I had everything under control," she mumbled as they left the patio, "but I'm falling apart."

"It's a delayed reaction," I heard Javie say to Allison. And in that second, my stomach cramped and my mouth became salty. "I need a cracker and some water," I told Ian. "I'll be fine. Just going back to the kitchen."

"You sure? You're as white as a napkin."

"I'll be okay."

Three crackers later, and the cavalry arrived. Deputy Travis Vincent and his new partner, along with a handful of firefighters, stormed into the building as if it was a warzone. Following them were two forensic technicians who looked vaguely familiar.

As the chief deputy walked into the kitchen, I saw that nothing had changed. He still sported the same five o'clock shadow and perpetual scowl.

"Miss Aubrey. Why is it no surprise that I find *you* here?"

I gulped. "Luck, I suppose. The Char-Board is one of the library caterers."

He nodded and motioned for the forensic techs to go to the patio. "Wait there until the fire department gives the 'all-clear.' Water and electricity don't mix. The coroner should arrive any minute. According to the office, it's Orin Tosler on duty. Meanwhile, cordon off the entire area."

Then he looked at us. "I hope you haven't made plans for the afternoon because I'm afraid they'll have to be cancelled."

So much for getting home at 2:00, I'll be lucky if it's 2:00 A.M.

And then, the mint green haze. "What about my plans? Doesn't anyone think about my plans?"

"You have no plans." My voice was dry and monotone.

"I beg your pardon?" Deputy Vincent crinkled his nose, and I swallowed. "I mean, all of our plans have changed."

He nodded. "Indeed."

Chapter Twelve

Sunday

With the expediency of a well-orchestrated drill team, the techs cordoned off the area and asked those of us in the vicinity to remain in the kitchen until further notice. Midway into the process, the marshal's office responded with its own staff, and they, in turn, collaborated with the sheriff's office.

"All we need is the police department's Black Mountain Precinct to send officers over here, and the three-ring circus will have reached capacity," Ian remarked as we watched everyone from the open door. "Then again, I suppose they'll need 'all hands on deck' because they've got sixty or more people to interview."

"I thought it was an accident." My mouth suddenly went dry.

"It might be, but the sheriff's office needs to make that determination. What if the victim got pushed? Or was he poisoned and keeled over into the water? I hate to envision that sort of thing, but let's face it, winding up face down in a decorative waterfall isn't something that happens every day."

No sooner did Ian make that comment when Deputy Vincent thundered back into the kitchen from the patio. "All right, folks. Listen to the plan. Most likely it was an accident, but the coroner will need to conduct a post-mortem, run a toxicology test, and well… you know the rest of the drill. Notwithstanding, we'll need to identify the victim and notify next of kin."

"Does that mean we're free to go?" someone asked.

The deputy shook his head. "Our office will need contact information and statements from everyone. There are four smaller conference rooms in the library, and as I speak, the marshal's office is escorting people, by table, into those rooms. Someone will be posted to make sure that there's no conversation taking place. We want clear, accurate statements in order to avoid the possibility of collusion."

"Collusion?" the same person asked. "I thought it was an accident."

"It's protocol," was the deputy's response. Then he motioned for one of his assistants. "Deputy Rinestock will remain in the kitchen until we've received your information. Then, *and only then,* will you be free to go."

Ian squeezed my hand. "That poor person. Imagine coming here to enjoy author talks, only to wind up electrocuted."

"Shh!" Deputy Rinestock said. And that's when I knew it would be a long afternoon.

Through the open doorway, I watched as the coroner and his assistant loaded the body onto a gurney. Then, out of nowhere, I heard Rosaline's unmistakable voice, "Oh no! I knew I shouldn't have let Edith talk me into a gown fitting! I missed the moment he departed! Now it will take me forever to navigate that first maze into the beyond and find him."

Sure enough, I saw her form hovering over the gurney, but there was nothing I could do except watch. *Darn it, Edith. Where are you when I need you? Whose body is on that gurney?*

Without warning, my aunt must have broken free from her captivity in one of the conference rooms because she tore onto the patio like a hyena in search of a meal. "I'm looking for my gold bracelet with my name engraved on the back. It must have slipped off my wrist at the buffet last night. That bracelet has sentimental and monetary value. I'll only be a second." Then, the scream that explained why Rosaline was there. "Richard! It's Richard Bellmore! Goodness, he's bloated! Are those electrical marks on his neck?"

"You have to leave the premises, Ma'am," one of the deputies said. "Please return to your conference room and do not say anything to anyone."

Fat chance!

Town criers weren't as loud as my aunt as she rushed down the hallway, forgetting entirely about her gold bracelet. "It's Richard Bellmore! Richard Bellmore! Deader than a doornail."

Within seconds, we heard the rising sound of voices. Thank goodness Deputy Vincent was seasoned enough to plant an officer in each of the conference rooms.

"Guess the cat's out of the bag, huh?" Ian said. "How long do you think it will take for the TV stations to show up?"

I looked at my phone. "I'm sure they're on their way now. Most of them are in downtown Phoenix, and all of them have police scanners."

Sure enough, the news appeared on my iPhone app before the crews even pulled up to the parking lot. It was a brief announcement, indicating a body was found at the Desert Foothills Library in Cave Creek, and that the library would be closed on Monday.

"Once his family is notified, it'll be all over the news," I whispered." I looked at Ian and then at everyone else in the kitchen. When the deputy had turned his head, Lilly-Ann pulled her chair over and sat next to me. She mouthed, "This is a nightmare," and I nodded.

The next two hours were as slow as waiting for a pot to boil. One by one, people were interviewed and released. Unfortunately, those of us from The Char-Board and Randolph's Escapade still had cleanup to do. Not to mention returning food and supplies to our own establishments.

Deputy Vincent informed us not to breathe a word about the victim's identity because it was unsubstantiated. True, it was broadcast like the Super Bowl, thanks to my aunt, but still, unsubstantiated. The deputy made it clear that his directive was being given to everyone on the premises.

At a little past three, when most of the attendees had left, the deputies allowed Allison to enter the kitchen and speak with us.

"I want to thank all of you for the incredible catering job you did. It was magnificent in every way. Sadly, the tragic death of one of our esteemed authors has clouded over everything. And while his identification has not been released, sources from the sheriff's office informed me that, indeed, it was Richard Bellmore."

"Of course it was Richard!" Rosaline shrieked as she and Edith moved about the kitchen. "Why do you think I'm still here? I have to figure out how to find him up there." Then she wafted over to Edith, leaving a pinkish hue in the air. "He *is* going up there, don't you think?"

Edith sighed. "The black darkness didn't take over the patio, so I imagine so. And if you want me to help you locate him, then we need to discuss the Carole Lombard gown."

"Not that again!" Then I caught myself. "Having to wait for an official ID. Sorry, it's just so taxing."

"I understand. All of us are in shock.," Allison said. "I'll be in touch with you tomorrow, Katie." Then she stepped toward Ian and spoke in a low voice. "Mr. Moss is quite distraught in conference room B. He said that you'd handle the details for him. In fact, he requested you drive him home when you get the okay from MCSO."

A few minutes later, Ian gave directions to his crew and left to drive Sterling home. "I'll drive one of the restaurant workers back here to pick up his car," he said. He squeezed my hand and whispered, "Take care. I'll call or text you as soon as I can."

And then, as if I didn't have enough on my plate, Aunt Regina bounced into the kitchen and announced, "I overheard one of the deputies say it was foul play."

Chapter Thirteen

Sunday, Monday

By the time I got home, I was mentally and physically exhausted. The only saving grace was that Edith was nowhere to be found. I imagined she and Rosaline were traipsing all over who-knows-where in the great beyond to locate Richard and/or that Carole Lombard gown.

My aunt had arrived back before me and had made herself comfortable on the couch with Speedbump resting against it. "I can't believe it," she said when I walked in. "Richard Bellmore. Murdered!"

"We don't know that he was murdered. His death is under investigation."

"The short deputy with the wispy blond hair told the tall, good-looking one that the coroner questioned the bump on Richard's head and did not believe it was post-trauma."

"Aunt Regina, until they conduct a post-mortem, it's considered an accidental death."

"Richard didn't strike me as someone clumsy enough to trip over those cords and take the heat lamp with him. He seemed pretty adroit to me."

"I'm sure we'll get answers soon enough. Tell me, what are your plans for the remaining few days that you're here?" *And they can't be few enough.*

"I'm driving to your mother's first thing in the morning. We're going out for breakfast and then off to a spa day at some resort that she booked. After that, we'll shop and then join your father for dinner at an old-world

Italian restaurant they've been raving about. Too bad you can't join us for the daytime activities. Or the dinner for that matter."

"The Char-Board keeps me very busy, and when it closes, I still have catering to do. I'm sure you'll have a terrific time."

"Tuesday, we're going to the art museum. Then your brother is having us over for dinner at his place. I told him not to fuss, considering how hard he works, but he said it's the least he can do for his favorite aunt."

Yes. Least *being the key word.*

"Great."

"My flight leaves at 7:23 Wednesday morning, so I'll be up before the roosters and on my way by 4:00. I need to have a two-hour window at the airport. Not to mention time to return the rental car."

I nodded, and she continued.

"By the way, this may sound strange, but I have the oddest feeling I'm being watched when I turn in for the night. Not the peeping Tom your neighbor mentioned, but more like something hovering over me. It was particularly noticeable when I wore my burgundy silky-laced lingerie that I treated myself to."

Oh no. Now Edith is looking at lingerie. Good grief. She never stops.

"Yeah, that *is* strange. You were probably overtired."

"I suppose. Anyway, I'm going to nap for a while and then catch up on some reading. This whole business with Richard's death has gotten to me."

"I understand. If you get hungry, I've got lots of leftover cold cuts in the fridge."

And while my aunt read and relaxed for the remainder of the day, I caught up on emails, paperwork, and text messages, taking breaks to walk Speedbump and chat with Ian on the phone at the same time.

"I'm still in shock over Richard's death," I told Ian as I meandered down the block with the dog in tow.

"Yeah. Of all things. Sterling isn't handling it well. Not only did he idolize the guy, but apparently, he and Richard chatted with each other during the event, and Sterling had invited him to dine at Randolph's Escapade that night."

"Did you return his car?"

"Yep. And you won't believe who went along with me—Warren. The nephew. I think you made a better choice to date me." Then he laughed.

"That bad?"

"Not really. He's a nice guy, but totally fixated on his molecular work. Lost me on at least three strands of thought. It was only when he mentioned his Star Wars collection that I understood what he was saying."

"Yikes."

"When does your aunt leave? Boy, that was direct and to the point, huh?"

I chuckled. "Wednesday morning. Are you free that night to come over? We can grab a pizza."

"I'll make myself free."

"I'll text later. Speedbump is tugging to smell something a few feet away."

"Miss you."

"Me too."

When I finally pulled the covers down on my bed and crawled in for the night, I took a final look at the news app. Sure enough, Richard's death was still scrolling, but no name had been released. I figured the deputies were still trying to reach the next of kin. By seven A.M. the following day, they had succeeded.

"It's on the news, Katie," my aunt called out from the kitchen. "I turned on the TV and the announcer said that famed author Richard Bellmore succumbed to injuries caused by a fall at the library event this weekend. He said the death is still under investigation, but the likely cause appears to be accidental."

"You see, it never pays to listen to gossip. Even if the talkers are deputies."

"I wouldn't brush that off too soon. Television anchors always play it safe."

My aunt grabbed a quick cup of coffee, and a few minutes later, took off to meet my mother. Hallelujah. A quiet, albeit brief, few minutes to myself.

I plunked a Jamaica-Me-Crazy coffee pod in the Keurig and took out a box of Honey Grahams for breakfast. That's when a creamy haze filled the room, accompanied by the scent of gardenia. So much for a quiet minute.

"Remind me to thank Rosaline. This isn't Carole Lombard's gown, but it'll suffice. It's Greta Garbo's gown from *Camille*."

"Looks poofy."

"It's not poofy. It's acquired elegance." Edith spun around so I could see the lift of the gown.

"It's poofy."

"Never mind that. Rosaline and I had no luck finding Richard. She's still navigating up there."

"When she finds him, let me know if he says he was murdered or if he was just klutzy."

"I doubt that will be anytime soon. It's a veritable labyrinth if you must know."

"Much as I'd like to sit around and discuss the 'realm above' with you, I've got to get to The Char-Board."

"I can take no for an answer." And with that, an ice cube flew out of the refrigerator dispenser and onto the floor, and when it landed, Edith was gone.

"What a nerve-wracking weekend," Lilly-Ann said. She stood over the counter, slicing assorted cheeses while Javie prepared eggs and toast for a few customers. Matt was due to arrive any minute, and I was relieved since he handled our Monday deliveries from Brioche, Toast, and Most. They, too, would be here within the hour.

"Think someone killed Richard?" Javie asked. "That was the scuttlebutt I heard."

I shrugged. "Me too, but you know how rumors are spread. At least this is one murder that really doesn't pertain to us." Then I caught myself. "Unless, of course, the toxicology report says he was poisoned. Aargh! Let's not go there yet!"

I started on the ham salad when a text came in from Maddie. It was short and succinct: *Can't put it off. Must check out house with you today. I can stop by The Char-Board at 4:00 and get you.*

There was no way I'd let Maddie down, and she sounded adamant about the place. I texted back: *Sure, but there's no such thing as ghosts.* After all, what could I say? That I lived with one? Besides, how many of them can be haunting houses in Arizona?

We pushed through the breakfast rush, and no sooner did we catch a breath when the lunch orders began to pile up. By now, the four of us had reached our usual rhythm of preparing, serving, and cleaning up. News of Richard's demise was all over the place. Not surprising. He was a household name, and thriller fans were stunned.

The news media hyped the situation with hints of foul play, but nothing substantial. At a little before 2:00, when things were winding down, Deputy Vincent made a surprise visit to The Char-Board.

"You're still in time for lunch," I said when I saw him walk in. Only a few customers remained, and none of them paid attention. The deputy walked toward me and held out a piece of paper.

"Thank you, but I've already eaten. This is the information we have on Regina Aubrey. She indicated she was staying with you and gave us your information as well. I'll need to speak with her. Do you happen to know where she is? I tried your house first, but no one answered."

I gulped. "My aunt is with my mother. Somewhere. Um, museum or spa. I'm not sure. I wasn't paying much attention to her this morning. Wait a sec. It's the spa. Then dinner at an Italian restaurant."

"Do you know which spa? Which restaurant?"

I shook my head. "I can call her on the cell."

"We've tried that. Left two messages."

"She must be having a really long spa day. I'll let her know you stopped by. I thought she had already been questioned about Richard Bellmore's death."

"She was. Now we are compelled to get more information."

When he said the word *compelled,* I froze. I'd been through this before. Compelled meant my aunt was no longer an attendee at a function where someone died unexpectedly. It meant they thought she might know more, or worse yet, might have been involved.

"Please don't tell me you think she's a suspect." I stood still and stared at Deputy Vincent's five o'clock shadow.

"A suspect, no. As of now, your aunt is a person of interest."

Chapter Fourteen

Monday

"A person of interest? I don't understand."

Deputy Vincent pinched his shoulders back and took a breath. "It's imperative we speak with her. When do you expect her back?"

I shrugged. "Hard to say."

"Fine. When she does return, please have her report to my office tomorrow morning at nine. I'd rather not send a deputy to your house."

"I understand."

With that, he nodded and left The Char-Board.

"What was that about?" Lilly-Ann asked in a low voice. Her arms were loaded with dishes. "I caught some of the conversation, but not all. I wanted to get these in the dishwasher."

"I'm not sure what it's about, but I'm sure it's not good. My aunt is now a person of interest in Richard Bellmore's death. They haven't officially deemed it a murder, but Deputy Vincent wouldn't have trekked over here if it was accidental."

"Try not to get ahead of yourself. You did say she was his editor, right? Maybe the sheriff's office thinks she may know something."

"Why then would Deputy Vincent say she was a person of interest? Something else is going on, but it'll have to wait until tomorrow. I'm texting her and my mother right now."

Lilly-Ann shuffled the dishes to one hand and, with the free hand, tapped my elbow. "Wait! No sense ruining her day with your mother. Besides, there's nothing she can do right now except worry. Tell her when she gets back to your house later."

"Ugh. I suppose you're right."

"And don't let it ruin the rest of your day, either."

"I doubt anything else could ruin it." *Except maybe that house of Maddie's.*

When the final customers left and we had cleaned up, it was 3:45. I locked the door behind the crew and poured myself the last cup of coffee. Maddie was insistent I see that listing of hers, but one ghost in my life, uh, make it two with Rosaline, was more than enough.

A few minutes later, she knocked on the door and I let her in, making sure our closed sign was visible. "Wow. Four pm on the nose. I'm ready to see this house of yours."

"Good, because the listing is driving me and my office bonkers. I dismissed it when clients said they thought it was haunted, but when the building inspector concurred, that was the last straw."

"Did he or she say why?"

"It's a he, and no, he didn't. Not yet anyway. He said he'd have his report to me this week."

"Where's the house located?"

"On East Highland Road. Not far from the library. It's priced at 2.5."

"Million? Million dollars?"

"Oh yeah. Expansive views, five acres, top-of-the-line construction, thick walls, four bedrooms, two of them master suites, gourmet kitchen, state-of-the-art bathrooms with rain showers and soaker tubs. Small lap pool and jacuzzi too."

"Heck, if I had the money, I'd move in. Ghosts or not."

"Let's hope not. Come on, we'd better get moving before it gets dark. I hate this time of year with the early sunset. Besides, I thought we could grab a bite to eat when we get done. Unless you've got other plans."

"Only my aunt. Better make it a fast-food meal." I then proceeded to tell her about Deputy Vincent's visit and my aunt's relationship with Richard Bellmore.

"That's not good, Katie. I hope it doesn't mean you'll be stuck with her past Wednesday."

"Bite your tongue. It's bad enough Ian and I have been like ships that pass in the night, or whatever that quote is. He's planning on coming over Wednesday night, and I better have the house to myself." *More or less.*

"The news said it was an accident. Social media is a whole other story."

"Why? What's trending?"

"Facebook? Instagram? X? Where do you want me to start?"

"Anywhere. I haven't had time to look."

"I'll give you the CliffsNotes. Rumors abound about Richard cheating on his newly engaged fiancée as well as hints of rivalries between him and other thriller authors."

"That's it?"

Maddie laughed. "That's enough. The threads on social media could be woven together to form a good romance novel." Then she paused. "Or murder mystery."

By now, we had gotten into her car and were turning onto North School House Road.

"I hope my aunt doesn't go off the deep end tonight when I tell her Deputy Vincent has summoned her to the sheriff's office. Aargh. I probably should go with her. Hold on a second, I need to text Lilly-Ann to let her know. The appointment is for 9:00, and that's smack dab in the middle of our breakfast rush."

"Your crew can handle it. Besides, it'll probably be a short meeting. In and out."

"I hope." Maddie turned onto East Highland Road, and I widened my eyes. "Oh my gosh! The view! It's spectacular!"

"Like the commission. *If* there's a commission." She pulled into the long driveway and turned off the engine. "I'm sure there's a reasonable explanation why it's not selling."

"Maybe that house next door scared them off. The yard is full of weird metal art and bales of hay. Do they have farm animals?"

"I have no idea. These acre-plus lots are zoned for it, but only horses. Not pigs or chickens. Ugh. Too bad it's November. I'd want to get into that lap pool of theirs. It happens to be heated."

We walked to the ornate security door in front of the house, and Maddie punched a code into its lock. Seconds later, she opened the lockbox, and we stepped inside. The first thing I noticed was the textured white and gray tile that gave the house its elegance, followed by a tastefully decorated living area that opened into the gourmet kitchen.

"Is that an atrium?" I asked.

Maddie nodded. "It connects the master suite with the main living area. Everything seems to crisscross in the house. It was designed by a Dutch architect, and if you ask me, his teacher was M.C. Escher."

She led me through the house like someone leading a child through a corn maze. All the while, I made sure to take in each room in terms of its scent and overall vibe.

"I don't feel anything at all that would indicate this place is haunted," I said. "I mean, it's not as if I expected a Bela Lugosi kind of thing, but still, shouldn't it come with the creep factor?"

"Not in this case."

"Did the clients give you any specifics?"

Maddie opened the large walk-in, or in this case, "live-in" master bedroom closet that was larger than my bedroom. "Funny, but they all said the same thing. That the house 'felt wrong.' They said something was 'off' but they couldn't pinpoint it."

"I take it there was no lipstick on the mirror that spelled out 'LEAVE WHILE YOU CAN.'"

"Nothing that overt." Maddie laughed. "But strange smells waft through it from time to time. Something *has* to be going on." Just then, her phone rang and she looked at caller ID. "It's my office. I need to take it. Walk around."

I left the bedroom via the door into the atrium and crossed to the opposite side, where I slid a patio door into a media room. Then I called out for Edith. "I know you're lurking around here somewhere. This time I really need your assistance. Materialize or something, will you?"

"You won't find her," came a voice I'd come to recognize. It was followed by a peach haze. "They just opened up Vivien Leigh's wardrobe from *Gone with the Wind,* and Edith is pushing her way through the line. That woman shows no restraint when it comes to these things. If she doesn't watch it, she'll wind up with the dress from the potato scene at the end of Act 1."

"Uh, yeah. Whatever. Listen, Rosaline, I really need help from your spirit world."

"My spirit world or me?"

I sighed. "You. I need your help."

"You should have just asked. What do you want?"

"Can you tell if any other spirits are occupying this house?"

"They're not."

"That was quick. You didn't even look."

"I don't need to. I'd know if there were any spirits lurking around. And this house is ghost-free."

"Are you sure?"

"I may be dead, but I haven't lost my marbles. Of course I'm sure. Why?"

"Because my friend's clients and the building inspector think it's haunted."

"Poppy-cock. It's as haunted as Mother Goose's shoe. If you want my opinion, someone's gaslighting you."

"Gaslighting?"

"From the Ingrid Bergman movie. Think of it like a murder, only instead of the body you get to figure out what's going on. And you still get to determine motive, means, and opportunity. Ta-ta. I've got to get going. Edith's probably snatched the green curtain dress by now. She's borrowed it before, you know."

"Wait, I—"

Too late, the peach haze was gone, and I heard Maddie call for me.

"I'm in the media room, or den," I shouted. "Where are you?"

"Turn around."

Maddie stood a few feet away, and I gasped. "How'd you do that? Get here so fast."

"There's a walk-through from the master bedroom to another closet that opens in here."

"Boy, this place is full of surprises. But I don't think ghosts are one of them. I think someone doesn't want this place to sell, and they're doing all they can to prevent it."

"Then why would they list it?"

"Not the owner. But someone with a motive."

"You've been too embroiled with all those murder mysteries you read."

"It *is* a murder. Someone is killing off your commission."

Chapter Fifteen

Monday

Maddie crossed her arms and walked into the atrium. "I don't get it. It's not as if this place has any historical value, or happens to be located on a mineral-rich plot of land." Then she stood for a few seconds before speaking. "Katie, you don't suppose one of those clients is deliberately sabotaging it so they can drive down the value and purchase it at a cheaper cost, do you?"

"It's possible. How many offers did you say you had?"

"Three signed contracts and one verbal commitment. They were about to sign but backed out. Is it possible all of them were in cahoots?"

"Not all of them, but it only takes one. See if you can find out if they knew each other. Maybe the real interested party paid off the others to keep the ruse going. Or, maybe they were threatened by another interested party. And no, *that* theory didn't come from one of my cozy mysteries."

"What about the building inspector?" Maddie opened the property folder that was in her hand and glanced at it.

"I'd want to know what connections he had with the buyers."

She smiled, "I knew I brought you here for a good reason. Come on, no sense wasting time when we could be eating, even if it is fast food."

We left the property and drove to the nearest McDonald's, where we scarfed down double cheeseburgers and fries before my brain even had a chance of registering that I had eaten. "That's the trouble with fast food, by the time your body registers that you've eaten, it's too late and you ordered another burger or worse yet, more fries."

"You want to order another burger?" Maddie put the last French fry in her mouth.

"Nah. I shouldn't overdo it. I'll order a regular cheeseburger, not a double."

"You're a terrible influence. Order one for me, too."

I told Maddie about my aunt's situation on the drive back because I didn't want to take away her focus on that house. After all, that was the reason we drove there in the first place.

Maddie all but came to a grinding stop on Carefree Highway when I said my aunt was a person of interest. She adjusted the visor and glanced at me. "Deputy Vincent always leads with the worst-case scenario. You know that."

"But he must have a reason."

"Sure. Your aunt knew the victim. Big deal. He probably said that to eke out information from her. I wouldn't lose any sleep over it."

The rational part of my brain said Maddie was right, but the "let-your-imagination-go-wild" part begged to differ. As it turned out, my imagination beat my rationalization by a long shot.

When we got back, she dropped me off at The Char-Board to pick up my car, and then we both headed to my place. We were bloated and miserable, with no real evidence of anything sinister going on in that house. Except perhaps on odd and unpleasant smell that Maddie hadn't caught prior.

"Strange," she said when we first noticed it, "I hadn't detected that odor before, and it's not as if there's any kitchen or bathroom garbage in here. The place was cleaned. I'll have the gas and water companies check it out. Yuck! Hope it's not a gas leak or a sewage issue."

"Maybe the heating system?" I offered at the time. "Those systems always have an odor when they first start up. And, it *is* November."

"I'll keep my fingers crossed that it's nothing. Meanwhile, I intend to formulate a plan to find out if any of the buyers sabotaged a sale or, worse yet, threatened someone. Anyway, I need to get going. I've got a super early showing in Tempe tomorrow morning. At seven. Can you believe it?

The buyer has to be at his lab by nine and wants to allow enough time to scrutinize the place. You know what that means, don't you?"

"Fussbudget."

"I'm sure." We both laughed and sunk into the couch where we commiserated for a good half hour before Maddie had to be on her way. I walked her out with Speedbump nuzzling her legs.

"Text me later when your aunt gets back." She bent down and rubbed the hound's head before taking off.

"Guess that's just us, buddy," I gave the dog another head rub, and he trotted behind me to the kitchen. I imagined by now my parents and my aunt were dining on authentic Italian food while I was left to scrummage through the fridge for mine. No matter. I doubted I'd be hungry after filling up on burgers.

Reaching for my phone, I texted Ian: *Call me if you're not too busy at work.*

Seconds later, he was on the line. "Hey, was going to call you later when I got home. Everything okay?"

"I suppose. I didn't want to call in case you were knee-deep at the restaurant."

"Monday nights are notoriously slow. Even worse is Sterling wandering in and out of the kitchen."

"Is that unusual?'

"It is when he stands in the middle of the prep area, lamenting about Richard Bellmore's death. He's been muttering, 'freak accident' every few minutes. It's like this night will never end."

"Um, it may not be an accident. Deputy Vincent paid me a visit. My aunt is a person of interest. They don't have persons of interest unless there's a criminal investigation. And accidents don't constitute criminal investigations."

"Oh no. Did he say why?"

"Nope. She's got to report to his office tomorrow morning. I haven't even told her. She's dining out with my folks, and I didn't want to ruin their evening. When she gets in, I'll break the news. Then she can break it to my parents."

"Let me know what happens. I take it you're going with her, right?"

"For sure. I'll be holding my breath she doesn't incriminate herself. Especially after all those verbal altercations she and Richard had. And I really need to be there so I can hear exactly what Deputy Vincent says, not Aunt Regina's stylized and exaggerated version."

"Good idea. Listen, I'm sure you've thought of this, but there may be a possibility she won't be able to leave on Wednesday. We'll have to play things by ear."

"Like me sneaking over to your place in the middle of the night like college kids?"

"I'll beat you to it! These past few days have been so weird. Uh-oh. Got to run. Sterling just made his umpteenth entrance. Miss you. I'll text and call you in the morning. Hugs."

"And kisses." I ended the call and plopped down on the couch. With an overhand reach, I grabbed the remote and turned on the late news in time for the weather report. Snow forecast for the high country and highs in the low seventies for the valley. My eyes drifted to the scrolling news that included a shooting in the West Valley and a wrong-way driver on the I-10. I anticipated more of the same and was about to channel surf when the next line rattled me worse than Edith in a foul mood.

The scroll read: *Author Richard Bellmore's death declared a homicide.*

I blinked, and it was off the screen but emblazoned in my head. *A homicide.* So much for clumsiness. I figured Sterling's 'freak accident' chant would now be replaced by 'murder.' I rubbed my temples and tried to organize my thoughts when the door flew open and I heard my aunt's voice.

"Katie! What a marvelous evening. The pasta primavera was spectacular, and their Sorrentino was to die for."

Not the best word, tonight, Aunt Regina.

I turned and faked a smile. "Sounds wonderful. What time are you meeting Mom tomorrow?"

"Hmm, mid-morning. We decided to sleep in before the art museum. We're not spring chickens anymore."

"Good. Because, well, uh, er—"

"What's the matter? You look as if you're about to deliver a death sentence."

"In a manner of speaking, yeah. Deputy Vincent came into The Char-Board today looking for you. I fielded him off, but you'll need to meet with him at 9:00 in his office tomorrow."

"Why on earth? I already gave one of those deputies my statement."

"Aunt Regina, he said you were a person of interest in Richard's death. Um, I don't suppose you caught the evening news, but it's no longer a death, it's a homicide."

"And they think *I* might be the responsible party? That deputy better have a darned good reason for ruining my museum day. A 'person-of-interest,' my you-know-what."

"There's one more thing. You'll need to tell my folks before they find out from the news. The fact you were Richard's editor will keep this thing in the limelight for quite a while."

"Not if I can help it. Heavens. Even dead, that man managed to get under my skin."

Chapter Sixteen

Tuesday

I woke up the next morning to find Edith admiring her nails as she sat at the foot of my bed.

"Good grief, Edith! How long have you been there?" I sat up and looked around. Speedbump was still sleeping next to me, oblivious to the third party who had joined us.

"Don't you just love this peach color on my nails? It's a perfect match for this little number." She stood and let the long peachy-cream gown fall in straight lines to the floor.

"Not at four in the morning. I've got to get to work and explain to the crew why I need to leave during the breakfast rush. And I have no idea how long my aunt will be detained."

"If by 'detained,' you mean one step away from the Fourth Avenue Jail, I'd be concerned too. Rosaline filled me in. Thought I'd fill in the missing details with you this morning."

"If you hadn't taken off to rummage through gowns, or whatever shiny objects caught your attention, you'd know she's being questioned as a person of interest in Richard's murder. Yes, murder. I think you missed that detail as well."

"I may be in spirit form, but I can't be everywhere."

"A murder under my nose should have been your number one priority."

"Not when my body itched from that burlap."

"Never mind. Is there any chance you can poke around and find out who fast-tracked him into the next realm?"

"Not really. It's a complicated maze up there."

"Ask around. Someone is bound to know something."

Edith let out a sigh as if I'd asked her to wear dungarees for a month. "I suppose."

"Did Rosaline mention the house Maddie walked me through? At least *she* had the goodness to show up and tell me it wasn't haunted."

"Rosaline is garnering Brownie points." Edith stretched out her hand and studied her nails again.

"She's doing a good job." I threw the covers off and started for the bathroom. "Boundaries. I need to get ready for work. Next time, give me a 'heads-up' before you split."

"Okay, fine. I'm leaving now." And then, poof! It was just Speedbump and me. And I had to hustle to The Char-Board.

"These jalapeño and cheese turnovers are practically flying out of here," Javie said. "What do you think about adding a few more variations? We've got an assortment of cheeses, meats, and veggies."

We were in the middle of the breakfast rush and moving at breakneck speed to get everyone served before the next onslaught. I had just taken a few orders and handed them to him.

"Uh, sure."

"You don't sound convinced."

"It's not that. I can't seem to focus, given my aunt's predicament. Trouble is, she refuses to take it seriously."

"Ten minutes with Deputy Vincent and she'll take it seriously," Lilly-Ann called out from the other side of the kitchen.

"I really hate leaving all of you. Especially since Matt won't get in until ten."

"We'll be fine," Javie and Lilly-Ann replied in unison.

"I know. And I appreciate it."

It was hard to believe that in the short time I'd been running The Char-

Board we'd have a crew that worked so well. I was fortunate that Lilly-Ann and Matt had been employed here when it was a sandwich shop, so they knew their way around. As for Javie, I still marvel that I came across such a burgeoning chef, even though he was less than a year away from graduating college and looking into business schools for graduate studies.

I loaded a few plates into the dishwasher, hung my apron on the peg near the back door, and threw on my fall jacket. "If I'm not back by noon, send for the militia."

"Deputy Vincent *is* the militia," Javie laughed.

"Don't remind me." Three seconds later, I was out the door and headed to my car. It was a quick drive from the restaurant, and my aunt assured me she'd be at the sheriff's office on time. And I assured her that she wouldn't have any trouble finding it. It was a large complex on North Cave Creek Road just below East Skyline Drive on one side, and East Paseo Drive on the other. Easy-peasy. I also told her that it was across the road from Oreganos restaurant in case she needed a focal point.

My phone pinged just as I slid into a parking space a few yards from the entrance, and I was relieved that it was Ian: *Text me after your aunt meets with Deputy Vincent. Tell her if she thinks it's getting dicey to stop and request legal counsel.*

I texted back: *Thanks. Already one step ahead. I had her call her attorney from New Jersey just in case.*

Ian: *And?*

I left before she called

Okay. Keep me posted. Miss you!

Me too!

The November chill was more bracing than I remembered from last year, and I wished I'd taken a scarf. Instead, I speedwalked into the building and once through the metal detector and sign-in, asked if there was a vending machine that sold coffee.

The deputy on duty looked at me as if I requested a dose of castor oil. "You may want to just get a Coke. Same caffeine but recognizable."

"Thanks for the warning." I smiled and proceeded to Deputy Vincent's office, keeping my fingers crossed my aunt would be there. The signage in the corridor was crystal clear, and I found myself in the waiting area of his suite in less than a minute.

I introduced myself to the receptionist behind a glass window, signed another sheet, and perused it for my aunt's name. No such luck. Fidgeting with my phone apps, I considered texting her, but just as I was about to open the app, she walked in.

"Hi Katie! This better not take too long. I could go for a cappuccino and a fruit-filled turnover or maybe a nice scone. I only had time for a quick coffee from the McDonald's drive-through."

That's more than me.

"I hope so, too, but something tells me it may be somewhat complicated. Did you speak with your lawyer?"

"With his paralegal. She said to wait until I get an official notice that I'm being charged with something."

Better keep her on speed dial.

Before I could respond, the deputy called out my aunt's name. "Deputy Vincent will see you now. It's straight ahead." He pointed to a door directly across from the desk, and I stood as if I was being directed to the principal's office. My aunt, on the other hand, bounced across the room like a gazelle.

Cappuccino my foot! She'll be lucky with tap water.

Deputy Vincent's office was as austere and unwelcoming as it was the last time I was here. Posters warning about drug abuse, a large MCSO calendar, and furniture in varied shades of military green and gray. He stood from behind his desk and motioned for us to take a seat in front.

"Good Morning, Ms. Aubrey," he said to my aunt. "I see you've brought your niece with you." Then he nodded to me.

I smiled. "Yes. I trust that will be all right."

"For this meeting, it will be. I'll try to be as clear and succinct as possible. As you're aware, my office is investigating the death of Richard Bellmore, which is now classified as a homicide."

My aunt shifted in her seat. "I don't understand what that has to do with me. I already gave my statement to one of the deputies at the time of the incident."

Deputy Vincent donned a pair of disposable gloves and opened a manila envelope, pulling out a gold chain bracelet with a small circular charm on it. "Does this look familiar?"

My aunt reached out to grab it. "My bracelet! Where did you find it? Is that what this is about? I thought I'd lost it. True, it's 18 karat gold, but it has sentimental value as well as its monetary value."

"Are you sure this is yours?" He held it in front of her so she could look at the charm.

"It's mine. My name is on that charm. Regina. On the back, there's a date. The date I got my first job as an editor."

The deputy returned it to the envelope. "When did you notice it was missing?"

"Not until I got home Saturday night. I went to remove it and saw it was gone. The clasp must have gotten undone. Why?"

"Ms. Aubrey, that charm was found at the bottom of the waterfall at the library where Richard's body was discovered. Right now, it is considered evidence."

"Evidence?" I thought my aunt would jump out of her seat. "Evidence of what? A clasp that came apart? I was seated near the waterfall and must have walked past it to the buffet. I probably got too close to the water, and the bracelet slipped in. Can you return it now?"

The deputy shook his head. "I don't think you understand. That bracelet is considered evidence of a possible altercation that led to Richard Bellmore's demise."

"Are you saying you think I killed him?" My aunt looked at the deputy and then at me.

"I'm saying that this is a criminal investigation, and you are considered a person of interest. Unless further evidence can be obtained, that is where it now stands."

"Um," I gulped. "What further evidence?"

Deputy Vincent returned the bracelet to the envelope. "That is for the forensic office to determine. In addition, we are still awaiting the full toxicology screen."

"What about my bracelet?" Aunt Regina asked.

She's worried about her bracelet? When she could be a suspect in a murder? Good grief! I'm not a suspect so why does my heart feel like it's about to bounce out of my chest?

"It will remain as evidence for the time being. You'll need to fill in a property claim at the front desk before you leave. Now then, if you don't mind, I have a few more questions."

My aunt lifted her shoulders and let out a sigh. "Fine."

"What was your relationship with Mr. Bellmore?"

"I am, er, *was,* his editor. He was under contract with my publisher."

"I see. According to information I've gathered, you were observed having words with Mr. Bellmore on at least two occasions at the library event. Care to expound on that?"

I tried to shoot my aunt a look that would indicate *no,* but she didn't pay attention to me.

"It was a professional discussion regarding the sloppy work he delivered to my desk. The man objected to my edits and said they were 'insane.' His word, certainly not mine. Frankly, if we, as editors, don't step in to address these things, the reputation of our publishing houses would drop like the New Year's Eve ball on Times Square."

"I understand. Now then, I'd like to go over the timeline with you. When was the last time you saw Mr. Bellmore?"

My aunt shrugged. "I suppose when we had that last conversation at the banquet. Hmm, it was actually in the corridor by the restrooms. I neglected to mention that. Again, it was business-related. I suggested he use a ghostwriter, and the man went ballistic. Verbally ballistic."

"Is that all?"

"If by *all,* you're implying something physical, you can forget it. It was a verbal disagreement. Nothing more."

"What about when the banquet ended?"

"I went my way, and I assumed he did the same. I didn't find out about his death until the next morning."

"One last thing, Ms. Aubrey. One of the attendees said they heard you say something about wanting to shove the deceased into the waterfall if you had been seated next to him. Is that true?"

"I may have said something of the sort. We were having words, that's all. And we were in the hallway, not near the waterfall."

The deputy jotted down something and looked up. "At this time, you're free to go."

"I'm scheduled to fly back to New Jersey tomorrow," my aunt said.

Deputy Vincent's response was well-rehearsed. "Unless criminal charges are filed against you between now and then, you're free to leave the state."

I kept my sigh of relief to myself, but inwardly, I did somersaults.

"Come on, Aunt Regina, I need to get back to work."

My aunt stood and leaned over the table. "Don't lose my bracelet. One can't put a price on sentimentality."

The deputy pinched his shoulder blades. "Or a price on evidence."

Chapter Seventeen

Tuesday

That was the morning, and while I held out hope that there wouldn't be sufficient evidence to move my aunt from person-of-interest to genuine *suspect,* the logical side of my brain screamed for me to do something. I cowered at the thought Aunt Regina would remain at my house while the investigation continued.

Someone once said that guests in your house are like fish. They begin to stink after three days. And that's under normal circumstances. This wasn't. It was as if someone put shackles on my wrists and not hers.

I texted Ian when I got back to The Char-Board. Meanwhile, my aunt drove off to spend her museum day with my mother, seemingly unperturbed about her conversation with Deputy Vincent.

My text was as direct as could be: *MSCO is making a case against my aunt. DV didn't say it outright, but I knew what he was doing. Call me when you can.*

Ten minutes later, Ian phoned. "It doesn't sound good. Tell me what happened."

I explained about the bracelet, the questioning, and the fact my aunt was overheard making a threat about shoving Richard into the waterfall.

"She really needs to get legal counsel. These things have a way of escalating fast."

"If we're lucky, she'll be on a plane to Hoboken tomorrow night, and if she has to return, she can stay with my parents."

"I'll keep my fingers crossed, but let's not get ahead of ourselves. She and Richard had a stormy relationship, albeit a business one. Still, murder is murder, and that's all the sheriff's office cares about. What's worse is if they set their sights on one person to the exclusion of other possible suspects."

"Are you saying what I think you are?"

"I guess so. Time to get our hands dirty with a little sleuthing of our own. I've got a few hours off until five. Any chance we can meet at a Starbucks between Randolph's Escapade and The Char-Board?"

"For sure. Let's do the one on East Lincoln Drive in Scottsdale. It's closer for you, and I don't need to get back to work like you do."

"Thanks, hon. Sounds good. Three thirty, okay?"

"Perfect."

I let my crew know what happened, and everyone agreed that I needed to do something before "the you-know-what" hit the fan.

"If there's anything we can do," Javie said. "Let us know."

"He's right." Lilly-Ann looked up from the peppers she was chopping.

"Yeah," Matt chimed in. "As long as I don't have a class at that time."

Lilly-Ann reached for a dish towel and swatted him. "Big help you are!"

"All of you are a great help," I said. "And I'll need it."

At three fifteen, I pulled into the Starbucks parking lot. The sun had come out, and it was the warmest part of the day. Nonetheless, I still needed a jacket and a scarf. Ian was already inside and seated to the left in a small alcove.

"I ordered you a hot mocha latte with whip. Hope that's okay."

"Anything mocha is more than okay." I leaned over and gave him a quick smooch on the cheek.

He smiled and pointed to my notebook. "Good. The trusty murder map book has arrived."

"This used to be for recipes. So much for that." I planted myself next to him and pulled out a pen. "Might as well list the suspects and go from there."

No sooner did I jot down Arist Arnet, Wilsetta Frum, and KC Camplin when Ian's name was called and he stood to retrieve our drinks.

"Add Jessica Loundry to the list," he said. He handed me my drink and sat. "Lots of grumbling about coming in second for the Claremont Award. Blamed Richard."

"She made an accusation that Richard bribed the judges. Javie and I overheard them in the corridor during the event."

"You two weren't the only ones. One of my crew overheard them as well and shared the scuttlebutt."

"It's not exactly a burning hot motive for murder, but then again, people kill for any number of reasons. Who else do we think is a suspect?"

"What about Richard's fiancée? Trouble in paradise?"

"We'll put her name down. It's Arist's ex-wife. That's why I put him on the list. Jealousy and all of that."

"Anyone else?" Ian widened his eyes and looked at me.

"Not that I know of. This list is substantial enough. We've got five players. Now we've got to figure out how to go about finding the truth."

"Figure it out quickly. I want my room back." In the blink of an eye, a mossy green haze enveloped the table, and when Edith's form gradually materialized, she was wearing Vivien Leigh's iconic green "curtain gown." I kept all remarks to myself as Edith continued to speak. "And 'by quickly,' I mean get moving on those suspects who'll be flying the friendly skies back home. That's right, Missy. You'd better check them out before they check out. And you can thank me later."

"You okay?" Ian asked. "You've got a glazed look on your face."

"Deep in thought, that's all. We'd better find out where they're staying or if they've already headed home. Let's hope not all of them reside in other states, or countries, like Dame Judith Symth. I read she resides in London, but no matter. She was never a suspect. No motive that we know of, and besides, she's in her nineties. I doubt she'd have the physical strength for a strong shove." I took a sip of my latte and pressed my lips together to absorb the whipped cream.

"How do you propose we do that? Other than going through the back jackets of their recent books. You know, 'the author resides in Hurst, Texas, with his wife and two Irish wolfhounds,' or something to that effect."

"I'll stop at Desert Foothills and find out from Allison. I'll also see if she's heard anything else." I opened the notebook and listed the five names to the left of three vertical columns—motive, means, and opportunity. Below that, I drew a circle and listed the names again, this time for a connections diagram. That's when I heard Edith's voice again.

"You're not sketching out a charcuterie design, you're figuring out who's connected to whom. Just draw lines like you did in grade school. And put your notes on the bottom. Legible, this time. Your murder maps give me eye strain."

"Eye strain?" The words just slipped out.

Ian glanced at the notebook. "Nah, I can figure out your writing. Take a camera shot and text it to me later."

Just then, my phone vibrated, and the caller ID read MCSO. I showed it to Ian and bit my lower lip before answering. If he did begin the call with a greeting, it didn't register, because all I heard was, "…could not reach your aunt. Please inform her to cancel her flight tomorrow. She will need to reschedule it. Our office has acquired some new evidence. Have her call me ASAP."

"I heard that," Ian said. He reached for my hand and squeezed it. "He didn't use the word *arrest '* or the word *suspect.* I suppose that's a good thing."

"For who?" Edith shouted into the air. "It means that overbearing, fastidious woman will be sleeping in the guest bedroom indefinitely, and I'll be relegated to the couch."

"Don't say indefinitely."

Ian placed his palm on my chin and moved my face toward him. "Not if we can help it."

Chapter Eighteen

Tuesday

I swallowed and took in his words. *Not if we can help it.* "At least one of our suspects lives right here in Cave Creek—Wilsetta Frum. The crazed fan that Richard tried to avoid during the entire event. It's a possibility, you know. Obsessed fans live in an alternate universe when it comes to their idols. Maybe she found out about his engagement and decided that if she couldn't have Richard, no one should, or could."

"Yeah, I've seen that plot on more TV dramas than I care to admit, and, believe it or not, in the news when it involved domestic situations that turned deadly. Wilsetta certainly belongs on that list, but since she's a local, let's see if Allison knows how long the others will be in town."

"I'm on it, right now." I took the last sip of my mocha, and he did the same with his drink.

"And I'm on my way back to Randolph's. Um, you *are* aware that my boss falls under that crazed fan category as well, but he's as harmless as a cottontail bunny."

"A neurotic cottontail bunny, but yeah, harmless." We walked out together and agreed to catch up on the phone later. "I'll text you what I find out about the other authors and where they're staying, but we'll have to figure out a way to eke information out of them. And do it in a way that doesn't have Deputy Vincent hauling us in for hindering an investigation."

Ian winked, and I knew he'd be onboard with most anything. "I seriously wonder how the Hardy Boys did it."

"I don't. They were fictional."

We both laughed and headed to our cars. Minutes later, I was at Desert Foothills Library, chatting with Allison in the comfy reception area. Given the dark circles under her eyes that the concealer missed, I knew she hadn't slept well.

"I'm still in shock, Katie, and trying to process this. It's been a strange scenario, especially fielding calls from patrons who want to know if it's safe to come to the library, as well as curiosity seekers who want to know what I know, and that's not much. I finally decided to put a message on our phone line explaining that the library was deemed safe and that all questions about Richard Bellmore's unfortunate demise need to be directed to the sheriff's office or the marshal's office. Anyway, how can I help you?"

I explained the situation with my aunt and the fact that the sheriff's office has deemed her a person of interest. "She's bold and often tactless," I said, "not to mention bossy and self-righteous, but she's no killer. She'd rather annoy you to death with her sarcastic comments."

Allison chuckled, and I continued. "I'm really concerned she'll be MCSO's primary suspect due to the circumstantial evidence. And now, I believe there might be more."

"The forensic technicians have been in and out of the patio area for the past day and a half, but I have no idea what they may or may not have discovered."

"I was hoping some of the authors at the event may still be in town, and I really need to see what they may or may not know." *Or if they had a motive for murder.* "It may help my aunt."

"As I recall, they were pretty open about where they were staying. Hold on a minute, I'll pull it up on my phone. As far as I know, only Dame Judith Symth has left the area. We were so fortunate that she was able to make an appearance. She's got a gala in London later in the week."

"How were you able to get her to accept the invitation? She's practically iconic."

"As a matter of fact, it was KC Camplin who was in touch with her. Seems he did her a favor once when they were at a mystery conference in Toronto two years ago. He convinced her that her presence at our author event would enable a small library to reach more readers. Frankly, no one was more surprised than me when she said yes."

"I see." *That must have been one heck of a favor to get her to leave London.*

I looked at the entrance doors and watched as two ladies entered. They moved slowly and cautiously as if they were crossing a minefield. Allison was right. People were edgy.

"Here it is. The information on where the authors are staying." Allison pulled up her notes from her cell phone. "Did you want to write it down or put it on your phone?"

I reached for my iPhone. "Got to love technology. Better than scraps of paper."

"For sure. It's like my second brain. Here goes: Kleo is staying at the Prickly Pear Inn right down the block. He leaves on Friday for Wyoming."

"Kleo?"

"Oh, I'm sorry. KC Camplin. The pen name for Kleo Carl Camplin."

"I forgot about pen names."

"That's the only one. Jessica Loundry and Lida Singleton are rooming together at the Scottsdale Fairmont Princess. They're leaving on Saturday for Minnesota. Barbara Beau-Wilton has quite the summer home in Castle Rock, Colorado, but she winters near Lake Pleasant, so she's in the area."

"What about Arist Arnet?"

"Hmm, how about that? He's at the Prickly Pear as well, but he didn't say how long he'd be in the area. Not that I'm telling you what to do, but the Prickly Pear has a happy hour that begins in a few minutes, and I wouldn't be surprised if you find one or both gentlemen there."

"Excellent idea. Thanks. I just don't need the worry hanging over my head. Although my aunt seems unperturbed about it."

"Yes. I got that impression from her as well."

I looked around and leaned toward Allison. "Do you have any idea who could have killed Richard? Could it have been something he wrote that hit a nerve with a reader?"

Allison shook her head. "Not that I'm aware, and I've read all of his books. They're the boilerplate thrillers. Nothing that would raise an eyebrow. Just a lot of suspense and page-turning. No mention of anything controversial or any characters who could be thin disguises for someone prominent."

"I appreciate your help. Like I said, I need to take a broader look before my aunt gets pigeon-holed into a corner."

"Good luck. And let me know if there's anything else I can do."

"I will. And please, visit us at The Char-Board. Breakfast will be on me."

As I walked to my car, I kept my fingers crossed I'd see KC or Arist at the bar. I needed a venue where conversation would come easily, especially after drinks. As I started the engine, I pulled out my phone and texted Ian: *Off to good start, I hope. KC and Arist are down the road at the Prickly Pear Inn. Time for happy hour!*

He texted back with a fingers-crossed emoji and the words: *Order a Coke.* Then a laugh emoji.

The Prickly Pear Inn was a western boutique inn on Cave Creek's main drag and featured southwestern-style rooms with modern amenities. It also boasted an amazing view of Black Mountain and easy accessibility to shops and restaurants. Its patio area was vibrant and welcoming to tourists as well as locals. Taking a breath when I parked behind the building, I walked past the mercantile shop and headed directly for the inn's patio and bar.

"How do you intend to break the ice, Missy? If you're not careful, those lechers will think you're coming on to them."

The green haze intensified, and I spun my head to see Edith a few steps behind me.

"Don't sneak up on me like that? In fact, don't sneak up on me at all!"

"I'm not sneaking up. I'm offering advice. What did you plan on doing?"

"I, um, er…"

"That's what I thought. You don't have a plan. Well, lucky for you, I do. I've been around the track more than once, so take notes."

"Edith, your track got you in limbo, or whatever you call it. I'll play it by ear."

"Better get a tuning fork because that's KC over there, guzzling a draft."

Sure enough, Edith was right. Kleo, or KC, sat at a corner table on the patio, and lucky for me, he sat solo.

"Now or never, Miss 'Play-it-by-ear.'"

I approached the bar, ordered a toxic water with lime, because I thought it could pass as a "real drink," and walked to KC's table, drink in hand. He looked up and tilted his head. "You look familiar. Have we met?"

"I catered the library event this past weekend along with other restaurants. I'm Katie Aubrey from The Char-Board."

"Oh yeah. Those charcuteries. Good stuff."

"Thanks. Mind if I sit for a few minutes? I thought I'd catch an afternoon break."

KC motioned to the seat next to his. "Make yourself comfortable. And tell me the real reason you're here."

The guy didn't waste any time. "Fine," I said. "I need to rid myself of a house guest and the only way I can do that is to find out who murdered Richard Bellmore."

"Go on. Sounds like an interesting plot if you ask me. I'm sure my agent would agree. Sid's always on the lookout for a new twist."

"In a nutshell, my aunt's bracelet was found in the water underneath his body. Naturally, she's a person of interest."

"Was she acquainted with Richard?"

"And then some. She was his editor."

It was only a nanosecond, but KC winced, and it was unmistakable. "Regina, right?"

I nodded as he continued. "Richard mentioned her. Followed by the words *harpy, she-witch, and harridan.*"

"Did he say anything else?"

"Uh-huh. Said she'd sacrifice him to the gods if she didn't get her way on his edits."

"He had to have been joking."

"Don't think so. I've known him for a long time, and trust me, the guy was dead serious. *Dead* serious. Too bad he had a contract that stipulated he couldn't change editors. Yeesh! Truth be known, I got burned once. It was early on in my writing career, and after that, I made sure Sid put in a clause that allowed me to change editors if the situation was untenable."

"Live and learn, I suppose."

"Got that right."

Chapter Nineteen

Tuesday

I took a sip of my drink and prayed KC didn't relay any information to one of the deputies during the questioning. "People make all sorts of comments and threats, but rarely do they come to fruition."

"Well, not saying your aunt had anything to do with it, but something sure happened."

Just then, a waitress walked by and he flagged her down. "Bring me another draft, will you?" KC opened his wallet and handed her a twenty. A purple and maroon business card was clearly visible on the opposite side with a book logo on it. I figured it had to have come from one of the other presenters, most likely in the cozy category due to its whimsical design.

"Did you know the other authors well?" I asked.

"I've done signings with Jessica before, and as you've probably surmised, Richard and I go way back. Conferences, media events, book signings, that sort of thing. As for the others, I've chatted with them at events, but that's about it."

"Do you know of anyone who had it *in* for Richard? Other than my aunt."

"Richard's bravado was a bit of a turnoff, but that wouldn't justify killing the guy. It had to be personal. And the only personal thing that comes to mind is his engagement to Arist's ex. Who knows? Maybe Arist is still holding out hope they can reconcile. He's staying at this inn, you know. Maybe you can wrangle it out of him. Doubt the deputies got anywhere."

"Thanks. Does he show up for happy hour?"

"He's not a drinker. More than likely, you'll find him in the open mercantile area, reading the paper. He's one of the few throwbacks who do that. Me? I prefer my news short and sweet on a phone app. I may be a baby boomer, but I'm not a dinosaur."

"I like my news the same way I like my coffee—ready to go!"

He laughed, and I thanked him again for his time. *One down, four to go.*

Stepping out to the mercantile area, I moved to a corner and shot off another text to Ian: *Chatted with KC. He pointed to Arist. And now the game begins. Later. Hugs!*

Ian followed up with a gif that showed a chaotic kitchen. Then another gif of a man crying a river. It didn't take a genius to figure out Sterling was not handling Richard's death well.

Muted lamp light made the mercantile area look like a postcard scene touting the southwest. Ocotillos in planters, assorted cacti, and a few decorative planters in the shapes of desert animals. A few guests were enjoying the evening sunset, and I perused the area in hopes that Arist would be one of them.

Sure enough, KC knew Arist's habits. In the far corner, wedged between a bronze statue of a javalina and a small barrel cactus, Arist sat at a bistro table with a newspaper spread out in front of him. On the wall behind him was a hanging light that gave off enough illumination to read every word. I thanked my lucky stars he hadn't left town since Allison wasn't sure of his plans.

"Be direct. No sense lollygagging around, Missy. I suggest a simple sentence like, 'Guess you don't have to fret about the competition anymore.'"

"That's horrible. Perfectly horrible. Who would say a thing like that?" I kept my voice low and hoped no one saw me converse with no visible party in sight.

"Anyone who wants to solve a murder without waiting for the next millennium."

"Don't hover over me. I did perfectly fine with KC."

"Wouldn't know. Rosaline wanted me to scour the intake area with her."

"And?"

"No sign of Richard."

"Do you think he went straight down to—"

"Doubt it. Usually, they stick around if their departure was hastened. Take me, for instance. I had the unfortunate—"

"No. I *had* the unfortunate…oh never mind. I'm going over there. Stay back."

Fat chance.

I ambled over to Arist and tried not to sound too lame. "Hi! Anything exciting in the news? Other than Richard Bellmore's death. I was at the library event this weekend and recognized you."

Arist looked up from his paper as if he was about to swat a fly that annoyed him. "The usual. I don't remember seeing you at any of the sessions. Then again, all the faces begin to blur after a while."

"That's because I'm not a reader. I mean, I *do* read, but I was there for my business. I catered the charcuteries. You know, the large boards with assorted cured meats, cheese, and other accoutrements."

"Yeah, I know. My wife used to make cheese boards all the time for social gatherings. Nothing as fancy as yours, but pretty good with crackers, cheeses, and pepperoni. Sometimes even salami and olives."

"Used to? She stopped making them?"

"She stopped everything. We're divorced."

"Oh, I'm sorry."

"Want to hear the kicker?" He went on before I could respond. "She got hooked up with Richard Bellmore. Met him at one of the writers' conferences we attended, and who knew? They were seeing each other behind my back three months later."

"Ew. That's awful."

"What's really awful is that they got engaged. Now I suppose all eyes are on me for his murder since I had the jealousy motive going."

"I take it they weren't wrong?"

"Oh, I was jealous all right, but not so jealous as to murder him. Stupid, I'm not. Why would I want a life behind bars? That's what I told that craggy deputy who questioned the daylights out of me. Travis something or other."

"Vincent. Travis Vincent. He's the lead deputy in this area. Um, by any chance did he request you stick around Cave Creek?"

"Nope. Said he had my contact information, and if they needed me, they'd know where to find me. I'm staying here a few more days before I fly home. Figured I'd get away from the winter cold for a while."

"Where's home?"

"Colorado Springs. And get this—Richard resides, um, *resided* in Castle Rock. That's only forty miles away. A really doable drive."

"Have you spoken with your ex-wife since Richard's death?"

Arist nodded. "I called her. Figured someone should break the news. Long story short—she already knew but didn't share that info with me. She flew out here yesterday, but we haven't talked since."

"Did she say where she's staying?"

"Boulders Villa in Carefree. We stayed there once before for a friend's wedding."

Boulders Villa. That's not too far from Ian's condo.

My mind clicked off information like a grocery checklist. "Mr. Arnst, do you have any idea who would want to kill Richard?"

Arist fiddled with the sharp tip of his turquoise bolo. Typical western attire, only Arist didn't fit the profile, especially with the style he had chosen. Then, with a shake of the head, he answered my question. "He was a haughty sort of a guy and thought his you-know-what didn't stink, but no, I don't."

I told him about my aunt, but he was already acquainted with her. At least on paper, via a manuscript rejection she had given him a few years back. Still, not a motive in my book.

"If you can think of anything that may absolve my aunt, please call or text me." I handed him The Char-Board's business card and invited him to drop in, promising a free meal.

"Thanks. Nice talking with you. Miss..."

"Aubrey. Like my aunt."

When I finally got home, Speedbump was all over me. Wasting no time, I fed him and put him on his leash for a quick walk. Aunt Regina was with my folks, and I relished the small window of time I had without her in the house.

As I closed the front door and walked down the block, the billowy beige haze that I'd come to recognize as Rosaline's appeared, followed by her lighthearted voice. "Edith spied Richard and slipped into a different realm or layer to have a tête-à-tête with him."

"Can she do that?"

"Apparently, she did. Now let's see if she can get out."

Chapter Twenty

Tuesday, Wednesday

Exhausted, I crept into bed early but left a note for my aunt and taped it to the guestroom door. "See you in the morning. Reschedule your flight! Deputy Vincent contacted me. They have new evidence and need to see you again. Let your lawyer know. Pleasant dreams."

The next morning, I found my aunt at the kitchen table at the tail end of a conversation. I heard her say the words *bail bondsman* and *retainer*. Maybe she took it seriously this time.

"Good Morning, Katie," she said when she put her cell phone on the table and picked up a donut from the Entenmann's box. "You'll be happy to know I called my lawyer. Honestly, I can't imagine what new evidence that office came up with."

"It could be something a witness saw. I chatted with KC and Arist yesterday in the hope that one of them might have had a more compelling motive to do away with Richard."

"And?" my aunt looked up from her coffee.

"No such luck. But Richard's ex is in town and I intend to snoop around."

"That's so sweet of you to step in and exonerate me if it comes to that."

"I'm not exonerating you. You haven't been charged." *Yet.* "I'm trying to find the real killer so we can get on with our lives."

"Oh, I intend to go on, all right. Before I called my lawyer, I called my building's superintendent. She's shipping me a number of things from my office that I'll need in order to continue my work here. Darned good thing Loralee is conversant with flash drives and Word docs. She's overnighting a number of files. Which brings me to another question—Do you have a computer I can commandeer for as long as I remain here?"

All I heard was, "Continue my work here."

"Huh? What?"

"You know, I'll need my own office space. It's really a shame this is a two-bedroom house. We'll have to think of something."

Yes! Find her guilty! Guilty as charged. Lots of work space in the Fourth Avenue Jail.

"Let's not get ahead of ourselves. You need to find out what Deputy Vincent alluded to. Call his office while I grab a coffee and get ready for work." I plopped a K-Cup in the Keurig, tossed some kibble into Speedbump's bowl, and changed his water. Then I got into the shower and got dressed for The Char-Board.

"That deputy is driving over here right now. At least I have foundation on and got dressed early." My aunt announced it as if a friend was dropping by and not someone with a possible arrest warrant in hand.

"Right now? Right this minute?"

"That's what I said. I get the feeling he thinks I'll skip town."

We should be so lucky.

"Give me a second." I texted Lilly-Ann and asked her to open The Char-Board and let Javie know what's going on. Matt would be in later, and I doubted he'd arrive before I did. Then, I grabbed a donut and braced myself for what was to come.

Sure enough, no sooner had I consumed the chocolatey treat and washed it down with coffee when I heard the rap on the door. "Remember, Aunt Regina, don't divulge anything at this point. See what he has to say."

"I don't have anything to divulge."

I opened the door and let the deputy inside. My aunt called out, "Good Morning!" and he returned the greeting, not budging from his spot.

"I'll be brief, Ms. Aubrey," he said as he looked directly at my aunt. "The completed autopsy on Richard Bellmore revealed something that wasn't initially seen at the preliminary post-mortem. And while Mr. Bellmore succumbed to electrocution and drowning, the coroner discovered a possible reason for this, other than the victim tripping over the lamp cords."

"Not poisoning!" I blurted out.

"You can take a breath, Miss Aubrey. He wasn't poisoned. He was, however, found to have a loss of hair follicles on the side of his head, indicative of someone literally pulling the hair out of him."

"Couldn't he have just been going bald?" I asked.

"Not according to the coroner."

My aunt, who had been quiet up until that moment, all but leapt from her seat at the table. "And you think I pulled his hair out, causing him to trip and fall?"

"Actually, our forensic lab discovered two strands of Richard's hair wrapped around that gold bracelet of yours. They sent it for DNA testing, and it was confirmed to be his. That begs the question—how did two strands of hair get wrapped around your bracelet, Ms. Aubrey?"

"Poor drainage in that waterfall pond? I didn't put them there. Like I told you, my bracelet's clasp must have gotten undone, and it slipped off my wrist when I was near the waterfall."

"I'm afraid, Ms. Aubrey, the evidence, coupled with witness statements, classifies you as the prime suspect in the murder of Richard Bellmore. And while it is insufficient to charge you with Richard's death at this juncture in time, it *is* enough to detain you."

"That's ridiculous. I'm calling my lawyer immediately."

"Yes. Do so."

"I thought you couldn't arrest me." Aunt Regina's voice was louder than usual. And with piercing overtones that shot through my ears.

"As a person of interest, no. But your status has changed. My office is reviewing witness statements and will follow up with those parties. To quote an old adage, 'Don't leave town.' My office will be in touch." Then he looked at me and said, "Have a nice day," turning away and closing the door behind him.

When a few seconds had passed, my aunt stood, went to the sink, and proceeded to rinse her coffee cup. "Well, that went better than expected."

"Better than expected? You're one step away from jail. Call your lawyer back. Get the name of a bondsman because you're going to need it."

"No need for drama. They can't prove anything because there's nothing to prove."

"True, but they can, and will, make a case."

"I suppose I'd better let your folks know what's going on. I planned on packing and seeing them before driving to the airport, but now, there's no rush."

"Oh, there's a rush all right. You don't know Deputy Vincent, but I do. Trust me when I tell you that you can't take this lightly."

"I'll be fine, Katie. Everything will get sorted out."

Yeah, in the prison laundry.

"Text or call me later with your plans, okay?" My voice was shrill and louder than usual.

"Okay. Have a nice day!"

I gave Speedbump a pat on the head and took off for The Char-Board, unaware that more trouble would be greeting me there. The second I walked through the door, Javie motioned me over, and given the look on his face, I knew he wasn't about to deliver good news.

"Don't worry, Lilly-Ann and I have got everything under control, but someone left a message for you on the phone. The light was blinking when we got here."

"Someone cancelled an event order?" It wouldn't have been the first time, and even with non-refundable deposits, it still cost us money.

"No. It wasn't business-related. It was more personal. And more of a threat than a message."

For the life of me, I couldn't imagine who would be threatening me. I mumbled something to Javie and raced over to the phone to replay the message. It was short and sobering.

"This message is for Katie Aubrey. I understand you're harboring the woman who murdered my fiancée. If she knows what's good for her, *and* you, she should make a full confession now."

That was it. No mention of a name, but I didn't need one. Richard only had one fiancée as far as I knew, and that was Arist's ex-wife. Somehow, word must have gotten out to her that my aunt was a person of interest in Richard's death. And since the message was left before Deputy Vincent escalated my aunt's status to *suspect,* she must have gleaned her information prior. But where? And from whom?

I knew Arist had contacted her, but she was one step ahead of him regarding Richard's murder. And that was on Monday. Too soon for MCSO to contact her. That meant one thing—someone at that author event couldn't wait to share the unfortunate news. *Wonderful.* Now I've got an unhinged woman gunning for me and offering ultimatums.

"Everything okay?" Lilly-Ann asked as she walked past me with an order of egg and cheese muffins. I followed her out to the dining area to continue our conversation.

"Sure, if you like cryptic messages and early morning threats. Although this message was recorded last night, according to the machine. It's Richard's fiancée, and she's demanding I get a full confession from my aunt."

"Or?"

"That's the million-dollar question. It could have been a line from a TV drama as far as I'm concerned. You know, the usual non-specific threat implying something but not specifying."

"You should let the sheriff's office know."

"Maybe later. But right now, I need to track her down and have a little chitchat."

Lilly-Ann placed the order in front of the customer and gave me a quick head-nod. "I don't think that's necessary."

"Huh?"

"That svelte woman on your left, who I've never seen before, doesn't appear to be interested in sitting at a table."

Sure enough, Lilly-Ann barely finished her thought when the woman approached us. She was tall, good-looking, and tanned. I judged her to be in her late forties or early fifties. Layered bob with bronze highlights and a tad heavy on the kohl liner.

She wasted no time speaking. "Can either of you direct me to Katie Aubrey? I understand she's the owner of this establishment."

"I'm Katie. What can I do for you?"

"It's what you shouldn't do. Perhaps we need to speak in a more private area."

Lilly-Ann took the hint and hustled back to the kitchen, leaving me with the woman whom I presumed to be Arist's ex-wife and Richard's recently widowed fiancée.

The expression, "Seek and ye shall find," sprang to mind, coupled with, "Be careful what you wish for."

Chapter Twenty-One

Wednesday

"There's a table on our left by the window. We can speak there." I motioned to the furthest spot in the dining area and then took the lead. She followed me without saying a word until we were both seated.

"I'll make this brief. I'm Dorrie Arnst, Arist's former wife and the late Richard's fiancée. But you've probably surmised that already."

I nodded. "I take it you were the one who threatened me earlier today by phone."

"Not a threat. Advice. I understand the sheriff's office has tangible evidence that your aunt had some sort of altercation with Richard that most likely led to his death. Voluntary manslaughter or murder, the result was the same. My fiancée's corpse floating and bloating under a waterfall."

I tried to get the image out of my head. "Then you know the evidence is circumstantial. And the assertion that there was an altercation is speculation at this point."

"Let's cut to the chase and save everyone some time and aggravation. Convince your aunt it would be in her best interest to go for a full confession. Heat of anger. Intoxication. Mental instability. It really doesn't matter. Better to be upfront with a plausible excuse than to be convicted of first-degree murder by a jury."

"Whoa! Aren't you racing to a finish line when the horse hasn't even been saddled up?"

Oh my gosh. I can't believe I said that.

Dorrie looked down and inhaled. Then she let out a slow breath and clasped her hands as if she was formulating a response, but I continued to speak.

"Why are you in such a hurry to convict my aunt?"

"Because I know she's the responsible party. To say that she and Richard had an adversarial working relationship would be an understatement. If she hadn't been responsible for his demise at the author event, most likely he would have succumbed to a bleeding ulcer from all the grief she gave him."

"A miserable working relationship does not equate to murder, if that's what you're implying."

"I'm not implying. I'm stating the facts. But fine, have it your way." Dorrie shifted in her chair and leaned forward. "For your information, I have every intention of tracking down any and all credible witnesses. In essence, documentary evidence. And when I do, it will be too late for your aunt to get a reduced sentence. Chew on that while you make your charcuteries."

With that, Dorrie stood and walked out, leaving me with my mouth wide open and no words. At least none, until I walked into the kitchen.

"I take it the conversation didn't go well with that woman." Lilly-Ann had just put something in the fridge when she and I were face to face.

"That woman is Richard's fiancée, and she's a snake in designer clothing."

"What did she want?"

"For my aunt to confess to a murder she didn't commit. And pretty obstinate about it, too."

Lilly-Ann crinkled her nose. "Why?"

"That's what I'd like to know. I'm no expert on grief, but isn't denial usually the first step according to the model we all learned in high school?"

"Yeah, I think you're right. Along with bargaining and depression."

I rolled my eyes. "She wasn't depressed, Lilly-Ann. She was a fuming maniac. But maybe that was an act. For my benefit. Maybe it's about another word altogether."

"What word?"

"Deflection."

"You should make Deputy Vincent aware of it."

"Don't worry. I fully intend to do so. Meanwhile, I'd better get going on those breakfast orders. The dining area is filling up."

"You overcooked that egg. When that man bites down on his egg and cheese muffin, it will be like biting on a hockey puck." Edith wafted past me and leaned her filmy self against the counter. No gown this time, but a decent teal and gold kimono.

"What are you doing here?" I whispered.

"What I always do. Offer you advice and direction."

"Make an offering somewhere else."

"Huh?" Javie called out. "I didn't hear what you said. Something about making an offering?"

I thought fast. "Make multi-grain fruit granola bowls as another breakfast offering. What do you think?"

"Good idea. Lots of health nuts around here. We can do a granola variation with dried figs, cranberries, blueberries, and pecans. And we can offer it with plant-based milk as well as dairy products."

"Notice how helpful I am after all." Edith wafted past me in a whirl of teal before vanishing.

Helpful? Like a mule in heels.

Javie moseyed over to the prep area and tapped my shoulder. "I've been watching you and you seem stressed. Really stressed. Is it about that murder?"

"That, and the fact my aunt may turn out to be my permanent house guest —*other than Edith*—if things don't change fast."

I explained about Dorrie's not-so-veiled threats, and followed it up with my aunt wanting to usurp my living space for her new office. "I feel so selfish. Concerned about my own self-preservation." *And my relationship with Ian.*

"You mean your sanity? Katie, you know what you have to do, don't you?"

"Yeah, I suppose. I really wanted to be the good guy, or gal, in this case, for my family, but this is untenable. Hmm, seems I remember seeing a movie about this."

"It was an old SNL skit with John Belushi—*The Thing That Wouldn't Leave.* Pull it up on YouTube. Christopher Lee was the host that night."

"My gosh! How do you remember that stuff? That was before your time."

"Not on YouTube. It kind of renders time unimportant. So, what's your plan?"

"Either a direct talk with my mother or an extended stay at the Marriott."

"Call your mother. Matt should be in any minute, and Lilly-Ann and I can cover the orders."

I looked around and everything seemed calm and orderly. Unlike the phone call I was about to have.

"Thanks for listening, Javie."

"Hey, your self-preservation means ours as well." He smiled, and I stepped outside the back door, cell phone in hand.

Chapter Twenty-Two

Wednesday

"Mom?" I didn't wait for a response. As soon as the call went through, the words flew out of my mouth. "You have *got* to take Aunt Regina to your house. That tile job must be finished by now. Did she tell you what happened? Did she mention wanting to set up an office at my house? If they're still tiling, put her in Dad's dental office!"

"Calm down, Katie. Your aunt called a little while ago and explained her predicament. I seriously doubt any charges will hold, but yes, we invited her to stay with us."

"And? Is she going tonight? Please tell me it's tonight and not tomorrow. I don't think I can stand another day."

"Hmm, that may be tough. Seems Regina enjoys staying with you and thinks the setup should work well for her editing."

"Well, it doesn't work well for me. Or my social life."

"Your social life? Are you seeing anyone? You didn't mention seeing anyone. In fact, all you talk about is how many hours you're putting into that business of yours."

Uh-oh. Not the time to mention Ian. She'll flip if she finds out he's seven years younger than me.

"I have friends and a life outside of The Char-Board. Listen, you have *got* to be convincing where my aunt is concerned. I'm serious. I can't take another moment. Or day, for that matter."

"All right, sweetie, I'll ask your dad to speak with her."

"Thanks. I've got to get back to work. Love you."

"Love you, too."

I was doomed. The minute the call ended, I knew I was destined for Aunt Regina purgatory. Looking around, there was no one in sight, so I edged closer to the trash container and called out, "Edith! Are you nearby? Edith! Can you hear me? Edith! I need you to appear. Pronto!"

"I'm not a genie in a bottle!" Edith rasped. "Or that witch who can snap her fingers and voilà! I'm an intangible spirit."

"Intangible and irritating. Listen, I really need your help. I'm desperate."

"Oh. So now you need my advice and direction."

"More like your skills. I need you to unleash them on my aunt so that she'll pack up and get out of the house. And the sooner, the better. She can give the word *nuisance* a whole new meaning at my parents' house."

Edith sniffed the air and moved away from the trash container. "What did you have in mind?"

I shrugged. "I honestly don't know. She doesn't scare easily. And she's not put off by appliances or lighting going wacko. Heck, Edith. I'm at a loss, but there must be something you can do to drive her out of my house."

"You mean *my* house."

"Yes." I tried not to roll my eyes. "Your house."

"I'll see what I can do tonight, but I may be delayed."

"Delayed? What could possibly be going on in your world?"

"More of Grace Kelly's wardrobe is being released, and I need to get to the front of the line."

"*That's* how you spend your time in the hereafter?"

"Not the hereafter. More like the here-for-now-I-better-move-on-up."

"Maybe Rosaline can put dibs on one of those outfits for you."

"Fat chance. She'll nab the best ones for herself."

"I'm sure other movie stars will pass on and you can snag their clothing."

"Not with Grace Kelly's sense of style and design."

I sighed. "Edith, my sanity rests on this. Be at the house tonight. Please?"

"Just remember that when I ask to visit Imogen."

I recoiled. "Fine. I'll remember."

"Hey, Katie!" Matt opened the back door and called out. "A strange lady just came in and dropped off an invitation for you."

"Is she still there?"

"Nope. She caught me just as I arrived and handed it to me."

"How strange?"

"Not serial killer strange, but kind of kook-and-nutcase strange. She wore a long scarf with cats on it and a matching skirt. Also cat earrings. Did we ever cater an event for her? Like for the animal shelter or something?"

"Not that I know of. Hang on, I'm on my way in."

Matt handed me the envelope with the word "Invitation" written in large gold script letters on the front. I tore it open as I walked inside.

"Was I right?" he asked. "An animal shelter fundraiser?"

"Um, not exactly."

In the same gold script lettering, the invitation read: *You are cordially invited to participate in a mourning vigil for the late Richard Bellmore. Light a candle. Chant a death song. Bring yourself closer to his spirit.*

At first, I thought it was some sort of a joke, but as I kept reading, I realized it wasn't. The letter detailed the time and place—this Saturday night at six at the home of Wilsetta Frum, 1701 E. Highland Road, Cave Creek. At the bottom was a handwritten note in blue ink that read "As a caterer for his final event, I'm sure you'll want to participate."

Who invites caterers to funerals or celebrations of life, or whatever this was, unless they're serving a meal? And the address. It was the same road as the house Maddie thought was haunted. Darn. If only I remembered the house number for her "mansion from hell."

"Hey guys," I called out to whoever was in the kitchen, "has anyone ever heard of a mourning vigil?"

"A morning vigil?" Javie asked. "Is that like early calisthenics?"

"Not morning as in a time of day. Mourning as in grieving for someone who died."

"Oh sure. We light candles and luminaries. And people bring tributes to the deceased. Like stuffed animals if it was a child, or favorite items if it was an adult. And flowers. Lots of flowers."

"What else goes on?" Suddenly, it didn't seem that weird.

"That's about it. People drop off things and hug each other. Usually, the items are placed in front of the house or at the scene of an accident if the person was killed."

"So, uh, no seances or anything, right?"

Javie shook his head. "Not that I know of. Why?"

I handed him the invitation, and he perused it. "Oh. I see what you mean. And I wish I hadn't. That's an awful poem on the opposite side of the card."

"I think it's supposed to be a song."

"Then it's an awful song. You don't intend to go, do you?"

"Go where?" Lilly-Ann entered the kitchen with an armload of plates from the dining area as a result of us installing a new dishwasher and buying Corelle ware.

"To a…uh, um, mourning party. As in mourning for a deceased person."

"You mean a funeral?"

"Here!" I thrust the invitation in her hand once she put down the dishes. "Read it yourself."

"Ew. That's downright creepy, Katie. Do you know that woman? I take it she was at the author event."

"She was the woman Richard tried to hide from. That fanatic fan of his."

"You're not going, are you?"

"Under ordinary circumstances, no. But I need to find out who really murdered Richard, and maybe Wilsetta's vigil or whatever it is, may be a good opportunity to pry and listen in on conversations."

"Don't go alone. Not that I'm offering, because those things really give me the heebie-jeebies, but maybe Ian will go with you." Then she looked at Javie. "Or Javie."

Before he could respond, I replied, "Ian will be all over it. No problem." Then I winked at Javie, and he mouthed "thanks."

Chapter Twenty-Three

Wednesday

During the early afternoon lull, I stepped outside and phoned Maddie to ask her what the address was for that house we saw.

"East Highland Road, number 1715. Why?"

"The neighbor is throwing a party."

"Huh? What?"

"How much time do you have? This could take a while."

"I'll make time," she said. "What's going on?"

"A lot in the past two days." I then proceeded to inform Maddie that my aunt had moved up the crime scale from *person of interest* to *suspect*. Then I told her about how she wanted to set up an office in my house and that I had to find a way to get her over to my parents' house before I lost my mind.

"Couldn't your parents call her and insist she go there?"

"They did. Seems Aunt Regina likes my house."

"Hmm, too bad it's not the one I'm trying to sell. The so-called *hex* is still on it. So, tell me about the neighbor. And the party."

"I'll do better. I'll read you the invitation."

When I finished, Maddie was flabbergasted. "I'd join you, but you'll never guess what."

"What?"

"Remember that chemist who was looking at a condo in Tempe? He's buying it. Not only that, but he asked me to dinner Saturday night and I said yes."

"You don't know anything about him."

"I know he has a degree and a good position at ASU. And he qualifies for a mortgage. Which, by the way, was more than you did when you had Ian stay over when you barely met him."

"That was different. I was in shock."

"You were lucky he turned out to be a decent guy."

I smiled and felt the heat rush to my cheeks. Even after dating him for months, he still had that warm effect on me. "Tell me about the chemist."

"He's not what I'd call handsome, but he's not a toad either. He's funny, smart, and endearing. I've given up on manly supermodels who turn out to be jerks. Besides, I haven't dated in ages. It's way too scary out there. Almost as bad as that albatross of a house I need to sell. What's the neighbor's address? I'll Google it."

I shot off the number, and Maddie responded in a split second. "It's the one next door. The one with all those cats roaming around. If I didn't know any better, I would have taken it for an animal shelter."

"Could that be the odor we smelled? Cats?"

"No. It didn't smell of cat. It was something else. Like a cross between electricity and dead fish. And it fluctuates."

"Oh my gosh, Maddie! I almost forgot. Arist's ex-wife came into The Char-Board to see me. She wanted me to convince my aunt to give herself up. Was more than insistent."

"Why? Did she say?"

"She used intimidation tactics but gave no explanation. I told her Regina was innocent, but she wouldn't take no for an answer. Left in a hurry."

"Boy, the nutcases seem to be crawling out of the woodwork. First, the cat house lady, and then—"

"Dorrie. Dorrie Arnst. I plan to let Deputy Vincent know about her visit."

"Good idea. I'm still trying to wrap my head around a mourning party, or vigil. Do you have any idea who else was invited?"

"Not a clue. But no one's off the hook for Richard's murder, even Wilsetta

Frum, who's hosting this, this…whatever-you-call-it. And don't worry. I won't go alone. Ian put in so much time for the head chef, he'll be able to get Saturday night off. At least that's what he said when we talked about dinner."

"Well, now you can talk about cats and a dead author. Maybe even find out who had a motive to knock him off."

"That's the plan."

"If Wilsetta knows anything about the house next door, pry it out of her."

"Will do. I've got to get back to the kitchen. Talk to you later this week."

We ended the call, and I charged back to the kitchen. The breakfast rush was still on, but not as frenetic as the prior hour when most of our patrons had to get to work. Midmorning, I phoned Deputy Vincent to inform him of my conversation with Dorrie. He responded by telling me that since no actual threats were made, there was little I could do. However, he also added that he would keep our conversation on record, should the matter persist to a greater extent. Whatever *that* meant.

The remainder of the day was non-eventful, but my drive home made up for that. No sooner did I start the motor when a peachy pink haze engulfed the car, and through the rearview mirror, I could see Edith sprawled out on the backseat.

"I'm about to take a siesta," she announced. "But don't worry. I'll be up in plenty of time to drive that compulsive aunt of yours out of my house."

"Oh. About that, whatever you do, don't conjure up those insects. You know, the no-see-ums. My aunt will waste no time calling an exterminator, and I don't want any chemicals sprayed in or around the house."

"Fine. No gnats or no-see-ums."

"And don't do anything with flickering lights. Or appliances. She'll be on the phone with an electrician, and they charge seventy-five dollars just to pull into the driveway."

"Fine. No electricity."

"And none of that business with sudden drops in temperature. I don't need to freeze my buns off. It's November. Sixty degrees might as well be sixty below zero."

"Look, Missy, you're not leaving me a large berth for my skills. Do you or don't you want that woman out of there?"

"Of course I do. I just don't want to be inconvenienced in the process."

Edith sat up for a brief second, leaned forward to catch a glimpse of herself in the rear mirror, and then stretched her arms and reclined directly behind me. "To reiterate, no insects, no electrical manipulations, and no drops in temperature."

"You got it."

"In that case, we're done."

"Done as in you won't do it, or done as in you have a plan."

"I always have a plan. And trust me, this one is a doozy."

"What? What are you planning?" I spun my head around, but Edith was gone. And in that brief moment, I almost wished I never mentioned the bugs, the lights, or the temperature, because those three things would pale compared to what Edith had marinating in her head.

When I stepped into the house a few minutes later, my aunt was measuring the walls and jotting the information on a small pad.

"I may have a solution," she said, before I could even muster a "hello."

"A solution? To what?"

"Why, my office, of course. If we have a contractor remove this wall on the left and rebuild it three or so feet in, it would enlarge the guest room so as to create an office nook. And besides, who needs all that living room space? It's not as if it's a classroom or anything."

Forget what I said earlier, Edith. Bring on the plague if you must!

"I need it. I need that space. And besides, I don't own the house. I rent it. Um, let's talk about that later. Have you heard anything more from Deputy Vincent or your lawyer?"

"Not a word. But a lovely box of chocolates was delivered here a little bit ago."

I froze. "You didn't eat any, did you?"

"No, I thought they were for you. The delivery boy didn't know."

"Delivery boy? Not a service like Amazon or a company car?"

"A boy on his bike. I figured it was a local delivery."

CHAPTER TWENTY-THREE

"Where's the box?"

"Right behind you in the kitchen. On the counter."

I was at the counter in a split second, eyeballing the box of See's Candies. True, it appeared to be sealed, but I wasn't about to take a chance. I put on a pair of food handler gloves and thrust the box into a plastic bag. "I'm dropping this off at the sheriff's office."

As I reached for my phone to text Deputy Vincent, awful thoughts raced through my head. And all of them involved a maniacal killer who had me next on his or her list. As I opened the cloud-shaped app, I noticed a small red dot at the bottom of one of my messages. It was from an unknown number, but I went ahead and tapped it.

The text read: *The candy order you placed for the Greater Phoenix Women's Shelter fundraiser last month was delivered to your address today. Thank you for your support.*

The Greater Phoenix Women's Shelter Fundraiser. Oh my gosh. I had forgotten all about it. It was a booth that I stopped at during a farmers' market I went to with Maddie. I removed the gloves, tore open the box, and brought it back out for my aunt.

"On second thought, help yourself, Aunt Regina. These should be fine."

Chapter Twenty-Four

Wednesday

At a little past ten, I turned off the light by the side of my bed and whispered, "Edith, if you're listening, tell me what you're up to. And on second thought, you can bring back the insects."

Dead silence with the exception of Speedbump's snores. Not knowing what Edith had planned in order to extricate my aunt from the guestroom was more frightening than Wes Craven, John Carpenter, and Quentin Tarantino with a new horror script in their hands. I turned on the light again and resumed where I left off with Lena Gregory's *Mistletoe Cake Murder* from her All-Day Breakfast Café series. No sense forcing myself to sleep with the likes of "Little Shop of Horrors" taking place down the hall. Not when I had a good cozy mystery in my hand.

An hour passed and nothing. Maybe Edith got waylaid with a new gown shipment. I muttered a few choice words to myself and once again, turned off the bedside lamp. I must have dozed off because when I woke, the digital clock read 12:51. Still nothing from the guestroom.

"Come on, Edith, Aunt Regina's intruding on your privacy, too," I whined.

"Shh! She'll lose her concentration."

I sat up and saw Rosaline perched at the foot of my bed. And behind her were two other specters, both women and both dressed like Cinderella's stepsisters.

"I'm not throwing a party, Rosaline. And what did you mean by 'Edith will lose her concentration?'"

"She's trying a new skill. And sometimes things go wrong. That's why I convinced Merrilee and Faye to pitch hit if need be. They've been around longer and have developed more skills."

Speedbump stopped snoring and looked up from his spot at the foot of the bed. Then, he yawned, shifted position, and curled back into a ball.

"But why would they help Edith?"

"They lost during a poker tournament."

"You can gamble in the netherworld? Oh, never mind. You can tell me later. I need to know—" And just then, I heard a loud shriek coming from my aunt's room. *Go for it, Edith!*

I tossed back the covers, threw a sweatshirt over my top, and charged down the hallway. "Aunt Regina!" I shouted. "Are you all right?" Without waiting for an answer, I threw open her door and looked inside. Objects were moving everywhere! Books sliding off tables, a hairbrush moving back and forth across the dresser, and what appeared to be a dust devil or vortex of sorts spinning around in the center of the room.

The wooden desk chair crashed to the floor and was joined by a small lamp I picked up at a garage sale for three dollars. I stared at the vortex and watched as it sucked it writing papers and crumpled up Kleenex. Ew!

My aunt plastered herself against the wall next to the bed. "Do you hear that noise, Katie? It's whistling in my ears. You know what I'm saying, don't you?"

"Um, ghosts. Like maybe the house is haunted?"

"Don't be ridiculous. No such thing as ghosts."

As soon as she said that, she put her hands over her ears. "The noise is deafening. Deafening! Can't you hear it?"

"That's *my* special touch," Edith announced from her spot on the armoire. Her legs were crossed, and she leaned over like someone admiring a view. "I can't take credit for the centrifugal force. Faye came up with that. But she's had decades to perfect it. Decades, mind you. I don't plan on leveling out up there for much longer."

As Edith droned on about the politics of the great hereafter, my aunt shouted, "Don't you realize what's happening?"

Before I could answer, she did. "It's a vortex! Like the ones in Sedona. Only I don't think this one is conducive to yoga or meditation. Look at it! The energy is pulsing and wobbling. Stay back before we get sucked into another dimension. Like *The Twilight Zone.*"

Hmm, I was sure she would say it was a ghostly apparition.

"Another dimension?" My heart was racing, and I wanted to give Edith a hug.

"Rod Serling knew what he was talking about in those episodes. They were based on science. And we're experiencing it right here in your house. Were you aware of it? I've read about this sort of phenomenon. Unexplained and uncontrolled energy. The consequences could be deadly."

"Deadly? Are you sure?"

The dust devil continued to whirl, but it lost its tornado-like shape and morphed into a lopsided blob that wobbled and rocked.

"I'm getting tired," Edith grumbled. "Got to step this up before it all goes puff!"

"Yes, do that!"

"Do what, Katie? I'm not sure what we can do except get out of here."

"It's probably a fluke. You know, something wrong with the air currents from the heating system. I turned it on recently."

"That's no fluke, and I suggest you contact one of those theoretical scientists from the university in the morning. In the meantime, I'm throwing together a few things and driving straight over to my brother's house. Do me a favor and let your parents know. I don't have time. I'll collect the rest of my things tomorrow."

Then she grabbed my wrist and shook it. "Maybe you should come, too."

"I'll be fine. Speedbump and I can always camp out at The Char-Board if it gets really scary."

"If you say so."

With that, my aunt pulled out one of her rolling luggage bags and proceeded to toss in items from the dresser. Suddenly, all energy stopped, and the room was back to normal.

"I'm completely worn out. Worn out, I tell you. You owe me, Missy. A nice visit to Imogen. Maybe I can duplicate this at her house."

"Look," my aunt said. "Maybe it's over for good. Maybe all that energy was used up, and whatever crack there was between dimensions sealed itself. Hmm, maybe I was being too rash about leaving."

I darted my eyes around the room and mouthed the word HELP to Edith and her friends.

"Fine," came that familiar raspy voice. "I'll do what I can."

"Good! That's the spirit!"

My aunt puffed her chest, and I realized she thought I meant her and not Edith. Then, without warning, she put her hands over her ears and shrieked. A sharp, chalk-on-the-blackboard shriek. "That noise! It's back with a vengeance. Katie, I think the vortex and that noise are related. I'm sorry. I have to leave. Now!"

She didn't bother to get out of her dressing gown. Instead, she put on a bathrobe and threw her camelhair coat over her clothes before stepping into a pair of loafers she had by the bed. "I'll call you in the morning. Call your folks. Tell them I'll be there in forty-five minutes. Maybe they could brew some coffee and set out a few cookies or cakes."

"I'll do that. Drive safe, Aunt Regina."

When my aunt reached the front door, she turned and said, "Please let that miserable deputy know I haven't left town, but I'm not staying in Cave Creek. For all I know, that vortex could be just the beginning."

No, Deputy Vincent's investigation is just the beginning.

At the sound of my aunt's car door slamming, Edith announced, "You should pack up the rest of her things now and get them over to your parents' house before she changes her mind."

"It can wait until morning. I'm exhausted."

"Oh, so now *you* know the feeling. Trust me, utilizing new skill energy is not easy. And now I'm sure Merrilee and Faye will want to have another round of high-stakes poker."

I looked up and around the room. "Thank you, Merrilee and Faye, wherever you are. By the way, watch Edith's thumb and forefinger. She twirls them when she has a bad hand."

"Not funny, Missy. And for your information, they've gone back to the beyond already. Left as soon as the dust devil stopped. Now you *really* owe me!"

I laughed. "When haven't I? Well, I don't know about you, but I'm going back to sleep. A nice, peaceful sleep."

"Aren't you forgetting something? And they say seniors are forgetful. Harrumph. You were supposed to call your parents and give them the warning. Also your aunt's food order. Ha! And you think *I'm* the demanding one."

"Oh my gosh! My parents! Rats? Where did I put my phone?"

Seconds later, I tapped the number and took a breath. As soon as my mother answered, I spoke. "Aunt Regina's on her way over."

"Why? What happened? Is everything all right? Does she have any idea what time it is? And I'm whispering because your father is still asleep."

"He probably won't be once she gets there. And yeah, everything's fine, but there was a problem with the furnace and the air currents. It sort of freaked her out. She was convinced it was a vortex. Like in Sedona. I suppose she wasn't used to old houses and the quirky heating systems. There was also a humming sound she didn't like. Guess I'm used to those things."

"I don't suppose you have any idea how long she'll have to stay in Arizona?"

"It's not looking good. Mom, she's the number one suspect in a murder case. And if she *is* charged, it could be months until a trial. She'll post bail and set up a permanent camp here! And the worst part is that it hasn't sunk in as far as she's concerned."

"She mentioned a lawyer."

"She also mentioned a manicure. Look, I'm trying as best as I can to snoop around and see if I can pick up any information. Someone at that author event had to have a real motive."

"You be careful, Katie. As much as I'd like to see your aunt on the next flight back to New Jersey, I don't want you to be the next target. That author was murdered, and that means a dangerous killer is out there."

"Uh-huh. Oh, before I forget, Aunt Regina wants cake and cookies with some coffee when she arrives."

"On second thought, if you must snoop, do it from behind your desk. Not as if someone's going to jump out at you from the computer. Cake and cookies, she said? It's the middle of the night. I may be the one jumping. From our second-story window!"

Chapter Twenty-Five

Thursday

"You look like you were up all night," Lilly-Ann said when I opened the door to The Char-Board and let her in. I had arrived super early in order to get caught up on orders and come up with a plan to make the most of my invitation to Wilsetta's mourning vigil.

"Um, yeah. I was. A heating glitch with the furnace that sent air all over the place."

"Liar!"

"Shh!" I eyeballed Edith, who stood a few feet away, and gave her "the look."

"Why are we being quiet? No one's here." Lilly-Ann looked around as if to verify the fact.

"Sorry. Habit, I guess. Not wanting to distract the customers."

"Did you call an HVAC company? I've got a good one."

"It sort of worked itself out, and the best part was that the noise and the dust sent my aunt scurrying to my parents' house. Too bad it couldn't have happened sooner. Listen, at around nine, I'm going to call Allison at the library and see what she can tell me about Wilsetta, so it will be just you and Javie for a little while."

"No problem. That vigil of hers may be your best chance to find out who crossed paths with Richard by that waterfall. Other than your aunt. What's Ian's take on all this?"

"We haven't had the chance to talk that much, but he's even more into the cloak and dagger stuff than I am. It's like dating a younger version of Shawn Spencer."

"Too bad he's not psychic."

"Neither was Shawn."

Just then, Javie walked in. "Hey guys, did you catch the news this morning? The sheriff's office said they were making progress on Richard Bellmore's murder and should be making an arrest soon."

"How soon?" I all but started him. That's how loud my voice got.

"They weren't specific. But hey, you know… 'soon' could be anything from a few hours to a few weeks. It's the sheriff's office." Then he saw the look on my face. "I'm sorry, Katie. Didn't mean to frighten you since your aunt is a suspect. But it could be anyone. Really."

"I wish I was that optimistic. That's why I need to chat with Allison at the library and find out what she knows about that vigil Saturday. Anyway, we better get going. The customers are going to arrive before we know it. And please, keep your ears out for anything you might overhear."

"Got it!" Javie said, followed by a nod from Lilly-Ann.

When nine rolled around, I left the kitchen, cell phone in hand, and walked to my car, where I'd have some privacy. No need to have curious customers pick up snippets of my conversation. Thankfully, Allison took the call but needed to close her office door. I figured I wasn't the only one who wanted to avoid being overheard.

"I was going to call you, Katie. I imagine it's about that invitation from Wilsetta. I just got off another call from Deputy Vincent about it. Seems the wife of one of his deputies got that same invitation, and the deputy showed it to him."

"Is Wilsetta some kind of a nutcase?"

"A nutcase with a family fortune and deep pockets. You wouldn't know it by looking at her or her house, for that matter, but she's got deep pockets and connections to places none of us would think of. That's why the situation with Richard was so delicate at the event. I knew she was stalking him, and I'm ashamed to say it, but I didn't step in soon enough for fear of alienating her and her money. Awful, huh? But we're a small library and our resources need all the help they can get."

"You don't suppose she was the one responsible, do you? Jealousy is a strong motive."

"Wilsetta may be camped out on the lunatic fringe, affectionately speaking, but she's harmless. She's lived in this community for years and has been an integral part of the library's book clubs and social events."

"Has she ever held a mourning vigil?"

"Not that I'm aware of. But then again, we've never had an author murdered in our library. I imagine this is how she's dealing with the shock. Anyway, I'll be in attendance along with some of the library staff. Wilsetta asked me to say a few words about Richard. I imagine it will be like a celebration of life, only with Kleenex."

"You wouldn't happen to know if any of the authors at that event got invites, would you?"

"As a matter of fact, I do. KC Camplin called me when he got the engraved envelope. Wanted to know if I thought it was, and I quote, 'for real.' And he wasn't the only one. Lida and Jessica got invitations as well. Somehow, Wilsetta found out they were staying at the Scottsdale Fairmont Princess."

"I take it they were shocked."

"More like amused. And curious. Same with Barbara. Only she wasn't so amused to find that Wilsetta knew where she lived in Lake Pleasant. Between you and me, I don't know if I'll ever host another author event."

"Doesn't that go with the territory?"

Allison sighed. "I suppose. Along with papercuts."

"Think any of them will attend?"

"They all will. Well, all except KC. He was rather non-committal. Then again, I doubt he'd pass at an opportunity to check out the crowd. That's just how he strikes me. If I were you, Katie, I'd go. You may pick up information you might need to help your aunt's case. Not to sound like a rumormonger, but Regina's name has been flying off the walls around here."

"If you were to wager a guess, who would you suspect?"

Allison's line turned quiet for a good twenty seconds, and then, "Someone who knew they could get away with it."

When the call ended, there was only one pressing question on my mind—did Wilsetta plan to serve food, or should we arrive after we eat? While I still had the courage, I wasted no time phoning her.

"Wilsetta? This is Katie Aubrey from The Char-Board. I got your invitation to Richard's, um, uh, vigil, and wondered if you needed to hire us to prepare a charcuterie board."

"You've become quite the brazen little food hussy, haven't you?" The voice came from directly behind me, but there was no need to turn around. Edith, draped in a hideous floral caftan, was perfectly visible in the rearview mirror.

"I don't wish to replicate the crime scene. Thank you anyway, but I plan to serve Richard's favorite food—meatball sliders. And of course, funeral potatoes."

"Uh, sounds yum—I mean, very appropriate." *And weird.*

"I plan to say a few words about him and have everyone write something that we will attach to helium-filled balloons and send them off into the night sky. Then, a lovely poetry reading and a few soul-filled songs in his memory."

"He must have meant a great deal to you."

"I lived for that man. His writing, his style, his presence. And Arist's ex-wife did not deserve him. I know that gold-digger has been prying around, but she's persona non grata as far as I'm concerned. Oh, did I mention our weeping room?"

"Weeping room?"

"Yes. I've designated a special room in my house for those people who wish to simply sit and cry."

Sounds like my junior year prom, but without the gowns.

"Well, it's been nice chatting. I'll see you on Saturday."

"A weeping room?" Edith leaned over my shoulder and all but engulfed me in rose and pink haze. "That's a first if I ever heard of such a thing. You should have asked her if she planned to have everyone listen to dirges."

"It's going to be bad enough."

"Not for me. I plan to have some fun."

"Forget fun. Plan to listen to every conversation. Every little nuance that could bring us closer to exonerating Regina."

"It's always work with you, isn't it?"

"When it comes to murder, then yes. Always work."

Chapter Twenty-Six

Thursday, Friday, Saturday

"Do any of you know what funeral potatoes are?" I asked when I walked back inside The Char-Board's kitchen. "It's what Wilsetta plans to serve at her mourning vigil."

Lilly-Ann rinsed off a salad bowl and set it on the strainer to dry. "It's a casserole with potatoes and cheese. Sometimes cornflakes and potato chips. Guess it was popular at funerals. I thought you called Allison, not Wilsetta."

"I did. Then I decided to call Wilsetta and pry a bit. Other than KC, who wasn't very direct with her, the other authors plan to attend. Same with library staff and who-knows-who from the community."

"Did Wilsetta divulge anything of importance?"

"Yep. She has no use for Dorrie Arnet. Referred to her as a gold-digger who didn't deserve Richard. Oh, and she's designated a room for people who want to cry their eyes out. I may poke mine with a fork by the time the evening is done."

Lilly-Ann burst out laughing and resumed washing out salad bowls while Javie hustled to get the breakfast orders up. Seconds later, Matt arrived, and we were in full force until well after one.

It was the same the following day. Nothing notable from the sheriff's office or anyone else, for that matter. Even my mother. I fully expected a phone call and a myriad of texts, but nothing. Maybe Aunt Regina had her tied up in such a tailspin, she didn't have time to complain.

Sure enough, that night I got a brief text: *MCSO had a deputy stop by. More questions for your aunt. We told her not to answer without an attorney present. Any news at your end?*

I texted back: *Fingers crossed. Will eavesdrop at bizarre vigil for Richard Saturday night. All the suspects will be there. Well, most all.*

Then, my mother's final text: *Good! It will be like Hercule Poirot or whatever investigator they have on Death in Paradise. Those British mysteries change investigators all the time. Or maybe it's the actors...*

That night, when I told Ian about her message, his response was that she had an awful lot of faith in my sleuthing abilities or had watched too many TV shows and movies.

"It's the latter," I said, "but one thing for sure, both of us should have a good opportunity to poke around. I'm thinking Wilsetta may not be as innocent as she appears. Rivalry, jealousy. That sort of motive. We just need tangible evidence."

"And a good distraction. Maybe if enough people go into that crying room."

Suddenly, my mind flashed over to Edith. What better distraction? Provided she didn't go overboard. Then again, if ever there was a time and place, that would be it.

"Let's make it happen," I said.

"Sounds better than eating funeral potatoes."

Ian was able to get off work on Saturday night and arrived at my place an hour before Wilsetta's death vigil/mourning party. It was the first time we had been with each other since my aunt had rolled into town, and all we could do was hug each other and kiss.

"At this rate, we'll never get our plan in place," Ian said. "Let's try to contain ourselves and focus. We can pick up when we get back from Wilsetta's."

"Good! About time! I was getting nauseous watching the two of you!" Edith pranced back and forth behind us as if she was a dancer in a Broadway musical. I shot her a look at least two times when Ian wasn't watching, but it didn't make a difference.

"While the both of you were playing 'kissy face,' I came up with a plan.

And don't poo-poo it. I'll cut the power in the crying room so everyone will be in the dark. Then I'll do whatever springs to mind."

Oh no. Not the "springs to mind."

"Meanwhile," Edith went on, "you and your boyfriend can go about your business snooping in her office and bedroom. Those are the likely places where she's kept a journal. Obsessed fans always keep journals. Find it, and your aunt will be one step closer to New Jersey."

I smiled at Ian. "Maybe we can snoop in Wilsetta's bedroom and office while everyone is occupied in the crying room or eating. Or maybe even outside launching those balloons."

"Works for me, babe." Ian squeezed my wrist. "And let's go one step further. I'll bring a flash drive and see if I can copy her Word docs while you root around."

"My gosh, we're getting to be old hands at this."

"Better than cuffed."

"Bite your tongue. I have every confidence it will work." *If Edith doesn't get distracted by a new shipment of vintage gowns.* "Hang on a second before we head out. I need to grab a sweater. It might be cold in her place. You never know."

There were a couple of zip-up hoodies on coat pegs by the living room door, and I grabbed the nearest one. Then, I patted Speedbump on the head and went out with Ian through the garage. We drove in his car to Wilsetta's house on East Highland Road, making one quick stop to take in the view.

"Someone must be looking at that house for sale over there," Ian said as we approached Wilsetta's driveway. "I could have sworn I saw the lights go on and off for a split second."

"Could be a timer. No bites on the place yet. Just saying the word *haunted* sends people running."

Just then, a large gray cat raced in front of us, followed by two smaller ones. "Hope no one's allergic," Ian mumbled under his breath. "Got a feeling the place will be filled with felines."

"And Speedbump will be sniffing the daylights out of us when we get home."

Cars were lined up alongside the driveway, and Ian was able to wedge his in between an SUV and a Volkswagen Beetle. Ground-level solar lights lit up the walkway to the house, and I took a deep breath before knocking at the door.

I anticipated background music, but nothing prepared me for the dark and deep dirge that most likely came from a mobile device. Ian must have thought the same thing because he whispered, "I didn't know that kind of music was on Alexa's playlist. Or Google Nest."

Wilsetta greeted us, dressed in a long, black sheath that did absolutely nothing for her large hips and well-rounded stomach. "Welcome. Richard would be honored to know that his caterers cared so much for him. Please join the other guests in the living and dining rooms and help yourselves to my offerings. And you can put your coats and jackets on the table over there."

"Thank you," we both said at once, but before Wilsetta could respond, another guest arrived and Wilsetta ushered her into the living and dining rooms as well. She was one of the library staff members and recognized us immediately.

"I wasn't sure what to expect," she said to Ian and me as we walked toward the dining room. "But I felt I should make an appearance. Wilsetta is the financial backbone of our library."

Ian nodded. "Yes, so we've been told."

Then, the woman moved closer and spoke softly. "Wilsetta's also a bit on the eccentric side, but you probably figured that out already."

I smiled. "And then some." I took off my hoodie and tossed it on the table when I noticed something—it wasn't mine. An embroidered 'Regina' was on the left-hand side in big, bold letters.

"Oh no. This is my aunt's hoodie. She forgot she left it, and I didn't notice at first. Dark hoodies all look the same. Oh well. No big deal."

Suddenly, we heard a crash from the living room and raced over to see what happened.

"It's only Sir Sidney," Wilsetta called out. "He knocked over a water pitcher. Good thing it was silver and not glass. I've learned to avoid glass. Cats may appear agile, but they're really little demons who take great pleasure in their own antics."

"Do you need any help?" I walked toward her.

"No. I'll grab a towel and refill it. Meanwhile, please mingle and share loving thoughts about Richard. So many people are here already."

Wilsetta was right. There were at least fifteen people buzzing about the living room, with a few of them offering to help with the water spill. Some of the faces looked familiar, including Jessica and Lida. I glanced at the large buffet table in the dining room and noticed two chafing dishes with food warmers and no takers. *Must be those funeral potatoes.*

Then, Lida approached us. "Strange event, huh? But how could I say no? Our fans are what keep us in business. And while Jessica and Richard had a rather prickly relationship, he and I got along splendidly. Such a loss for the mystery community."

I studied her expression, and one thing came to mind. She may be a well-known author, but she's a lousy actress. Next thing I knew, she pointed to the buffet table. "Too bad Wilsetta didn't ask you to prepare one of those marvelous charcuterie dessert trays. I'm not so sure of what's in those chafing trays."

"Funeral potatoes."

Lida chuckled. "The woman sure knows how to carry off a theme."

"Katie," a voice called out. "I didn't expect to see you here." It was Colleen Wexbly of all people.

"Colleen? I didn't know you were a fan of Richard's or that you knew Wilsetta."

"I'm not exactly a fan of Richard's. I only know what I read in the tabloids, but Wilsetta and I are on the same 'Save the feral community cats page' on Facebook. We message often, and she invited me to this event. Rather odd, isn't it?"

"Uh, yeah. Odd, all right."

Ian, who was still chatting with Lida, turned and mouthed, "Will wander and listen in."

I winked when Colleen turned away for a second and watched as Ian moseyed over to a mixed group of men and women by the alcove near the living room. Seconds later, something brushed against my leg, and I jumped. It was a fat orange tabby who made its way to a line of food dishes under a credenza.

I was about to say something when Wilsetta's voice cut through the air. "May I have everyone's attention, please? We are about to begin the orchestrated portion of tonight's vigil. To my left, down the hallway, is the designated quiet room of sorrow. There, you can sit, weep, and reflect over a life cut short. Please feel free to go there at any time during tonight's vigil and remain there as long as you need."

Sixty seconds in there and that'll be enough sorrow to last me into the next decade.

"And now," Wilsetta continued, "Please take a seat and we will begin the poetic reflection of Richard's life. After that, we will create our balloon eulogies and go outside."

Worried that Ian and I wouldn't have enough time to snoop, I burst out, "Let's read our eulogies out loud. Maybe our words will resonate throughout the night sky."

"Now I'm really going to puke," Edith said. She pulled a black veil over the peacock and purple fascinator on her head and crossed her arms. "But I've got to hand it to you, you certainly know how to spice up a party."

Chapter Twenty-Seven

Saturday

Wilsetta's living room was certainly large enough to entertain family or friends, but given the number of "death vigil guests," it was cramped and crowded as we bumped into one another while trying to adjust our seating. The fortunate ones were the people who nabbed room on the couch and wingback chairs. The rest of us had to contend with fold-up chairs, and in some cases, small ottomans.

In our case, the fold up chairs were actually an advantage. Ian and I moved ours to the rear of the room so that when poetry hour ended, we could scoot off to our poking and prying. As for Edith's whereabouts, it was anyone's guess. *Please don't tell me she's chasing after eveningwear.*

A chime sounded, and the room conversation stopped for a moment. Then, Wilsetta spoke in a slow, monotone voice. "And now, everyone, our poetic reflections on Richard Bellmore will begin. I shall start with my own ode to Richard in Pindaric form."

Ian stifled a groan, and I tried not to laugh as Wilsetta stood in front of her fireplace and began.

"There once was time, when thought was thine,

And mystery clouded sense.

Thy words unveiled the trials and trails

Of all that gave suspense."

"I don't think that's Pindaric," someone whispered, loud enough to be heard. "More like Horatian. You know, quatrains."

"Shh, I don't know, Edna," someone else said. "And no one cares."

Wilsetta droned on and on for what seemed like an eternity. When she finished, there was a small applause, and she asked if anyone else cared to read a poem. I was positive the reading would end right then and there, but no, I was wrong. Apparently, that library crew must have had lots of time on their hands, because one by one, people read all sorts of mind-numbing poems.

Ian leaned over and pressed his face close to my ear. "I forgot to tell you something. Sterling got an invitation to this event, but came down with a bad sore throat and swollen glands yesterday. He was beside himself. Mentioned something about grieving amidst fellow literary fans."

"Did he write a poem?"

"The man couldn't write a grocery list, let alone a poem."

Just then, another reader took center stage. This time with a lengthy epic that made Beowulf sound like a nursery rhyme.

"I don't know how much more of this I can take," I whispered to Ian.

"Me either. Want to try to sneak out of here?"

"They'll see us. We'd better wait."

"I can move her along if you want." A beige haze rose from the floor to my waist.

"Rosaline!"

"Who? Who's Rosaline?" Ian looked around.

"Sorry, I thought I recognized someone."

The epic "Richard" poem continued, and next thing I knew, Edith stood directly in front of me minus the veil and peacock fascinator. "I thought you wanted me to get things going once the party moved outdoors."

I thought for a moment and answered in a way that Ian and Edith would both think it was meant for them. "On second thought, we should start now. We need to slip out of here unnoticed."

In that instant, the lights flickered and the room went dark with the exception of the flame from the fireplace.

"Move it, Missy. You can thank me later." Edith managed a gust of air in my face and it took all my will power not to utter an expletive. Wordless, I stood, and Ian followed suit. We exited the room just as the lights flickered back on.

"Quick!" Ian said. "Luck is on our side. We've got to figure out where her office is as well as her bedroom."

Luck, all right. Spelled E D I T H.

As if she could read my mind, Edith answered as she hovered around us. "Office is next to the guest bathroom, and master bedroom is across the hall on the right. Unlike you, I didn't need a Google map."

I pointed to the hallway. "Um, the guest bathroom is over there. I saw a few people going in and out. Usually the other bedroom, which is probably her office, will be right next to it. Seems to be the style for one-story homes. You take the office, I'll find the master bedroom."

"Watch the time. We should hustle and get done in a half hour."

"I'm on it!"

Just then, a banshee howl pierced my eardrums, and I spied a large black tortoise cat wailing its lungs out by the kitchen. Then I heard Wilsetta's voice, "Shelli! You stop that! You're upsetting the guests. I'm sorry if you didn't like the salmon pâté."

I grabbed Ian's arm and the two of us charged into the guest bathroom. I locked the door behind us and caught a breath. "This might not be as easy as we thought."

Ian put his index finger to his lips and motioned for us to listen behind the door. We could still hear Wilsetta, only her voice now had a sing-song lilt. "I'm opening a can of minced cod. If you don't like that, you can go outside and hunt for mice."

The cat's wails now turned to loud meows, and seconds later, Wilsetta said, "I'm going back to my guests, Shelli. Behave yourself."

"Think it's safe to get out of here?" Ian asked. "I don't hear any sounds from the kitchen. Not even that cat."

"We should be okay. Come on, let's do it while we still have the nerve."

Ian tiptoed to the office and closed the door behind him. Then he re-opened it and whispered, "Don't turn on lights. Use your cell phone flashlight. Unless, of course, there are lights on in there already."

I gave him a thumbs-up and moved toward the master bedroom. Once inside, I closed the door, thankful that the en-suite had lights on which gave me enough illumination to poke around without juggling the cell phone.

Next, I perused the furnishings. Only one nightstand with a small drawer, a five-drawer dresser, and a three-drawer dressing table. All farmhouse style in dark, heavy wood that could have been mahogany or cherry. No electronics in the room, with the exception of a digital alarm clock on the nightstand. A crocheted duvet covered the queen-size bed and gave the room its only soft feature.

A copy of *The Cat Who Talked to Ghosts,* by Lillian Jackson Braun, was the only other item next to the bed. *No surprise there.* I yanked open the stubborn drawer on the nightstand, hoping to find a diary or a journal. Instead, I found a packet of tissues, a nail clipper, and a small skeleton key.

Moving on, I systematically opened all of the dressing table drawers, only to find underwear, scarves, pajamas, sweaters, and a variety of small cat beds. At that point, I prayed Ian was having better luck.

Last, I opened the top dresser drawer and stared at more mini-jewelry boxes than I thought humanly possible.

"Rats," I mumbled. "This could take all night. And we don't have that much time."

"I do. I have all the time in the world." I turned and spied Edith peering over my shoulder at the jewelry boxes. "Well, time in *this* realm anyway. Larken is lecturing on expectations for unsettled spirits, and he's downright boring. Don't need a snooze-fest. Don't say I'm not helpful."

With that, she vanished before I could implore her not to do anything outrageous. Then again, maybe outrageous was what we needed in order to accomplish our mission.

From left to right, I opened each and every box to make sure the only contents were jewelry and not notes or messages. Lots of QVC stuff and some from HSN. Bracelets, pins, earrings, necklaces. You-name-it. And most of it with cat motifs. Halfway through, I wanted to yowl like Shelli.

And not because I craved canned cod.

Twenty minutes had passed, but there were still two drawers to go, and maybe, with any luck, I'd find something incriminating. Sadly, I didn't. Only blankets and a well-worn quilt. I was so engrossed with digging around, I didn't hear the conversation outside the bedroom door until someone turned the knob.

Panic-stricken, I did the only thing I could. I climbed into the bed, and with the lights out, prayed whoever it was wouldn't notice. Unfortunately, Wilsetta used woolen blankets, and within seconds, I began to itch. Seriously itch. But that was the least of my problems.

I recognized one of the voices and knew I was in trouble.

Chapter Twenty-Eight

Saturday

"Shh! Hurry up and close the door before anyone sees or hears us." It was Arist, but I had no idea who he was talking to. I held as still as I could and listened as he continued.

His voice was raspy and hushed. "Too many people in and out of that bathroom, and her office is too close to the kitchen. This is probably the safest place to speak, and whatever you do, don't turn on a light. That nightlight is enough."

"It's enough, all right. Something's moving in that bed. The covers are moving up and down. That much I can see with the nightlight."

Of course, the darn covers are moving. I'm breathing! Wait until the itching gets out of hand.

"Probably one of her cats under the covers. Don't go near it or the thing might yowl."

"What was the big deal that we had to sneak away from that balloon launch? Not that I care, mind you, but our hostess might."

It was a woman's voice, but it wasn't Lida or Jessica. And definitely not Allison. The speaker's tone was more guttural. That left Barbara or any number of library workers or volunteers. Not to mention Wilsetta's friends and neighbors.

"I need you to keep your ears open and let me know if there's anything I should be concerned about. Fact is, I'm second in line after Regina. It doesn't take a genius to figure out I abhorred the man."

"I still think you're overreacting."

"No matter. We agreed on a price for your assistance, and if they question you harder, tell them I was in one of the conference rooms during the time of the murder. That's part of our arrangement."

"No worries. Extra cash always comes in handy."

At that moment, a sudden urge to sneeze overtook me, and I forced myself to hold it back. Unfortunately, it resulted in an exaggerated rise and fall from the blanket over my face.

"Do you think that cat can breathe under that blanket?" The woman asked. "Maybe we should check." I heard footsteps approaching and then, the worst reaction—an intense burning and itching all over my body. Most likely nerves, but it didn't matter. In a nanosecond, the cat would be out of the bag—literally!

I had to think of something, but my mind drew a blank, and the footsteps got closer. Then Arist called out, "Leave well enough alone. I think there are two of them under the covers. They can probably breathe through the material."

I let out the breath I held, but it was short-lived. Whoever that woman was, she was definitely persistent. "I need to be sure."

No, you don't!

And then, "What the heck? Did you feel that? Got a gust of air right in my face. Must be Wilsetta's heating system. Talk about antiquated."

Hallelujah! Edith's on the case.

"Come on, last thing we need is for Wilsetta to walk in here for one reason or another."

"Fine. I'm sure everyone's still writing their messages on those balloons. We've got time."

"Not that much. Look out the window. Those are balloons in the air. She's got glowsticks attached to the strings. For all we know, that cat-crazy lady has a check-off list of her guests."

"Just tell her we were in the crying room or whatever she called it."

"The mourning room, I think."

Then, as if the itching on my extremities wasn't enough, my head began to itch as well. Seriously itch! Only now I pictured head lice. I tried a stealth arm move to scratch my scalp and hoped it would go undetected.

It didn't.

"Arist, look," the woman said. "I think one of those cats is trying to get out and is trapped under that blanket. Give me a second."

Again, the footsteps. This time faster. At that point, I forced myself to remain like a Buckingham Palace Guard, hoping she'd change her mind.

"Leave it be. You'll make things worse."

He's right, whoever you are. You'll make things worse. For me, that is!

By a stroke of luck, she listened and they exited the room. I waited until I heard the door close. Then I tore off the covers and brushed my arms and legs. Thoughts of mites, ticks, fleas, and bedbugs blocked everything else out of my mind. Next, I shook my head, figuring that maybe, if there were lice, they hadn't attached themselves yet.

An instant later, Ian opened the door a crack and whispered, "Better get going. The launch is in full swing. I peeked out of the office window."

"I might develop a rash. Or worse."

"Huh?"

"I had to hide under the covers. Tell you once we get out of here." Then I turned and made sure the blanket was back in place.

I couldn't stop itching as we stepped onto the crowded patio, only to find ourselves face to face with Wilsetta. She handed us pens and hole-punched file cards. "Write your messages and attach them to your mylar balloons. One of the library volunteers is blowing them up over there. Oh, and be sure to grab a glowstick and bend it around the string. Makes for a poignant nighttime farewell."

"Uh, yes," I mumbled. "Poignant."

When Ian and I were a safe distance from Wilsetta, I told him what happened in the bedroom.

He crinkled his eyes and looked at me from the ankles up. "Doubt it was bedbugs, but still…as soon as we get back, head for the shower and I'll be right behind."

"You weren't exposed to anything in that office."

"One can't be too careful."

I laughed and squeezed his shoulder.

"Enough with the lovey-dovey stuff. Mill around. You don't see Miss Marple canoodling with anyone." Edith flitted back and forth between Ian and me.

"She's what? In her eighties?"

"Who is?" Ian tilted his head toward mine.

"Um, just thinking out loud about possible suspects from the library."

"Yeah, it really could be anyone."

We grabbed pens and began writing. I hadn't composed fiction like this since my sophomore English class, but I knew Wilsetta was going to have us read them before setting them adrift in the night sky.

Ian rolled his neck and scribbled something. And just as Wilsetta approached us, gesturing for us to read our cards, a blood-curdling scream echoed through the vast space behind her house.

"Coyotes killing something?" Ian asked.

"No, they'd be yelping," someone replied. "Sounded human."

"Could be a bobcat. They make noises like that." It was another voice from the crowd.

And then, the scream again. This time louder and with more intensity.

"Can you tell where it's coming from?" I asked no one in particular.

"Has to be behind the house next door. Look! Lights are flickering in the windows."

"Pay no mind," Wilsetta said. "It's probably an electrical short. As for the noise, it's most likely coyotes making a kill. Now, let's get on with the balloon launch. Dear Richard's memory needs to fill the air."

She looked at me, and I, in turn, looked down at what I had written. I took a breath and prepared myself to read the worst piece of dribble imaginable when someone yelled, "Listen! Sirens! And they're getting closer!"

Wilsetta put her hands on her hip and stared at the neighboring house—Maddie's prospective sale house that may never sell.

"Maybe it wasn't coyotes." I recognized Lida's voice. Deep and husky.

"Maybe it was someone screaming for their life. This town is beginning to resemble the fictional ones in my books."

"I don't think so." Ian nudged me and pointed to the window. "It's real enough for me. Look! Two sheriff cars and too soon. Besides, one of them just turned into this driveway."

Chapter Twenty-Nine

Saturday

"It's probably nothing with nothing," Wilsetta announced. "We'll continue with our mourning vigil shortly." With that, she walked to the side of the house where the sheriff's car had parked, blue and red flashers still on.

Meanwhile, the other car turned into the property next door.

"Maybe someone thought the screaming was part of Wilsetta's balloon launch, and they called the sheriff's office." I looked at Ian and shrugged.

"Doubt it. They wouldn't have sent two cars."

Along with the rest of the curiosity seekers, we skirted around the house to where Wilsetta and two deputies stood talking. As I got closer, I realized one of them was Deputy Vincent.

His overall demeanor wasn't exactly warm and fuzzy. "Miss Frum?" he asked. She nodded. "Our office received more than a handful of complaints emanating from your house and the house next door. Reports of wild shrieks that sounded as if someone was in jeopardy."

Wilsetta crossed her arms and didn't move. "Sounds of the desert, that's all."

Deputy Vincent didn't move either. "The desert doesn't sound as if it's fighting for its life. That was one of the 911 calls our office received. Tell me, what's going on at your place? Quite the crowd. And what are those things in the air?"

"Memorial balloons in memory of the late and great Richard Bellmore. This is a mourning party."

"It's nighttime."

"Mourning. As in death vigil."

I tried not to laugh and wound up making small choking sounds that Deputy Vincent heard. Next thing I knew, he strode toward Ian and me and cleared his throat.

"Miss Aubrey, you do seem to have a penchant for showing up to places you should probably avoid."

"I was invited. Along with everyone else here."

The deputy surveyed the crowd. "Anything unusual going on? As if I need to ask." He took a step back and watched as two women clutched copies of a Bellmore novel and sobbed. The light from his vehicle was enough for me to see him widen his eyes at the sight of those women.

"In spite of the circumstances," he said, "I tend to think you're probably one of the more level-headed people here."

"Thanks. To answer your question, there's nothing going on here that would warrant a visit from your office." *Unless bat-poop-crazy counts.* "Maybe something was going on next door in the empty house. We heard those screams, too, but thought they were coyotes."

"I've got another two deputies checking that place out. Local rumor has it that it's haunted. Bunch of malarkey if you ask me. Anyway, we'll have a look-see and get going."

With that, he walked to his car and drove to the house next door. I didn't think much about it and returned, along with everyone else, to the patio where I was compelled to read my tribute to Richard and launch my yellow balloon in the air.

When the outdoor portion of our mourning vigil concluded, Wilsetta ushered us back into the house for a final toast to Richard. I was still itching like crazy and positive that my body was infested with all sorts of despicable insects and mites.

Wilsetta took a deep breath. "Let us toast to Richard with flavored oat milk. I read on one of the book jackets that he was quite fond of it."

"I'm quite fond of Bourbon," a craggy KC called out. "Can't we toast with that?"

I poked Ian. "I had no idea he was here."

"First I knew. I thought I had studied that crowd, but I guess I didn't spot him. But someone said they were pretty sure they saw Richard's fiancée."

"Dorrie? She was here?" The small hairs on my arms stood at attention. "That doesn't sound right. Wilsetta despises her."

"At least your aunt is with your folks. I don't want to think what that would have been like if she were here."

"Me either. Let my parents deal with her for a while."

I looked to my left and saw Wilsetta handing out red plastic cups and pouring the dreadful oat milk into them. My next instinct was to see where I could dump mine inconspicuously. No luck. Once she poured it, I swished it around as if it was fine wine. Then I slipped outside when I thought no one was looking. In a flash, I dumped the contents off of the patio onto the lawn. That's when I realized, the deputy cars were still at Maddie's listed house next door. Not only that, but a third car had now joined them.

I pulled out my phone and texted her: *At Wilsetta's vigil. Your house next door has 3 sheriff cars in the driveway. We heard screams earlier.*

Maddie texted back: *Find out what's going on. Can't end my date. Best one in ages.*

I sent her a heart emoji and a screamer. I figured she'd get the message.

"I don't think it's coyotes," Allison announced. "I was outside getting a bit of air, and guess what? They've got three vehicles over there. All with flashers on."

"Make it four." Barbara, whom I hadn't seen since the event started, joined Allison and the rest of the guests as they sashayed onto the patio for what now became the "late-night entertainment."

"Four sheriff cars?" I squinted to get a better look at the berm behind Wilsetta's house that separated her property from the one Maddie was trying to sell. With no street lights, the red and blue flashers were easily identifiable. And yep, there were four of them, all right.

"Maybe coyotes killed a neighbor's dog or something," one of the guests said.

"Not four vehicles for a dog. Not even if it was more than one dog. It's got to be something worse. Maybe those shrieks weren't from an animal after all." Barbara gazed in the distance and rubbed her arms together. "I don't know about anyone else, but I think I've had enough for one night. I'm going home."

"Aren't you the least bit curious?" the same guest asked.

Barbara shook her head. "Nope. My imagination will do a fine job before I even get to the highway."

As she turned to walk back inside, a sheriff's car pulled into Wilsetta's driveway for the second time.

"Uh-oh," I whispered to Ian. "Trouble in paradise?"

"Trouble, period."

Sure enough, Deputy Vincent returned for Act II. No one made a move as he slammed the car door shut and thundered back to the house, stopping for a brief moment to have a few words with Wilsetta, who was now in the kitchen. Next thing I knew, he directed everyone to gather on the patio for an announcement. Lucky Barbara. She had already made it to her car.

"Will someone make sure there are no criers in that sobbing room or whatever you call it. I need everyone's attention, and I need it now."

Terrific. Another Deputy Vincent moment.

"This definitely doesn't sound good." I edged closer to Ian, and he put his arm over my shoulder.

The cacophony of voices ended abruptly when Deputy Vincent announced, "There's been an unsettling discovery next door. I'll cut to the chase. Seems a body was found a few yards from the rear of the vacant house. Could have been the cause of those screams."

The chatter turned to gasps until Wilsetta asked, "Was it mangled by coyotes?"

That was followed by KC, who shook his head. "Doubt it. Coyotes usually don't mangle people. Had to be javalina. They're unpredictable as hell."

"What about—" But the female voice was cut off by Deputy Vincent. "We're not here to speculate, although I do concur that wildlife usually does not behave that way. The evidence will tell. Anyway, our office responded to numerous emergency calls, and that's what brought us to the victim. Now then, since all of you were at this crying party, or whatever you call it, and you're in close proximity to the scene of the, the…well, body, I will need written statements from every one of you."

"You don't think one of us was responsible," Allison asked. "We've been here the entire time."

"This is an investigation, and like I said, 'I will need statements.'"

At that moment, there was a rap on the door, and another deputy announced himself before stepping inside. Deputy Mikkelson, to be precise. Tall, sandy hair, and recently out of puberty.

Deputy Vincent studied the faces around the patio. "Find a place to plant yourselves and get a statement sheet from Deputy Mikkelson. A pen, too, if you need it. I want names, addresses, phone numbers, and emails. Understood? And no one leaves until you are directed to do so. This is a very disturbing situation."

"Definitely not javalina or coyotes," KC whispered. "Unless he plans on questioning them as well."

I tried not to chuckle and wound up choking. "Frog in my throat," I said out loud, but no one paid attention. No one except Edith, who sat on a cushioned bench, admiring her fingernails. "Wake up, Missy, and ask if everyone's here. Don't need another author on the fast-track to the Great Unknown."

"Don't you know?"

"Know what?" Ian asked.

"I meant, 'Do you know if any of the authors are missing?'"

"Hmm, no. But that's a really good question."

Chapter Thirty

I completed my statement, handed it to Deputy Mikkelson, and texted Maddie: *Dead body found on property next door.*

The text read "delivered," but I didn't think I'd be hearing back from her until tomorrow.

Then, I perused the patio and counted off the authors—KC, Lida, Jessica, Barbara, and Arist. Whoever departed from this world wasn't one of them. Allison sat a few feet from us and must have had the same idea. She leaned forward and called out, "All of the authors are here. So are my staff members and volunteers. Don't know about the patrons though."

My next thought was Colleen, although I doubted she would have ventured next door. I stood and took a few steps when Deputy Vincent directed me to remain seated, but that didn't stop me from blurting out, "I'm looking for my neighbor, Colleen Wexby. I haven't seen her, and the thought that she might be the body on that property over there is downright chilling."

"She's not," he said. "I have her statement right here. She went inside for a glass of water. Something about the taste of oat milk in her mouth."

"Can you tell me if the body was a man or a woman?"

"No, I cannot. Not until the initial review of the scene by our forensics team is complete. I suggest that you, along with everyone else, wait until information is released to the news media."

Under ordinary circumstances, local news vans would already be on the scene. However, given the late hour and the distance from Phoenix, I figured it wouldn't be until morning when they covered the situation. Just as well. Didn't need my aunt to hear about it and grill me for information I didn't have.

It was another forty or so minutes before Deputy Vincent collected the last of the statements and informed us that we were free to go. He told us that his office would be contacting each of us for follow-up information, and that if we thought of something that we did not write down on our statements, to call his office after nine the next day.

When he and Deputy Mikkelson left, a number of us moved closer to the edge of the patio and watched as the victim was loaded onto a gurney. The forensics crew had set up portable lights so it was as if we had our own private showing of "the grim discovery."

Wilsetta stared at the scene and shuddered. "Dreadful. I hate to think Cave Creek will become the next Phoenix crime pocket."

"I doubt that," someone said. Then the man approached Wilsetta. "Thank you for inviting us to Richard's farewell. He was an incredible author, and he will be missed." With that, the man took off, followed by a few more guests who shouted their thanks and appreciation to Wilsetta for "a night we will always remember and cherish."

"I doubt the body next door will cherish it," Ian said as we headed inside so I could grab my hoodie from the pile of jackets and coats on Wilsetta's side table. I'd placed it there when we first got here and should have retrieved it before going to the patio, but everything happened so fast.

"Rats! My aunt's hoodie is missing. Someone must have taken it by mistake. I'll let Wilsetta know in case they return it. Maybe even ask Allison to post it with the library news. Guess I'll have to get her a new one. Embroidered no less. Who does that? I thought personal names on clothes went out in the seventies."

"Yeah, that's what I hate about hanging up coats and stuff at gatherings. Half the time, someone winds up with the wrong one."

I told Wilsetta and thanked her for including us in her tribute to Richard.

"By the way," I said, "If you find out anything about what happened next door, can you give me a call at The Char-Board? I'd appreciate it. My friend is the listing agent for that property."

"Hurumph. After tonight, I doubt there will be many offers."

"Thanks anyway."

Ian and I followed Lida and Jessica to our cars. By now, only a few vehicles remained in the driveway and on the road.

"This is certainly good fodder for my next novel," Lida said to all of us. "A mourning party and another dead body. You can't make this stuff up."

"Who'd want to?" Jessica looked around and shuddered. "I like to keep murder between the pages, not looking me in the face. Honestly, Lida, 'good fodder?' It's one thing to fabricate this stuff, but quite another when it's dead-on real and smacking us in the face."

"I'd like to keep it as far away as possible," I said, "but I have a funny feeling this may be just the beginning."

"That was optimistic," Ian laughed when he started the engine. "At least the victim wasn't anyone we knew."

I gulped. "I hope you're right."

As he pulled away from the house, I could still see two sheriff cars next door and decided to text Maddie again.

The body's been removed, but the crew is still on the property. Call or text me when you read this.

Unfortunately, Maddie didn't read it until the next morning, and by then, news of a body being discovered on the property she listed was all over the news. Not only that, but the victim's gender as well—female, late forties/early fifties. No other information was given, other than a request for Silent Witness if anyone knew anything.

Ian and I had just finished our first cup of coffee and were glued to the local Sunday news while Speedbump continued to wolf down his kibble. Since my parents and my aunt were aware that I had attended the so-called "party," which took place a stone's throw from a possible murder victim, I worried they'd phone. With fingers crossed, I prayed they'd wait until the victim was identified. Then, pending results, I'd have to share what little I knew.

Lamentably, I didn't have to ponder longer than a day. No sooner did I flip the Open sign on the door to The Char-Board the following Monday morning when I was greeted by none other than Deputy Vincent. Thankfully, none of our customers had arrived yet, but Javie and Lilly-Ann were within earshot and heard every word.

"Miss Aubrey, I need a word with you." The deputy's voice was stiff and mechanical.

I shrugged and widened my eyes. "Sure. Does this have something to do with Saturday night? Because if does, it was all over the news yesterday. I caught it at noon. The news anchor said it was a woman and—"

"Yes. Yes. I'm perfectly aware of that. What I'm not aware of, is this." He opened a large black bag and revealed my aunt's hoodie. Up close and personal, the name "Regina" blazed in front of my eyes.

"My aunt's hoodie! Did someone turn it into the sheriff's Lost and Found? That's wonderful."

"So you admit you recognize this sweatshirt?"

"Of course I do. It belongs to my aunt Regina. It even has her name embroidered on the front."

He reclosed the bag and stuffed it under his arm. "I'll need to speak with your aunt immediately."

"There's no need. I can fill out a claim form or whatever your office needs."

"What my office needs is to have a word with your aunt. Let me be succinct. This item was found a few feet from the victim's body."

It took a second or two for the words to sink in, and I think I may have mumbled them to myself before speaking coherently. "My aunt was nowhere near that body. Or that house. She's now staying at my parents' house. Long story. Hates the ventilation at my place. Something about dust whorls." Suddenly, I realized I was jabbering but couldn't seem to stop.

"Deputy Vincent," I babbled on, "I wore that hoodie to Wilsetta's house. I grabbed it from my coatrack, thinking it was mine. Didn't realize it until much later on, but figured my aunt would never know. I threw it on Wilsetta's side table with all the other jackets and sweaters from the guests. Then, when I went to get it when I left, it was missing."

He looked at me as if I had just described a field of aliens dancing to the Macarena. "Indeed."

"I'm telling you the truth. My aunt wasn't at that mourning party. She and Richard were not on the best of terms, and Wilsetta certainly didn't invite her to honor his passing."

"I understand you may feel the need to protect your aunt, but failing to disclose the truth to an officer of the law constitutes obstruction of justice, which can lead to fines or even prison time."

Just what I need. Prison time.

I bit my lower lip and exhaled through my teeth. "Believe me, I'm not covering for my aunt. Whoever snatched that hoodie from the pile of outerwear, had to be the person who was responsible for committing murder. And maybe, just maybe…they recognized the name 'Regina,' and set her up to take the fall."

"Or maybe, your aunt snuck into that party. It was dark, and from what I gathered, there was quite the crowd. Who is to say she didn't find her own sweatshirt in that pile of clothes?"

At that moment, three customers walked in, and two more followed a second later. I motioned them to the tables and told them we'd be right there. Then I looked directly at the deputy and asked, "Are you going to arrest me? I was the last person to have worn that hoodie."

His voice was stern and steely. "I am going to return this to our forensics lab for further testing, but rest assured, given the preponderance of evidence against your aunt, I strongly suggest legal counsel. And one more thing, I shall need the address where she is now staying."

I recited my parents' address and watched as he took a pen from his pocket and wrote it down on a small pad. It was now inescapable. I'd have to let my aunt and my parents know about Deputy Vincent's newest possession, emblazoned with the word, "Regina." And more pressing than that, I had no recourse but to find out who stole it. Yep, stole it. It was no coincidence that my aunt's black hoodie wound up in the vicinity of a dead body.

Chapter Thirty-One

Monday

"We heard everything," Lilly-Ann said when I walked into the kitchen. "Javie raced out to take orders, and I've been back here getting them ready. Oh my gosh, Katie, what are you going to do?"

"I wish I knew. It's a stressor I don't need. Heck, all of this is getting to me. I never had trouble falling asleep, but now I've become the poster child for insomnia. I seriously do not have an inkling of what to do next."

"Well, I do. But did you ask? I'll have you know my skills aren't limited to the culinary world." Edith crossed one leg over the other and sat herself on a stool in front of the counter. "Begin with the victim. Find out who she was. If you wait for the news media, it'll be Christmas before you know it."

"Christmas," I muttered.

"Huh?'

"Sorry, Lilly-Ann. I'm thinking it'll be Christmas before the sheriff's office comes close to catching a killer. I need to find out who that victim was before I can even think of who might be responsible."

"Ah-hah! So you're following my advice after all!" Edith stretched her arms out in a twirling motion before settling back on the stool. I turned the other way in a desperate attempt to ignore her.

"I'm trying to be rational."

Lilly-Ann squinted. "Of course you are. And speaking of rational, do you think that woman's murder is connected to Richard Bellmore's?"

"I thought it was totally random. Maybe someone out walking, or a blind date gone bad."

"Or someone who didn't want that house to sell."

I froze the second Lilly-Ann said that. The thought had never occurred to me, but what if there was a diabolical person out there who would stop at nothing to prevent a sale? Even if it meant murdering an unsuspecting woman.

"Katie, are you all right? You look as if you've seen a ghost."

Seen one. Talked to one. Yelled at one. And the list goes on...

"Yeah, I'm fine. I'd better get going with orders. The place must be filling up. At least it'll take my mind off of my aunt and those murders for the next two hours. Oh no! My aunt! Deputy Vincent is probably on his way over there now. Rats!!"

"Call her. Javie's got a handle on things, and I'll go take orders. Besides, it'll take that deputy a while to drive to the other side of Scottsdale."

"Not with his lights and siren on!"

I moved to the corner of the kitchen and tapped my mother's cell number. *Yep. Let her deal with this mess.*

"Mom, I hate to bother you, especially if you're working, but there's a situation going on with Aunt Regina and you need to know about it."

"*Another* situation? How many more *situations* can she have?"

"Um, the same one but with more ammunition from the sheriff's office."

"I don't understand."

"Remember that vigil one of Richard Bellmore's fans held for him Saturday night? And I went because I thought I could snoop around? Anyway, Aunt Regina accidentally left her hoodie at my house, and I didn't realize it. I wound up wearing it over there."

"Is that all? You wore an old sweatshirt of hers?"

"It gets worse. I put it with the other hoodies and jackets when I got there, but when I went to find it later, it was gone."

"Oh dear. Guess you'll have to buy her a new one."

"That's not the issue." *I'd buy her Nordstrom's entire collection if it would make this all go away.*

"Then what is?" My mom began to sound irritated.

"The hoodie was found right near the dead woman's body on the property next door to where the vigil was held. The lead deputy just left here, and he's on his way to speak with her at your house. I had to give him the address. Something about withholding information."

"Oh dear. This is not good. Not good at all."

"It's worse than 'not good.' It's bona fide evidence, even if it's circumstantial. Plus, they already have evidence of her bracelet with Richard's hair that was found at the crime scene. If those two people are connected, Aunt Regina will be trying on orange jumpsuits."

"I'll call our lawyer right now. Hers is in New Jersey. A lot of good that does."

"Tell my aunt not to speak until a lawyer gets there. Or a paralegal." *Or anyone who's watched Law and Order.*

"I'll keep you posted. Good thing I'm working from home. And Katie, I know you. It was bad enough you snooped around at that vigil. Imagine, a murder yards from where you were. Don't put yourself in that kind of position again. I'm sure once a complete investigation is done, the authorities will realize your aunt is not culpable."

"I'm not so sure. But don't worry. I'll be fine."

When I ended the call with my mom, I texted Ian to let him know about my surprise visit from Deputy Vincent. No sooner did I tap the Send arrow, when a text from Maddie appeared: *MCSO sent 2 deputies to our office. Rookies. Wanted to know if the victim was one of our clients.*

I immediately texted back: *Who is she? It's not on the news.*

And then: *Keep this to yourself. It's hush-hush for now. According to her ID, it's Dorrie Arnst. Post-mortem results pending. Plus notifying next of kin. Will call you later.*

Wasting no time, I texted Maddie's message to Ian and grabbed the plated breakfasts to take them to the dining area. After three runs back and forth, Javie held out his arm, and I stopped dead in my tracks.

"What's going on?" He furrowed his brow. "I've never known you to work without talking. It's as if you're in a cloud or something."

"Worse." In the two or three minutes that followed, I told him everything that had happened, beginning with Ian and my arrival at Wilsetta's. "Share that with Lilly-Ann and Matt, when he gets here. I don't have the energy to repeat it," I said.

Javie nodded. "No problem, but what's the next step in your game plan? I know you have to have something brewing in your head."

"Shh—keep this to yourself. My game plan was to find out who the victim was, and I did—Dorrie Arnet. Maddie's office had a surprise visit from MCSO because they're the listing agents for the property where her body was found."

"Yeesh."

"For sure. But now that I know, I'm not sure where to begin. One thing for certain—those murders have to be connected. Dorrie was Richard's fiancée and was more than distraught over his death. Wanted my aunt to confess to something she didn't do."

"Are you thinking that whoever killed Richard, knocked her off as well?"

"I suppose. It's way too coincidental."

"What about her ex-husband? Also an author. Think he did the deed?"

"Revenge and jealousy are always solid motives. I doubt it had to do with money. Unless Arist had a mega policy on Dorrie."

"Or Dorrie had one on Richard that would go to the secondary benefi-ciary."

"Who?"

"That's the million-dollar question."

It was all but impossible for any of us to concentrate on charcuterie trays and sandwiches, but somehow, we made it through the day. The sheriff's office still hadn't released Dorrie's identity to the media, so I kept things to myself. It was that or I'd have to tell Matt I'd slice his tongue off and put it on one of our trays if he dared to let it slip.

At a little past four, I made myself a cup of coffee and sat at one of the empty tables to gather my thoughts. I grabbed a napkin, and with a pen that was in my pocket, drew my first "order of operations." Only it had nothing to do with math.

Instead, it was a step-by-step plan to poke, pry, and snoop out any information that would hopefully lead to an arrest that didn't involve anyone in my family, including me.

Once I finished, I photo'd it and texted it to Ian with the following: *Which Hardy Boy do you want to play?*

He texted back: *Slow down, Columbo. R U available for pizza and an action plan tonight?* Then: *Not that kind of action.* Followed by silly-face emoji.

My response: *With bells on!*

Chapter Thirty-Two

Monday

When Ian and I returned to my place, having consumed a meatball, mushroom, and pepperoni pizza from Brugos Pizza Company, we plopped ourselves on the couch in a full-blown pizza coma.

"I suppose we really should do something productive," Ian said. "I had all the best intentions, but that last slice of the pie literally did me in. At least we were able to brainstorm as we stuffed ourselves. Now all we need to do is finalize our action plan."

"My murder notebook is on the kitchen table. Hang on."

A few minutes later, I sat, humped over the coffee table, jotting down what we remembered from our prior conversation.

"Colleen is more than the eyes and ears of the neighborhood. Very little escapes her. I'll make it a point to mosey over there tomorrow when I walk Speedbump in the afternoon. She's back from work by then."

"Good." Ian rubbed the back of his neck and looked down at the list of names I had written. "I wager those authors were less than thrilled when Deputy Vincent informed them they'd have to extend their visit to Cave Creek while MCSO continued its investigation." He looked at his cell phone and then at me. "I know we're pooped but now would be a perfect time to chitchat with Arist and KC at the Prickly Pear. With nothing else going on, they'll be at the bar for sure."

"But they don't know the victim is Dorrie."

"I wouldn't be too sure about that. Artist is the ex-husband, and I guarantee someone already informed him."

"If that's the case, and he and Arist talk to each other, it won't stay a secret for much longer. Men can be worse about spilling out information. No offense."

Ian laughed. "None taken. So it's a yes?"

"I'll let Speedbump out for a minute and we can take off."

Once again, we found ourselves at the Prickly Pear's bar and no surprise that both authors had made themselves at home. KC on a bar stool near the restrooms, with a large draft in front of him, and Arist at a table by himself, staring at a pitcher. The word "despondent" immediately sprang to mind.

"Who do you want?" Ian winked. "The 'two-fisted drinker' or the 'crying in his beer' one?"

"Beer crying. I'll give him a soulful look and eke out what info I can. When he tells me he knows the woman was Dorrie, I'll crank it up a notch."

"You're beginning to sound ruthless."

"Nah, just overtired. What about you?" I really didn't have to ask because I could see it on Ian's face. He was as exhausted as I was.

"Yes too tired, but as far as KC is concerned, I'll need to tread carefully. His bravado isn't sitting too well with me."

"What do you mean?"

"Nothing I can pinpoint. Just one of those guys who's all show and hot air."

"Good Luck. How about twenty—twenty-five minutes, and we meet in the outdoor patio? The heaters are on, so we won't freeze."

"It's a plan." Ian gave me a thumbs up and turned toward the bar. I headed in the opposite direction and walked directly to Arist's table before I took a closer look and chickened out. Another woman beat me to it. Unsure of what my next move should be, I backtracked to the bar and ordered a Coke with lemon.

I couldn't tell who Arist was speaking with since the woman's back was to me and I couldn't very well scootch around them. I tried leaning to my side when I heard Edith's raspy voice. "It's the librarian, you chicken."

"I can't hover like you do," I said under my breath.

With her hair pulled up and dressed down in jeans and a fleece top, I didn't realize it was Allison.

"Walk over there and say something." Edith whirled around me, creating a light fog. I ambled over, Coke in hand, when the fog intensified and I stumbled forward, bumping into the table. The pitcher of frothy beer landed in Allison's lap, and I stood back, speechless.

"I couldn't think of anything else." Edith shrugged, and the fog evaporated. "Best I could do on short notice."

Allison stood, grabbed the linen napkin from the table, and blotted her top, but most of the beer had landed on the front of her jeans. Oblivious to the fact that I was only feet from her table, she rushed off, presumably to the ladies' room, while I took full advantage of the situation and snagged her place at the table.

"I'm sorry," Arist called out. "I'll pay for any dry cleaning." But it was too late. Allison was already halfway to the restroom.

"Jeans and cotton tops don't need dry cleaning," I said. "And some stains don't come out. Lucky for her, beer isn't one of them. I didn't know both of you were acquaintances. Mind if I keep you company until she gets back?"

Arist, who had used his napkin to sop up the liquid from the table, looked up. I could see his eyes were red, and I doubted they were from allergies. "Make yourself comfortable. Up until the event, the only correspondence she and I had was via email regarding the event. She stopped in here to grab a bite and saw me. What brings you here?"

"Pretty much the same thing. After making food for a living, it's nice to have someone else prepare it. Anyway, have you heard any news on that body they found next to Wilsetta's house? I've been at work all day and had errands to run. Never caught the news."

"The name wasn't released yet on the news." He rubbed an eye and blinked.

"But you know, don't you," I said, "I can tell by your swollen eyes."

"That transparent, huh?"

"Red, puffy eyes? It's not allergy season here. What do you know? Or should I ask, *who?* Although I can wager a good guess."

"Tell him. Tell him you know everything! Do it! Do it"

"Don't act like an impertinent child." I glared at Edith, but Arist jumped in.

"Impertinent? More like shocked and terrified rolled into one. That miserable deputy came to my room and dropped the bomb on me as if he was telling me about stock prices that fell, not my former wife being found dead a few yards from a get-together I was attending."

"That's terrible."

"What's terrible is having to identify the body."

"But they already knew."

"Circumstantially, yes. But nothing like an up-close and personal ID of a corpse."

I gulped. "Did they say how she was killed? Could you tell when you looked?"

Arist motioned for a waitress and asked for another pitcher. "I was informed that the preliminary post-mortem suggested death by strangulation. I couldn't tell. Her neck was covered. All I saw were scratches on her face." He bent down and rubbed his forehead.

"I'm sorry. Really, I am. Even though people divorce, it doesn't mean they still don't have feelings for each other."

"That's the same thing the deputy said. Only he followed it with the word *motive.*"

"Did he mention any other suspects?"

"No."

Hmm, Deputy Vincent must be playing this one close to his chest.

"What did you say to him?"

"That Dorrie had feelings for Richard."

"And?"

"And I was directed to keep mum and remain in Cave Creek as a possible suspect in her murder."

"What about Richard's murder?" I stepped closer in case he whispered.

Arist shook his head. "Nothing new, but I'm still on the list. Same as everyone."

"Arist, do you have any idea who would kill Dorrie and why?"

"Only one person—that aunt of yours. Regina."

"What? Why?"

"To silence her, of course. Dorrie must have confronted Regina at some point regarding Richard's death and maybe even threatened to blackmail her. It was no secret your aunt and Richard were not on the best of terms."

"Don't tell me you shared that ill-conceived theory with Deputy Vincent?"

"Never got the opportunity."

I unclenched my teeth and took slow, measured breaths. "What about the other authors? You must have heard something."

"Nope. It's a regular poker game around here, only with higher stakes."

"Did you tell Allison?"

"No. And I shouldn't have told you."

"Don't worry. I know when to keep quiet. Most likely, they'll reveal her identity in the next twenty-four hours."

At that moment, Allison returned to the table, and I relinquished my seat. "Sorry about the drink," I said, "I think I must have startled everyone."

"I'll be fine. Grab another chair, Katie. I didn't realize that was you. These things happen all the time around here. The bars are packed, and everyone bumps into people—literally and figuratively. We were just chit-chatting about the awful turn of events. Imagine—two murders within a week. And in Cave Creek, no less. Even though I'm a tad hesitant, I hope this doesn't deter our board from wanting to conduct more high-profile events once these are solved. *If* they're solved. I can't help but wonder if both murders are related."

With a slight tremor in his hand, Arist reached for the only glass of water on the table and took a long drink. "Go ahead. Say it. I know what you're thinking. I know what everyone must be thinking—that I murdered Richard out of anger and revenge. Well, I can tell you right now, I didn't. I may have disliked the man for reasons too innumerable to mention, but Dorrie was smitten by him. No matter my feelings for her, Dorrie had moved on."

His eyes welled up a bit more, and I watched as he took one of those small paper napkins and wiped it across his eyelid.

I glanced over to where Ian and KC were talking, and judging from Ian's body language, I still had time. "Allison, were you aware of anyone on your staff who harbored a grudge toward Richard or his fiancée?"

"Not a grudge, but Wilsetta was certainly star-struck with him. I wouldn't have been surprised if she threatened the fiancée prior to his murder. But after? What's the point? Besides, she was at her house the entire time. Wasn't she?"

"Can anyone document that?" Arist's demeanor shifted from "deer in the headlights" to accuser.

Allison looked startled for a second and then spoke. "That's something for the sheriff's office to ascertain. But as far as what went on at Wilsetta's place, no one kept tabs on anyone. People all over the place. Easy to slip in and out."

I really wanted to know if either of them had noticed Dorrie on the premises, but since neither of them offered it up, I was stuck. Even though a theory brewed in my head. Not yet, anyway. Dorrie *had* to have shown up at Wilsetta's and then left the property, only to be confronted by a killer.

"Um, I need to get going. Nice seeing both of you. Even under these troubling circumstances. If you hear anything, would you please call The Char-Board. It's no secret I'm concerned about my aunt."

"Absolutely," Allison replied, followed by a "Yeah, sure," from Arist.

I left my Coke glass on the table and walked outside. Ian was seated in front of a Ficus tree in the far left and I rushed over. "Arist identified the body. MCSO swooped in on him to confirm what they could ascertain from her cell phone. It was still with her, along with her purse. Her license said 'Dorrie Arnst' and believe it or not, Arist was listed as one of her emergency contacts on the phone."

"I can't believe he shared that with you."

"He may have had one beer too many. And right now, he's chewing his nails. His spot on the suspect list just moved up a notch."

"That may be good news for your aunt."

"Not necessarily. I asked him if he knew of anyone with a motive to murder his ex, and his response was Regina."

"She's going to have a hard time exonerating herself. Wish I had info to share from KC, but unfortunately, I don't. He didn't know a thing. Hadn't spoken with Arist, even though they're staying in the same hotel. The only thing he mentioned was that his publisher called, and after some tight negotiations, he landed a mega movie deal for *Don't Ride Alone.* Apparently, it's been a long time coming. He's anxious as heck to get out of here. Said he was so jazzed that he forgot to put on his belt when he left the room. Thought maybe I noticed."

I laughed. "Did you?"

"Heck no. That's the last thing I'd be looking at."

"I forgot to mention this, but Allison was the woman seated next to him when I arrived. I sort of managed to dump his pitcher of beer on her so I could speak with him privately."

"Forget Miss Marple. You've become a regular Stephanie Plum."

"Tell that to Janet Evanovich."

Chapter Thirty-Three

Tuesday

I tugged at Speedbump's leash the next morning as I walked down the block, hoping to run into Colleen before she left for work. I'd already phoned Lilly-Ann and asked her to open The Char-Board for me. Tuesdays weren't as frenetic as Mondays, due to deliveries, and with any luck, I figured I wouldn't be too long. Unlike Arist, Colleen didn't need to be coaxed in order to share whatever "news" passed her way.

Unfortunately, Speedbump had other plans. He spotted a rabbit that ran behind the house next to Colleen's and nearly yanked my arm off in an attempt to chase after it. Stumbling forward, I caught myself inches away from a nasty clump of barrel cactus.

Next door, Colleen had backed her car out of her garage and was about to drive off when she spotted me. "Are you all right?" She rolled down her window and leaned forward.

I caught my breath as I pulled the dog toward me. "Thanks. I'm fine. Still unnerved about Saturday's party and that body they discovered next door, but other than that, fine."

"Good job, Missy. You got right into it before she drove off." I clenched my hands and tried not to react to the swirling mauve haze that was Edith's telltale entrance.

"You and me both. All I know was that it was a woman, but the rumor mill has been stirring like mad. I heard it was Richard Bellmore's fiancée. Don't say anything, but that's the buzz around here. You know, she could have shown up at Wilsetta's that night. Who would have known? It was dark out, and it wasn't as if the place was locked or anything. What have you heard?"

I shrugged. "Nothing."

"Don't make eye contact. It's your tell. She'll know you're lying."

Again, I ignored Edith and let Colleen continue.

"I also heard your aunt is the prime suspect since she and Richard had a fractured working relationship."

"Where did you hear that?"

"Wilsetta mentioned it, but please don't tell her you heard it from me."

"Um, about the fiancée, what else have you heard? Motive? Enemies? Come on, Colleen, I won't breathe a word of it. Besides, your rumor mill is probably right and her identity is bound to be disclosed to the public. It's been three days."

"She was still having issues with her ex-husband, Arist Arnet. Korina, one of the library aides, told me that they almost didn't invite Arist because they heard about the situation and didn't want to risk an uncomfortable scene between Arist and Richard. Ha! Some scene. Two murders, no less. And here I was worried about peeping Toms in the neighborhood. Now I'll have to add murderers."

"I wouldn't go that far. Hmm, I wonder what changed the library board's mind about inviting Arist."

"The librarian, that's what. Or *who*. According to Korina, it was Allison who insisted the board invite Arist because his cozy mysteries are so well-known."

Or maybe something else.

"I see. Anyway, I should let you get to work. And I need to do the same. Got a late start this morning. Have a great day, Colleen."

"You too. And watch out for those rabbits. They come out of nowhere." She started to back the car out when something occurred to me.

"Colleen! Wait! Any chance you can find out for sure if anyone saw Richard's fiancée at Wilsetta's that night?"

"Hmm, come to think of it, I took lots of photos on my phone but haven't had the chance to look. I'll check during my break and let you know if I spot her. I've only seen her photo in publicity shots with Richard, but not many women can pull off a decent bob like hers."

"Thanks. I appreciate it."

"You don't have to say a word. I know you want to get your aunt off the hook. Everyone knows."

I gulped and watched as she backed the car out and headed down the street. Speedbump bumped my knee and I petted his head. "Good boy. Only next time, don't pull so hard."

If Colleen had tangible evidence of Dorrie's presence, it would open up the investigation to include more suspects. And if not? I tried not to think about it and instead, focused on Arist. For someone who had issues with his ex, he seemed genuinely distraught. Then again, it could have been nerves and fear. Nerves because he was her killer, and fear because he would be found out.

The trouble was, I couldn't prove a darn thing.

"How'd your snooping go?" Lilly-Ann asked when I walked into The Char-Board. I was a good hour later than usual, and the place was filled to capacity. Mostly the usuals, but a few tourists. She was busy refilling coffees, and I gave her a thumbs up as I rushed into the kitchen.

Javie unwrapped a few English muffins and put them into the toaster. "Just in time. I'll have these orders up in a jiff. Lilly-Ann said you were tracking down information from your nosey neighbor who went to that same mourning vigil or whatever you called it."

"A disaster. That's what I called it, and yeah, my neighbor, Colleen, is the proverbial eyes and ears of the county, plus the 'voice of the valley.'"

Javie choked back a laugh. "So what did you find out? Anything that could get your aunt out of the hot seat?"

"Not exactly. But hopeful. Oh my gosh, I'm not supposed to breathe a word of this, but I know who that female victim was."

"So does everyone else in the Greater Phoenix area. It was on the 'News at Nine' morning segment on channel 10. Also KPHO, channel 5. Matt called here to tell us. He'll be in shortly. Thought we should know it's Dorrie

Arnet. The fiancée and ex-wife. Not in that order."

"What else was on the news? Did Matt say?"

"Uh-huh. Preliminary autopsy indicated foul play. Deemed suspicious. They're waiting for toxicology results. Anyone who knows anything was asked to call Silent Witness."

"Anything more definitive? Stab wound? Ligature marks? Gunshot?"

"The news didn't say. Or didn't know."

I texted Ian as Javie spoke. Then I took Javie's orders into the dining room when something hit me like a paintball to the chest. I hadn't considered Jessica as a suspect, but she was more than peeved Richard had gotten the coveted Claremont Award she deserved. In fact, Javie and I overheard her accuse Richard of bribing the judges. Maybe in a fit of anger, she was the one who pushed him into that waterfall. I just needed a way to find out.

Then, as if Edith could read my mind, she appeared a few feet from me in a black mestiza bolero dress that would have looked darling on Taylor Swift. On Edith, no so much. A black dust devil circled around her legs, and I held my breath. Whatever she was up to, it couldn't have been good.

"You need to crank the heat up if you want your aunt to get back to the Garden State."

"What?" I looked around to make sure no one could hear me.

"Your so-called sleuthing is moving slower than a digestive track on a ninety-eight-year-old plumber."

"What are you suggesting? And by the way, that was a horrible image that will most likely stay with me all day."

"Gumshoeing may work in the detective novels, but nothing beats romancing to get the truth out of someone."

"What someone? What romance?"

"Don't tell me the thought hadn't crossed your mind? You fix up Jessica, of course. She all but had fire breathing out of her mouth when she and Richard got into it during the author talks."

"But how did you—? I mean, Jessica just came into my mind a few seconds ago."

"I can't help it if you're a slow thinker. Listen, I have the most ingenious plan that will either eliminate a suspect, or uncover a murderer."

Again, I looked around. "I'm listening."

"Javie. Javie Rivera. He's tall, dark, exceedingly handsome, and single as far as I know."

"Oh my gosh! What are you suggesting?"

"Really? I have to spell it out for you? You really are quite the Pollyanna."

"Are you okay, Katie?" Lilly-Ann asked. She had an armload of plates and brushed past me. "You look like you're in a daze or really deep in thought."

"Uh, the thought. Javie told me Matt called with the news about Dorrie."

"Yeah. Bizarre, huh? Those murders have to be connected. A famous author and his fiancée? That's no coincidence." She turned and raced back to the kitchen with the dishes. Wasting no time, Edith continued spouting off.

"Jessica's fairly young and in good shape. Granted, a tad older than Javie, but you're not one to cast aspersions on that."

The heat in my cheeks rose, and I knew it wasn't from the room temperature. "Spit it out. What are you saying?"

"Get Javie to ask her out. Romance her. Find out if she had means and opportunity. We already know she had a motive."

"That's preposterous. I can't ask him to do a thing like that."

"Fine. Then pay him."

"Oh, good grief! That's even worse! There's a word for that sort of work."

"Actually, it's two words—*undercover work*."

Chapter Thirty-Four

Tuesday

Edith continued to pester me at The Char-Board in spite of my attempts to ignore her. Finally, at a little before two, she decided to see what was happening in her unearthly realm and took off. But not without admonishing me first for my "eighteenth-century thinking."

It wasn't as if I hadn't exhausted every bit of energy I had trying to figure out who killed Richard and his fiancée. I simply was up against a brick wall. Worse yet, there were two murders, not one. And there was no common denominator as far as the weapon was concerned.

Richard had an unexplained bump to the back of his head, but it was the heat lamp in the water that electrocuted him. Dorrie was, well, dead. I supposed I could cross electrocution off my list, but it still left a laundry list of "means."

I stood at the sink, rinsing off some pans while Matt and Lilly-Ann handled the few remaining customers and their orders. Meanwhile, Javie checked the contents of the refrigerator and consolidated a number of items.

Tossing an empty jar of jalapeños into the trash, he glanced my way. "It's frustrating, isn't it? We're getting tidbits of information regarding murders that are close to home, and we have no idea if we're dealing with one or two killers."

I turned the faucet off and wiped my hands. "Duh! I need two murder strands, not one. With one strand, I'm forcing the information to line up."

"I'm not sure I understand."

"My murder maps. I always keep a murder map of suspects, motives, opportunity, timing. That sort of thing. Only in this case, I have one combo map, not two."

"Wow. I had no idea you were so thorough about your sleuthing."

"Yeah, well, a few dead bodies too many and it becomes a habit. The maps, I mean. Not the murders. But you've given me a better direction at least. Maybe by breaking it down, I'll find connections that were there in the first place. And if not, then I'll know we're dealing with two entirely different homicides."

"And you majored in tech with a penchant for culinary arts?" he laughed. "You should have studied criminology."

"Nah. That would take all the fun out of it. Although, this is anything but. I have horrible thoughts about my aunt in prison garb."

"Don't lose faith. They haven't even disclosed Dorrie's cause of death. That could be a tremendous clue."

"Or one that points straight to my aunt."

Javie went back to consolidating our foods while I pondered my next move. Usually I dismiss Edith's outrageous suggestions, but she did have a valid point about eking out information from Jessica. So much so that I texted Ian about it when I got home later in the day.

"Funny you should mention her name," he texted back. *"Sterling popped in and told me that she and Lida had made reservations for a late lunch here tomorrow and he wanted me to 'go all out,' since I'll be the one running the kitchen. Too bad I can't be a fly on that wall and listen to their conversation."*

Forget the fly. I had Edith. That is, if I could find her. Usually her jaunts didn't last that long, and I kept my fingers crossed I'd find her sprawled out on the couch before nine.

I texted back: *No, but I can. I'll take Lilly-Ann with me. Maddie's got a full schedule. Can you make sure we're seated in close range? And can I get the employee discount?*

He answered with a thumbs up and a heart, followed by *"It's on the house!"*

By quarter to ten, Edith still hadn't made an appearance, and I began to worry. Not that she *wouldn't* appear, but it would be after the fact, and without her to hover around, I doubted Lilly-Ann or I would pick up any pertinent information.

Unfortunately, that was the last of my worries. The next day, when I asked Lilly-Ann to join me for a gourmet lunch and a bit of conversation snooping, she all but burst into tears. "Oh, Katie, I'd love to, really I would, but I have a dentist appointment for a new crown, and it was a four-week waiting time. If I cancel at the last minute, it'll be another four weeks for sure. Or more."

I tried to hide my disappointment, but I was as transparent as Saran wrap. Enough so that Javie noticed.

"Hey, not that I was eavesdropping," he said, "but it's a small kitchen, you know."

I nodded. "No problem. I found out that Lida and Jessica are having lunch this afternoon at Randolph's Escapade, and I thought I might be able to glean something from their conversation. Ian found out at the last minute. Luckily, the meal will be a freebie."

Lilly-Ann tossed the towel she held into our wash bin and sighed. "The one chance I get to dine at a five-star restaurant, and instead, I'll be at the other end of tooth prep for a crown. Talk about a missed opportunity."

"Yeah, me too. Don't feel bad. It was last minute."

"Hold on," Javie said. "I can be your other set of ears. If you don't think it'll be too awkward."

Oh my gosh. Edith is getting her wish after all.

"Uh, no. This is simply work-related. In a manner of speaking. We're working to prove my aunt's innocence. True, she and Richard were at odds, but so were Richard and Jessica. In fact, Jessica had a really solid motive to get him out of the picture. She needed to win a literary award, and with him in the picture, that wasn't about to happen."

"So it's a go?" Javie smiled.

I nodded. "Uh-huh. And thanks."

I texted Ian with the update, and he texted back, *"Order the Argentine Red Shrimp in garlic sauce. It's amazing. Just like you!"*

Javie and I took separate cars when we drove to Randolph's since we both needed to go home and change into fancier attire. Ian suggested we park out back, which was closer to the kitchen and easier for him to escort us to our table.

"I know we're not doing anything wrong," I said to both of them when Javie and I walked into the kitchen, "but my stomach is doing twists."

Ian grabbed my wrist and squeezed it. "That's a good sign. Like stage actors before a performance."

"Please don't tell me to 'break a leg,' because I just might."

"See, you've got the drama part all worked out." With that, he leaned over and kissed my cheek.

"Showtime," I whispered to Javie. Then I took in the dining area and spotted Lida and Jessica seated at a table for four in front of a large fountain, complete with greenery that could hide an elephant.

Ian led us to the opposite side of the fountain, so we were able to avoid making contact with them. At least for a while. I figured once our "surveillance" was complete, I'd mosey to the restroom and act surprised to see them.

A young female server filled our water goblets and told us our waitress would be right over. Seconds later, another young woman greeted us and presented us with large, ornate menus. She inquired about our drink preferences, and both of us announced "coffee" at the same time. She detailed the specials on the menu and like Ian, suggested the shrimp.

"Guess it's a no-brainer," Javie said, making it a point to keep his voice low. "Argentine Red shrimp."

I nodded. "Ditto." Then I took out my phone and texted him: *Let's communicate by text so we don't miss any of their conversation.*

He texted back: *Good thinking.*

Ian must have spoken with the waitstaff because the other tables were far enough away so that the voices wouldn't blend into Lida's or Jessica's. The only problem was, neither woman spoke. At least not right away. But that was about to change. The greenery that separated our table rustled as if a gust of wind caught the leaves by surprise. Only it wasn't wind.

Chapter Thirty-Five

Wednesday

"Must be they've got one hell of a ventilation system here because that gust of air didn't come from the overhead fans," Javie texted.

Before I could text back, the verdant hue that surrounded the fountain had turned an ugly shade of mossy green, and I rolled my eyes. Edith resembled a thin version of Friar Tuck in a horrid brown hooded robe, and I had all I could to stop myself from laughing.

Her voice was snippy and sharp. "Do a favor for someone and see where it gets you? To that obnoxious wardrobe mistress of Larken's."

She waited for my response, but I clamped my lips shut.

"Fine, if you want to play that game, Missy. Rosaline got a lead on Richard's whereabouts and insisted I accompany her. It was off-limits for my level, and Larken pitched a fit! Talk about uptight bureaucrats. Meanwhile, Rosaline got off with a warning, and I got a wardrobe demotion."

Then, she focused her attention on Javie. "Ah-hah! You did listen to me after all. Dangle him like bait! That's why you came here in the first place, isn't it? Ian must have told you Jessica and Lida made reservations. Get up! Introduce him! Get the plan moving."

I clutched my phone and tapped a text that I wanted Edith to see. *"This no-talking, eavesdropping plan should work."* Then I held the phone out in front of me, hoping she'd peer over my shoulder and read what I wrote.

No such luck. Only Javie nodded. Edith continued to babble until the server reappeared to take our orders.

"Eyeball that shrimp!" she commanded. "And if you see as much as a trace of a dirt track, call the health department."

"Are you all right?" Javie texted. *"You seem jumpy."*

"Just anxious. I need a moment in the ladies' room."

"Relax. I'll keep my radar on."

I thundered into the restroom, intent on setting Edith straight about this afternoon's plan. I knew she'd follow me like a homing pigeon, and I was right. The mossy green haze rose from my ankles to my hips, and I brushed at it as if it were a swarm of black flies.

"I didn't bring Javie here to entice Jessica," I said. "My first choice was Lilly-Ann, but she had a dentist appointment. We're here because—"

And suddenly, the door to one of the stalls swung open, and a heavy-set woman stepped out and approached me. "Are you rehearsing lines for a play? It sounds intriguing. A plot with mixed gender romance. Is it Arizona Broadway Theater?"

"Um, no. Uh, college theater class."

"Oh dear. That's too bad. I would have paid to see it. Good luck." She washed her hands in the sink and left without another word.

"You don't have to bend down and look under the stalls. No one else is here," Edith said.

"Good. Javie and I are here to eavesdrop on Lida and Jessica. Lida and my aunt had words at the authors' event, and Jessica and Richard fenced off like nobody's business. No love lost there. Maybe they're not number one in Deputy Vincent's list of suspects, but I'm not about to dismiss them so easily."

Edith pushed the hideous hood off of her forehead and fluffed her hair. "That's all you're going to do? Listen to them and hope they'll reveal something telling?"

"That's it."

"Oh brother. Might as well look at a piece of bread and hope it turns into toast."

"What did you have in mind?" *Why do I ask these things?*

"Trust me. Whatever I figure out by the time you get back to the table will be far better than bland old snooping."

"Edith, wait!" But it was too late. Along with the mossy green hue, she vanished.

When I returned to my seat, our salads were already on the table, and Javie shoved his cell phone against mine. He mouthed, "Was about to send this."

The text read: *Your aunt is in worse trouble than we think. Their voices carried in between oohs and aahs about the food.*

I stabbed a plum tomato and put it in my mouth. Then I chewed slowly and listened to a conversation I wished I hadn't.

"Come on, you heard the news anchors. All of the evidence pointed to her. It's not as if she wasn't the prime suspect."

"It was circumstantial."

"Yeah, for now."

"What are you saying?"

I recognized Lida's heavy voice as the first speaker and texted Javie. The two of us held still, almost afraid to taste our food when our waitress reappeared. "How did you enjoy your salads?"

"Still enjoying them," I smiled.

"Wonderful. I'll be back with your entrees in a few minutes."

I looked at Javie and wrote: *Drat. We missed the rest of their conversation.*

When they resumed their conversation, I wasn't sure what I missed, but what I did hear was enough to raise my blood pressure.

"I liked your first idea. Cinch it by tossing in the final piece of evidence. Fabricated or not." It was Lida's voice.

"You don't think that would be too easy?"

"There's a timing issue involved."

"I suppose you're right."

Then, another familiar voice—our waitress. She asked if we needed more coffee and said she'd be right back with our Argentine Red Shrimp.

I texted Javie: *I think they're going to set up my aunt.*

He mouthed back, "I know."

I moved the salad around on my plate, pausing now and then to stab something and put it in my mouth. Surprisingly, I had eaten most of it by the time the waitress returned with our shrimp. The aroma was tantalizing and overrode the angst that bubbled up inside me when thinking about what those two women were up to.

But my angst wasn't the only thing bubbling up. Rosaline returned from who-knows-where, dressed like a 1920s femme fatale in a silky cream sheath. She stood inches from us with Edith glaring at her.

"I'm not finished," Rosaline said.

Edith studied her couture and glared. "Well, I am."

"Not so fast. I smoothed things over with Larken. See for yourself." She pointed to Edith's outfit, and within seconds, it evaporated and was replaced by a stunning peach and gold gown."

Javie nudged me and pointed to my phone. His text read: *Do you see something in that greenery? You haven't taken your eyes off of it.*

I texted back: *Admiring it, that's all. I wish Lida and Jessica would talk. They must be stuffing their faces with tiramisu or molten lava cake.*

"Not that fast," Edith said. "I need to take care of something. Right here. Right now."

No, you don't! Not here. Not now! Not at all!

Rosaline reached out and grabbed Edith's arm, taking her by surprise and sending her cascading into the greenery.

The waitress, who stood a few feet away, announced, "I've never seen those leaves flutter and blow so much. If I didn't know any better, I'd swear we have ghosts in here."

And then, a shriek from the other side of the fountain.

"My Swedish Princess Cake! It landed in my lap! There's raspberry jam all over my dress. And we just got back from the ladies' room."

I texted Javie: *That's why they were so quiet.*

Rosaline choked out an apology of sorts. "Oops! My fault. I meant to hustle you along and must have gotten my energy too close to—Oh goodness—that woman is Lida Singleton. And that's Jessica Loundry seated across from her."

"As if you didn't know," Edith said.

"I didn't. I don't make it a practice to stalk celebrities."

"Only when they happen to be named Richard Bellmore."

"Enough!" I shouted. It came as a spontaneous burst, and I immediately covered my mouth. By now, the waitress rushed to the other side of the fountain.

Javie straightened his back and looked around. "Enough what?"

"Forget the texting. I've had enough."

"Good. I was beginning to feel like I was back in the sixth grade, passing notes. Long before cell phones."

"Let's move to Plan B. The women went back to the ladies' room. I'll go in, act surprised to see them, and ask what they've heard regarding the murders. If they act as if they're covering up something, I'll know."

"Guess it's as good a plan as any. I'll peruse that dessert menu."

"Order the princess cake for me. The raspberry jam sounded good."

Chapter Thirty-Six

Wednesday

"Lida! Jessica! What a surprise. Isn't Randolph's wonderful?" I sashayed up to the sink and smiled.

"You're a regular Little Mary Sunshine," Edith laughed. She settled herself next to the hand dryer and leaned back. I looked around for Rosaline but didn't see her.

"It would be," Jessica said, "if we weren't being detained like outlaws."

Lida nudged her as she wiped her dress with a damp towel. "I'm sure that investigation will wind down soon enough. Besides, they already have a major suspect." Then she looked at my face and recoiled. "Oh no. I'm sorry. I forgot for a second that Regina Aubrey is a relative."

Sure, you did.

"I understand. But the evidence is circumstantial. They'll need more in order to make an arrest and have it stick."

The women glanced at each other before Jessica spoke. "It's only a matter of time."

"What do you mean? What have you heard?"

She paused for a breath and continued. "Seems most investigations go that route. First, the circumstantial evidence, and then someone comes forth."

"It had better be soon," Lida added. "I've got a book tour to continue, and my agent is pitching a fit. Plus, the publisher isn't going to pay for my sojourn much longer. I've got to produce results. The company watches sales numbers like a stockbroker checks the NASDAQ."

Lida rubbed the tip of her index finger with her thumb. I wagered she'd chew those nails of hers if she wasn't out in public.

"It looks like you still have some raspberry jam on your dress," Jessica said.

Grabbing a damp paper towel, Lida wiped the dress. "My cake dropped. Nerves, I guess. It's no big deal. The dress, that is. Not what's going on all around us. It's a wonder I can think straight. At least I don't have a manuscript deadline in the middle of all of this."

Jessica glanced at the mirror and fluffed her hair. "It's only fun when the murder count rises in our books, but not in our faces. Especially since we're remotely acquainted with the victims."

"Speaking of which," I said, "did either of you happen to notice Dorrie Arnet at Wilsetta's the night of the vigil?"

"I wouldn't have noticed the late Queen of England," she replied. "That place was so dark, and there were so many people. I only met the woman once at a book signing in Seattle. She was with Arist at the time. So yeah, remotely acquainted. Still…it's creepy."

"Don't look at me, ladies." Lida continued to dab water on her dress even though the stain appeared to be gone. "There were so many cats. I've never seen that many in one place. It was like a moving episode of Hoarders. And all that cat hair. It was everywhere. You can't even remove it, no matter what you do."

Jessica reapplied her lip gloss and turned to Lida. "If she *was* there, those forensic examiners would substantiate it by taking a look at her clothes." Then Jessica faced me. "Do you think she snooped around the vigil to overhear us? That doesn't explain how she wound up dead on the property next door."

Before I could respond, the conversation bounced back and forth between Lida and Jessica.

"At least we're not suspects in *that* homicide. I certainly didn't have a beef with her. Not like I did with Richard. That conniving stinker bribed his way to fame."

"Glad he didn't write in my genre. Competing against Arist was tough enough. Nope, the only one I had a beef with was Regina. No offense, Katie. Not only did she reject my books, but I had it on good authority she blackballed me with other publishers."

Sounds like my aunt, all right.

"Ouch. I'm really sorry. I'd better get going. Nice running into you."

I darted out of there, but remained in close proximity so that Edith could listen in to their continuing conversation.

"Give me a warning when they head out," I told her. "I'll rush back to the table."

And then, in a sing-song voice, Edith said, "You owe me."

"Just listen in. No shenanigans."

Like telling a fish not to swim.

A few feet away from the ladies' room was an alcove with comfy chairs and a small coffee table. I sat in one of the chairs and took out my cell phone to appear as if I was reading something. A few seconds later, Edith swooped over. "Move it, Missy. Back to your table."

Flash Gordon couldn't have been any quicker. I arrived back at our table in a nanosecond and nearly bumped into Javie as I sat down.

"Well? Get anywhere?" He asked.

"More or less." It was Edith, who answered before words could form in my mouth. "Those two are about to hatch something, and it won't be chickens. I gave them a bit of a warning. Anyway, I've got to find Rosaline before I wind up in eighteenth-century prison garb or worse." With that, she disappeared, and Javie motioned me for a response.

"Uh, sorry," Javie. "Thanks for being patient. Nothing definitive. Those women were cagey, that's about it."

And then, a shriek emanated from the ladies' room. We stood to see what happened and were astonished when both women emerged, totally drenched.

"The sink faucets went haywire!" Jessica shouted.

I rolled my eyes and stood still. *Haywire, my patootie! Yep, the warning, all right. Like telling a fish not to swim.*

Ian and a sous chef exited the kitchen and, along with the hostess, spoke with the women. When they were done, he stopped at our table and told us that theirs would be the second meal comped today and that he was just glad that "Sterling wasn't around for the melee." Then a quick kiss, and we'd talk later.

"If nothing else," Javie said as we walked to our cars, "your instincts are probably right. Those women may try to set up your aunt. At least she can be on her guard. Too bad you can't tell Deputy Vincent because overhearing snippets of a conversation may be the same as hearsay."

"They were both in a hurry to see the investigation wrapped up, but it was impossible to tell if that was because they wanted to get on with their own lives, or save their own butts."

"Hey, thanks for letting me accompany you. That was some fabulous lunch. Weird ventilation and all. By the way, I had the oddest feeling we were being watched. And most likely we were."

I froze and widened my eyes as he continued.

"Yeah, those surveillance cameras are hidden everywhere these days. Creepy, huh?"

Not as creepy as the two specters who were really watching.

"For sure. And I appreciated your help, too. See you in the morning."

By the time Ian got home from the restaurant and phoned, I was already in jammies and had revisited my murder map. It was linear and written with the premise that there was one killer with two victims. That meant finding ironclad links to both parties. Not *that* difficult considering the love triangle with Arist, Richard, and Dorrie. Still, it was contrived.

I tried another approach. This time, two separate maps with different motives for murder. Under Richard, the suspects were the same—jealous authors, furious ex-husband, and unhinged editor, according to Deputy Vincent.

Under Dorrie, it was a tad different—furious ex-husband or overzealous and possessive fan. At least my aunt wouldn't be on that list.

Then, a thought occurred to me that should have occurred a while ago—who would benefit monetarily as far as life insurance or wills were concerned? Only the sheriff's office would have access to that information, and Deputy Vincent wasn't about to share any of it with me. Edith would tell me to get my hands on it another way, but it wasn't as if I was talking about one of her coveted gowns. I was talking about breaking and entering a deputy's office. Most likely a super-high-on-the-ladder felony. Nope, no need to find makeup that would go well with orange attire.

Unfortunately, Ian and I wouldn't be able to get together until Sunday afternoon. He picked up the morning brunch, but thankfully had the evening off. That meant I had three days left to my own devices to get my aunt off the hook without finding it piercing my own mouth.

Chapter Thirty-Seven

Thursday

It was Thursday morning, and like every morning since that first murder, I awoke wondering what new fiasco would await me. No surprise, today's "Jack-in-the-box" hit me like a double punch as soon as I walked into The Char-Board.

"Katie," Lilly-Ann called out when she heard me enter, "Your neighbor Colleen called. She said to tell you that she texted you the photos from Wilsetta's vigil. They're on your phone. She didn't see Dorrie but said you might have better luck if you enlarge them on the screen."

"Thanks." I stepped into the kitchen where Lilly-Ann had just started the coffee. We were early, and Javie hadn't arrived yet. I pulled out my phone and went to my text messages. Sure enough, the attachment from Colleen was there. I sat on the stool by the counter and pulled it up. The first two photos were dark, taken in the crowded living room. Still, I enlarged it, but the only women were Lida and a few library volunteers that I recognized.

I pulled up another, this one taken in the crying room, but again, no sign of Dorrie. Then, three outdoor patio photos with quite the crowd scene. It was early in the evening because the sheriff cars hadn't yet arrived on the property next door, which was visible from the patio.

Slowly and systematically, I eyeballed every corner of those photos, and in all three, something, or I should say *someone,* caught my eye.

"What's wrong?" Lilly-Ann asked. "Is it something on those photos?"

I nodded because the words wouldn't come out. Not at first, anyway. I scanned the photos again, and this time I knew what I had seen was no illusion. The woman may have been wearing an ash blonde wig with a blue sash around her forehead, but make no mistake—it was my aunt Regina.

"I don't believe this. I don't want to believe this. It's my aunt. See for yourself." I passed the phone to Lilly-Ann and she squinted as she looked at the screen. "It's hard to tell, but yeah, doesn't your aunt have that beauty mark under one of her eyes?"

"Uh-huh. And not only that, but look closely at those pearl-drop earrings. It's her go-to piece of jewelry. I can't believe this. She was there! When I overheard Lida and Jessica yesterday, they hadn't noticed or they would have said as much. But if Deputy Vincent finds out, it's over for sure. They'll insist she was responsible for Dorrie's death. Add in a false testimony from Jessica or Lida, or both, and my aunt's editing days are done."

Lilly-Ann gulped. "Forget the editing days. All of her days will be behind bars for sure."

"What's with the sullen looks?" Javie bounced into the kitchen. "Don't tell me there's been another murder."

"My aunt's life, in a manner of speaking."

"Huh?" Javie hung his jacket on a peg by the outside door and walked over. I handed him my phone.

"See for yourself. She's incognito, but it's her all right. At Wilsetta's mourning party."

"Holy cannoli! You're right. That means—"

"Don't say it. I already know. Oh my gosh! I hope Colleen didn't share those photos with anyone else. I've got to text her." Javie handed me back the phone, and I wrote: *"Please don't share those photos, Colleen. We need to talk. Thanks, Katie."*

Seconds later, she texted back: *I didn't share them with anyone directly, but I did post them on Facebook under my weekend activities. No worries. Posted to my friends.*

I showed Javie her text, and he grimaced, followed by the words, "not good."

"Tell me about it. Friends share with friends, and next thing you know, that embarrassing photo of you with a canary on your head is plastered all over social media. I only pray no one looks that closely. Especially the authors in attendance who didn't exactly hold my aunt in great esteem."

"Now what?"

"I'm getting a hold of my aunt this very second. Let Lilly-Ann know that the two of you will need to hustle for a bit. I doubt I'll be that long on the phone with her."

Just long enough to read her the riot act.

My mother picked up the phone when I called and asked if everything was all right.

"No! It's not, Mom. Aunt Regina was in disguise Saturday night at that get-together next door to where Dorrie Arnet's body was found. I know because my neighbor was there and showed me the photos on her phone. For crying out loud, Aunt Regina's the prime suspect in Richard's death, and who's to say she didn't finish the job with his ex-wife?" My voice was loud and strained, and even though I made the call from the porch area outside the kitchen, I was positive I could be heard in the dining area.

"Calm down, honey. I'm sure there's a reasonable explanation. Hmm, I invited your aunt to join your father and me at the movies that night, but she wasn't interested. By the time we returned, she was here."

"What time was that?"

"Oh, eleven forty-five or so. The movie was over two hours and started at nine. Plus those never-ending previews."

"Is she with you right now?"

"I'm afraid not. She made an early appointment for a mani-pedi."

I'm biting my nails and she's getting hers done.

"Tell her to call me when she gets back, okay? I'll be here at The Char-Board."

"Stop worrying, Katie. I'm sure your aunt had a good reason to be there, and I doubt it was to murder someone."

The only thing she's murdering is my reputation and possibly my business.

My response was unintelligible, and it was probably just as well. When I got off the phone, I raced over to the counter to help Javie with the breakfast orders. Lilly-Ann rushed them to the customers, and we kept up the pace for a solid hour before catching our breath. By then, Matt bounded in with the energy of a twenty-year-old, something most of us had forgotten.

When we hit a lull, I told the three of them about seeing my aunt incognito at Wilsetta's vigil and the fact my mother dismissed it as if it was nothing with nothing.

"Maybe she doesn't understand the gravity of the situation," Lilly-Ann said.

I shook my head. "You'd think an intimidating visit from Deputy Vincent would have made it clear, but not with my mother. She thinks everything will 'right itself.'"

Javie put his hand on my shoulder. "It will, but I'm afraid it will fall on your shoulders. Just let us know what we can do."

"Thanks. That means a lot."

"What about me? For your information, I missed out on a Mary Astor gown while I was giving Lida and Jessica a wet wake-up." Edith's peach and gold gown was now replaced by a brown shirtwaist dress, circa 1953. I didn't bother to ask. In fact, I didn't even make eye contact.

"What do you plan on doing?" Lilly-Ann asked.

"Confront my aunt. Granted, there are a number of reasons why people dress incognito. To spy, steal—"

"Or commit murder. Oops. Sorry, Katie. It just slipped. I, uh, better see if any more customers arrived." She took off while the rest of us looked at each other, too afraid to say a word. Finally, I spoke. "Pray it was one of the first two reasons."

As the day progressed, I couldn't help but wonder if I was one of those people who simply couldn't accept the truth. Maybe my aunt did commit the unthinkable. Maybe Richard said something to her that pushed her over the edge, and she reciprocated. Then again, my aunt was never one to let things get under her skin. She gave people ulcers. She didn't get them.

At a little past two, the personal assistant for Danica Patrick phoned The Char-Board to request charcuterie trays for a family gathering in two weeks.

Matt took the call and was practically speechless when he charged over to me to "handle this one."

"Huh?" I picked up the landline as he spoke.

"It's Danica Patrick. The racecar driver. Well, not her, but her assistant. Danica Patrick. Wants us to cater. Said it's in Taliesin West. That's north Scottsdale. Nothing else registered."

I mouthed "okay" and then said, "Hello, this is Katie Aubrey. How may I help you?"

What sounded like a young woman's voice said, "This is Marjorie Jordan, Danica Patrick's assistant, and she's having a family gathering at her house two weeks from Sunday. Is it possible to order three large charcuterie trays, or is it too late of a notice?"

Danica Patrick? Too late. I'll stay up all night making them if I must.

I told her we'd be delighted, and she explained that they wanted two French-themed trays and one dessert tray that would "pull out all the stops."

As I jotted down the information, I asked how she heard about us, and she said it was from an article about the library event. Then she said something that stunned me—I had neglected to scope out a possible player in the murder scenario.

"I'm surprised those celebrity gossip sites didn't jump on those murders," she said. "Then again, it's probably too early. They like to dig up lots of dirt first."

It was only three words—celebrity gossip site—and I remembered where I'd heard them before. It was from someone on the book purchase line from Poisoned Pen Bookstore at the event. They said Barbara Beau-Winton and Richard were rumored to have had an affair. Or something of the sort.

Like a punch between the eyes, I knew what, or *who*, I neglected. And most likely, so did Deputy Vincent. Barbara kept a relatively low profile and scuttled out of Wilsetta's place without anyone as much as raising an eyebrow. Ha!

I caught my breath and nonchalantly asked for the details. I took notes furiously as my mind bounced between a terrific catering opportunity and another one that hinted at exonerating my aunt.

When the call ended, I told our staff about the event at Danica's and then launched into a new thread in my so-called investigation. Matt volunteered immediately to serve at the event and was disappointed to learn that all we were doing was dropping off the charcuteries. He then offered to "carry anything or everything."

As for pursuing Barbara's involvement in murder, all three of my employees offered to help in any way. And then, a question I never expected. From Lilly-Ann, no less.

"Does this mean we'll need to bone up on our equestrian knowledge?"

"Equestrian? Like in horseback riding?" I crinkled my nose and looked at the crew.

"Before she wrote cozy mysteries, Barbara rode horses for show. Jumped, too, from what I read," she said. "I did my homework. She has a stable at her winter home in Lake Pleasant and one in her summer home. Her seven horses are transported back and forth. Oh, and did I mention she has a full-time stable manager? I read that, too."

"Wow."

"The article said Barbara came into a substantial inheritance from her late husband, Montross Wilton. Now she supports all sorts of equestrian charities, as per an early passion. Hmm, that may explain some of her book titles…"

"Uh, very interesting, but what do horses have to do with information gathering?"

"Yeah, what?" Matt asked.

Lilly-Ann smiled. "It's a conversation opener. They do it all the time on those TV mystery shows. The investigators pretend they're interested in something, and then—Boom!—they ferret out information."

"As long as I don't have to ferret out information seated on a horse, I'll be fine."

Then Lilly-Ann looked at Javie and Matt before turning back to me. "I also read she only conducted interviews while riding."

Chapter Thirty-Eight

Thursday, Friday

"I've never ridden a horse before in my life," I told Ian that night when we spoke. "Apparently, if I'm going to pursue the only other avenue left as far as snooping, I won't have much choice. I mean, how hard can it be?"

"English or Western?"

"English or Western what?"

"Saddles. And style. They're different. Both hands are used to grasp the reins on English and only one hand on Western. The other hand holds the horn. That's the piece that sticks up on the front."

"Oh my gosh, I'm doomed."

"Hey, you don't even know if she'll agree to talk to you. If she does, ask her if the horses are trained in English or Western riding. Then maybe watch a few videos on YouTube. You're a quick study and you're agile as anything."

"Why couldn't she enjoy miniature golf? Or bowling?"

"You'll be fine. The horse does most of the work. Wish I could join you. That is, *if* you wind up going there. As luck has it, we're completely booked for the next few days, and Trenton got selected for jury duty, of all things. Then Sterling surprised the daylights out of me today. He gave me a raise and said he didn't know how he would manage without me."

"That's wonderful!"

"I still can't believe it, but I think Warren might have had something to do with it. We talked at length the night of Richard's death when he drove me back to get the car. I think he put in a good word for me. Anyway, let me know if you reach Barbara and what she says. It may be a long shot, but it's not out of the question. Boy, I can't wait to see you on Sunday."

"Me either."

I remembered that the library had the author emails on their program list for that event and spent the next fifteen minutes rummaging around my desk and drawers to find it. Then I sent Barbara a thoughtful and hopeful note before turning in for the night.

Once in bed, with Speedbump's head plastered against my side, Edith joined us. Only she sat at the foot of the bed with her arms crossed and a brownish haze that engulfed her upper torso.

Her voice was shrill and sharp. "Why didn't you run this by me first, Missy?"

I looked up. "I didn't know I had to." *What doesn't that woman listen in to?*

"In this case, you should have. For your information, I had English riding lessons all through my school years. It's a matter of rising and sitting according to the trot or canter."

Trot or canter. At least she didn't say gallop.

"What if Barbara's horses aren't trained that way?"

"Hold on to that ridiculous horn and stay put in the saddle. It can't be that difficult."

"Edith, I don't even know if she'll agree to see me."

"Oh, she'll see you all right. If she's innocent, she'll want to taut it. If she's guilty, she'll want to cover it up."

"But I'm not an investigator."

"Worse. You own an eating establishment with lots of customers with a penchant for gossip."

"Thanks."

"Ta-Ta. Remember, you owe me. And I'm getting itchy to bug Imogen."

With that, Edith vanished along with the brown haze.

When I got to The Char-Board the next morning, I grabbed a few seconds to scan my emails and was shocked as anything to see that Barbara had responded to my request. It was one sentence, but I read it over and over as if it was the Emancipation Proclamation.

"Be at my ranchette at three today, dressed for a heady ride."

A heady ride? I immediately asked Siri what on earth that meant, and the response gave me the chills—intoxicating, potent, strong, and exhilarating.

I'm dead. She said yes, but is planning a wild ride. I texted Ian.

He texted back: *Dress warm with layers of cushioning. Take hat and gloves. Wear sturdy shoes. Don't worry. The horse knows what it's doing.*

I returned the text with five screaming emojis and then informed my crew that I needed to leave early in order to eke out a confession, eliminate a suspect, or cross horseback riding off of my bucket list.

Everyone reassured me that I'd be fine. At least to my face. But I wasn't about to take chances. I pulled up a video on the proper way to mount a horse and watched it three times before I was reasonably assured I could do it.

"The video showed a mounting block," I told Javie. "What if Barbara mounts from the ground?"

He shook his head. "Doubt it. She's in her sixties. Not that limber. Besides, a mounting block will give her stable manager something to do." Then he laughed. "What other videos did you watch?"

"The Beginners Step by Step Method for Horseback Riding."

"And?"

"It's mind-boggling. Point toes up! Bend knee. Or was it *don't* bend knee? Keep thumbs up on the reins, Don't grip with legs. Use your core. Oh my gosh, Javie! I haven't even approached that horse, and I'm terrified."

"You'll be fine. Just watch what Barbara does."

"I have less than five hours to pull this off. Promise me you guys will run this place if I wind up in the hospital, okay?"

"You won't wind up in the hospital. Most likely, she has trail horses that will simply plod along on well-worn paths."

As it turned out, half of Javie's equation was correct. Barbara did have trail horses. Spunky trail horses. And the word *plod* was not in their vocabulary.

When I turned onto the long driveway that led to her house, I expected to see a typical Arizona ranchette—Santa Fe style with a shaded archway in front. What I didn't expect was the Ponderosa. True, the landscape was different from Virginia City Nevada, but other than that, I half expected the Cartwright brothers to come riding up. Instead, I was greeted by Barbara's stable manager, Cory, who introduced himself and walked me to the barn.

He appeared to be in his mid-fifties with solid muscles and a fast stride. A hint of a five o'clock shadow gave him a rugged, weathered look.

"I take it you've ridden before," he said. "Barbara always makes that assumption, and sometimes it doesn't work out as well."

I gulped. "I've been known to work my way around horses." *Merry-go-round horses, but he didn't specify.*

"Good. I've saddled up Pansey for you. She's a blaze quarter horse, eighteen years old."

Pansey. Sounds like a nice, gentle one. Thank goodness.

Corey motioned me toward the mounting block, and I tried to recall what I watched on that video. Pansey stood perfectly still for a few seconds before switching her head around.

"Lucky it's not summer. You won't have to worry about rattlers on the trail. But the flies are pesky as hell, and Pansey goes crazy when they get anywhere near her face."

Wonderful.

"If you get thirsty, there's a leather bottle holder hanging from the horn with Geyser Spring Water. Barbara's choice."

My choice is a nice Sangria, but what the heck.

As I leaned toward the horse, I remembered to move my fingers down the reins to tighten them and keep my toes up. So far, so good, until I nearly fell off the horse when I heard, "Shift your weight toward the front and make it a smooth motion, Missy!"

Oh no! Edith!

I looked straight ahead and sure enough, there she was, dressed in Iberian equestrian garb—traditional vaquero skirt and decorative jacket in shades of deep red and gold. My jaw dropped, and for a brief second, I froze.

"Lovely, isn't it? Now I owe a favor to Rosaline's friends."

"Go away," I muttered under my breath, but Cory heard me.

"Suppose that'll be all right if you don't need any help. Just head over to the fence line and wait for Barbara. She took a quick ride to warm up." With that, he walked away, and I was left on my own. Except, of course, for Edith.

"Don't do anything to spook this horse," I told her.

"No problem. I'll spook Barbara into spilling the beans if she's got anything to hide."

"No spooking. I have enough problems." With that, I tried to nudge Pansey to the fence line, but she wouldn't budge.

"Press into her with your thighs, not the knees, and make a clicking sound."

I rolled my eyes but took Edith's advice. In a nanosecond, Pansey took off and reached the fence line, which was about fifteen yards from the mounting block. I caught my breath and waited for Barbara to arrive.

Then, the sound of hoofs on the dirt road as Barbara trotted up to where I waited. She was a robust woman, dressed in jeans and a heavy sweatshirt. As she moved her horse toward mine, she reached out her hand and I shook it.

"Thanks for agreeing to see me," I said. "I wanted to run a few questions by you in the hope you might be able to provide—"

"Information about Richard Bellmore's unfortunate demise?"

"Um, yeah. That."

"Don't know what I can tell you that I haven't already told that grouchy deputy, but I suppose if you have different questions, then maybe you'll get the answers you want."

"Thanks. First off—"

"We ride!" With that, Barbara's horse took off like Secretariat. I gripped the reins until my knuckles turned white and then did what Edith told me. I pressed into Pansey's side and held my breath.

Please don't let me kiss the ground. Don't need to become the third casualty this month.

Chapter Thirty-Nine

Barbara remained a good thirty yards ahead of us, but not for long. Apparently, Pansey didn't like following another horse and shot out like a bolt, passing Barbara, even though it meant moving at full speed over boulders and scrub brush.

As we whizzed past her, Barbara shouted, "Did Cory tell you Pansey is unpredictable?"

Terrific. Now is a fine time to find out.

I had no idea if we were trotting, cantering, or galloping. All I knew was that Pansey was going fast. Really, really fast. I tried to block visions of me getting thrown off of her and landing on a boulder where I'd crack my skull off. And then, like that, Pansey slowed down.

Not only slowed down, but veered off to the left before heading down a gully. Behind me, I heard Barbara's voice. "Lots of fallen logs on that trail. Pansey loves jumping over them. Very invigorating."

Very invigorating? Is she nuts?

Then Edith, who hovered over the horse and me, put in her two cents. "She's a madwoman all right, but I don't think she's your killer. Why waste time shoving someone into a waterfall when you can invite them for a horseback ride and make it look like an accident?"

"Edith! I'm trying to stay on this horse! What do I do when she jumps?"

"Anticipate the jump! Bend forward and lift your butt from the seat. Shift your weight to the front. Ball up your hands and press them on the sides of the horse's neck."

"If I lean over her head, I'll fall off!"

"Anticipate the jump! Do I have to say it again?"

"How on earth do I do that? I can't read the horse's mind."

"Look straight ahead. If you see a log, the horse will see a log. The horse is smart enough to jump over it and not ask questions. Oh no!"

"What? What 'Oh no?'"

"Merrilee and Faye just told Rosaline that some of Catherine the Great's clothing is available. True, she was a big woman, but still, I am not going to miss out. Not like I did with Nefertiti's wardrobe. Good Luck!"

And then, no surprise. No Edith. Just Pansey and me on a downhill trail with more obstacles than sand on a beach. I took a breath and leaned forward, too scared to do anything else.

I adjusted to the rhythm of Pansey's jumps, mainly because I had no choice. Finally, after minutes of excruciating mental torture, not to mention the physical strain on my butt, we reached the bottom of the gully. Then, I fixated on what was in front of me—an uphill trail that I swear was ninety degrees.

My only other choice was to get Pansey to turn around and go back the way we came because that gully wasn't as steep. Unfortunately, the horse had other ideas. She bolted up the steep terrain with unbridled energy, compelling me to grip my thighs in even tighter, which, in retrospect, might have hastened her up the hill. I don't remember breathing, but I must have, because when we reached the top, I was panting.

Pansey, however, was in her glory. She reared her head and snorted a few times before slowing down and trotting down a circular road that led back to the barn. Cory looked up from the stool where he sat, checking something on his phone.

"Whoa! That's the first time someone beat Barbara back to the barn. Do you want to walk Pansey around to cool off, or would you rather have me do it? Some riders like to bond with the horses."

"I think we've bonded enough. I'll dismount if that's okay."

"Come on, I'll give you a hand."

My legs were like rubber when I hit the first step. Thankfully, Cory didn't notice, and by the time Barbara arrived on her chestnut quarter horse, I was seated on another stool, perusing my own email and text messages. She dismounted in a fluid movement, handed off the horse to Cory, who had just led Pansey inside the barn, and strode toward me.

"Must say, I didn't take you for such an exuberant rider. I suppose you've definitely earned what you came here for in the first place—information about my relationship with Richard."

"I, um, er…"

"I read the tabloids, too. But that was old news. Come on, my housekeeper made cranberry scones, and there's a pot of fresh coffee in the kitchen. This way."

She pointed to a well-worn path, and I prayed my rubbery legs wouldn't alter her opinion of my ability to ride a horse. I figured if I could keep her engaged in conversation, she'd be less likely to notice how off-balance I was.

"Actually," I said, "I was more interested in why you left Wilsetta's house so early."

"If you must know, I spotted Richard's gold-digging fiancée, Dorrie Arnet, early on in the evening. Wanted to hightail it out then, but decided to stick around for a bit longer. Harrumph! Thought no one would notice her with tinted glasses and a cheap chin-length wig, but I sure did. We exchanged cold glances but didn't say a word to each other."

What are the odds? My aunt and Dorrie in disguise. Go figure.

By now, we'd walked across the threshold of her house and into the kitchen. A plate of scones, along with assorted jams and small chocolates, sat in the middle of a large oak table, along with two carafes of coffee and large mugs.

Barbara motioned for me to take a seat as I took in the western décor in the room.

"I take it you and Dorrie weren't on speaking terms," I said.

"Not what you or the tabloids may think. Richard and I fizzled long before she wove her tight little spiderweb around him. But that's not to say we didn't have our moments. She knew I saw through her well-rehearsed charm and that she was only interested in climbing to a higher rung on the social ladder."

"Then why leave when you did?"

"I didn't want to risk a nasty encounter with her. I've had too many of those in my past, if you must know. That's when I threw my attention into horses. They offered me what men couldn't—emotional bonding, energy, freedom, and a certain sense of empowerment when I ride. Much better than washing some man's dirty socks."

I looked directly into her eyes. "So it was more of a 'Barbara thing' than a fading relationship with Richard."

"Face it, that woman had a penchant for drama. And apparently an ability to go undetected. Arist never knew Dorrie was at Wilsetta's. And frankly, I only saw her when I first arrived. My guess is that the little minx flitted off somewhere and wound up six feet under. Oh! Don't look so shocked. We all know the outcome. It's the in-between that's leaving those deputies baffled."

"They're not baffled. They're about to charge my aunt for a double murder. You're no stranger to both parties. What's your take on it?"

"Excluding your aunt, and I honestly wouldn't blame her if she did shove Richard into that waterfall, I can't come up with a single reason why she'd kill Dorrie. Arist had a motive—jealousy and revenge. That equals two homicides. And we all know that Jessica would kill for that Claremont Award, but now we're down to one. As for Lida, KC, and Dame Judith, nothing bubbled to the surface."

"That's an odd way to put it. Are you saying that maybe there's another motive? Something more sinister?"

"I wouldn't say *sinister*. Maybe an old-fashioned reason. Like bribery, blackmail, or the threat of publicly revealing something that would ruin someone's reputation. As for me, I've got nothing to hide, but I do value my privacy."

"I understand."

We spent the remainder of our conversation with lighter topics, and Barbara invited me back to ride "anytime I was in the mood." Which, in my book, was *never.*

When I got home, it was already dark and I was famished. I fed Speedbump, nuked a Trader Joe's curried chicken bowl, and texted Ian before I tossed my clothes in the wash and took a long, hot shower.

I heard the ping of his text when I dried off and looked to see what he had written. In a few short words, he managed to get my heart beating faster than a romantic kiss. The text read: *Have you seen the news? New evidence points to double murder. Arrest imminent.*

Suddenly, the curried chicken didn't sit too well in my stomach, and I raced to find my bottle of Tums.

Chapter Forty

Saturday

After a fitful night's sleep and a queasy stomach, I made myself a cup of ginger tea and ate a few saltines before I got ready to head to The Char-Board. By that time, Ian and I had spoken, and he told me that he had started to review what was on the files he copied from Wilsetta's computer.

He sounded somewhat optimistic, but I wasn't so sure. I visualized a spreadsheet on all of her zillion cats that documented their features, food preferences, health records, and whatever else she kept track of.

I held off sharing the details from my ride with Ian, figuring I'd give him the long version tomorrow. And I would do it complete with action sequences and a few expletives. What I did share, however, was that Barbara spied Dorrie incognito at Wilsetta's place, and that she and Richard broke up long before Dorrie's divorce from Arist and engagement to Richard.

Then I mentioned the three motives that Barbara alluded to—bribery, blackmail, and destroying someone's reputation. "That means we'll need to get our hands on other files," I said. "And that would be impossible. But we can do a little tabloid digging. After all, those magazines need a smidgen of truth in order to print their articles. All we need to do is figure out who hid what and why."

Ian was totally in, but we both knew that time was not on our side, and if we were to make any headway, we'd better be prepared to pull off our armchair investigation in a hurry. Midway into the morning, when it slowed a bit at The Char-Board, I asked Lilly-Ann if she knew what tabloid magazines were popular, and she rattled off a few.

"I only read them when I'm in a long line at the supermarket. Right now, I'm totally hooked on Deenie Alexandria. *Forbidden Nights* was by far her best. And I love how she infused some of those old-time words like malarkey or tommyrot."

Matt, who was at the sink, turned and said, "My mother's nose is glued to those things. If you want to know which ones to get, I can ask her."

"Would she be up to date on the celebrity gossip?"

"She knows it before they do. Uh, does this have anything to do with Richard Bellmore?"

I nodded. "Hold on. I'm writing down a few names. Ask her what she knows and take copious notes. Think of it as if you were in one of your college lectures."

Matt's eyes bugged out. "Seriously? The tabloids?"

"It's a start."

We bustled our way through a busy Saturday lunch and took three orders for charcuterie trays. Javie was more than happy to put in extra hours, and I was relieved he could pick up the slack. With my aunt in such a precarious situation and my mother in happy LaLa Land, my concentration was at an all-time low. So much so, that I had forgotten to stock a staple of assorted Bries and had to send Lilly-Ann to the supermarket.

At a little before two, Ian texted: *Glanced over Wilsetta's utilities statements late last night. Very odd. Her electric bill is off the charts for a house that size.*

I texted back: *Billing error?*

He replied: *Nope. On-going. Was looking for anything Richard related. So far, zilch. Gotta go. Sterling's headed to the kitchen. Miss you!*

It was signed with two heart emojis, a hug, and the image of a man running.

I returned it with a hug, a kiss, and a few cats to remind him of Wilsetta.

Then, an hour later, as we were cleaning up, Matt tapped my shoulder. "Got the skinny from my mom. You may want to take notes."

"What did she tell you?"

"Lots of rumors about a major motion picture based on one of KC Camplin's books. According to the person who wrote the article, Richard was seething since his latest novel was turned down by producers, so he badmouthed KC's novels during a TV broadcast. Is that a motive for knocking off someone? Geez, I hope not. I like KC's books."

"Who knows? Lately, breathing too hard seems to be a motive around here. Did she mention anything else?"

"Uh-huh. She said Richard's fiancée lost her shirt at a Las Vegas casino, and my mother wasn't referring to Dorrie's clothing."

"Did she say when?"

"A week or so before he was murdered."

"Thank her for me. She saved me a lot of time."

"Sure thing."

I texted Ian immediately: *Dorrie may have bribed/blackmailed someone. She was broke. And the tabloids offered up KC.*

He responded with a screaming emoji and left it at that. Since it was still early in the day when we closed up, I drove to the library in hopes of a quick chat with Allison, but my hopes were dashed when the library aide told me I had just missed her.

There was something oddly familiar about the aide's voice, and I looked at the name on her tag. It read, Korina Kashian. Where had I heard that name before? Or the voice, for that matter? It was deep and guttural, and seemed to match the woman's overall appearance- stocky, facial hair, and long, straight dark hair that hung limply past her shoulders. She had to be past middle age but not quite a senior.

I didn't remember seeing her at the author's event, but there were so many people, and I was totally preoccupied with the charcuteries and my aunt Regina. Heck, I didn't even notice Colleen at first. Colleen! That's where I heard Korina's name. Duh!

Colleen was the one who told me that Korina thought Arist shouldn't be invited due to the strife between him and Richard, but it was Allison who insisted he be given the invite. But that voice? I associated it with something offsetting, but for the life of me, I couldn't recall what.

Later that night, when Ian and I spoke, I told him about meeting Korina at the library today, and as I spoke to him, it all came back to me. "Oh my gosh! Good grief! I know where I heard that voice. Remember the night of the vigil when I was in Wilsetta's bedroom and you were in her office?"

"Impossible to forget. Why?"

"I overheard Arist's conversation with a woman while I hid under the blankets on the bed? It was her voice. *Her* voice. I'd take an oath on it. The woman is Korina. She was the one who got paid off to cover for Arist."

"But if he was innocent, why did he pay her off?"

"He had a compelling motive. Next to my aunt Regina, he would be the likely suspect. He claimed he didn't need the grief. Rats! Now it's too late to speak with her. The library won't open again until Monday."

"Hang in there. We've got a full plate as it is. Besides, I'm not quite done with Wilsetta's files. Who knows? Maybe I'll find something that links her to those deaths."

"I'll be happy if we link anyone except my aunt. And that includes her cats!"

Sadly, that never happened. Although one mystery was solved shortly before I turned in for the night. My father called at a little before nine to let me know the sheriff's office got two Silent Witness calls from two separate women, claiming they both had seen my aunt tousling with Richard the night of his demise. No surprise that both claimed she rapped him on his head with a candlestick from the table, before shoving him into the waterfall and wiping the candlestick clean. Yep—Jessica and Lida, no doubt. No need for Agatha Christie to figure that one out.

"Only the one murder?" I asked my father.

Even over the phone, I could tell he was aggravated. "Isn't one enough? Your mother is so distraught she can't speak."

"What about Aunt Regina?"

"Let's just say it's been a long, harrowing day. She was read her rights and escorted to the Fourth Avenue Jail. Fortunately, she was able to get a hearing and post bail. Talk about miracles."

"Now what?"

"An arraignment for a hearing. And that will be after a Grand Jury gives an indictment. Meanwhile, she's on house arrest with an ankle monitor."

"What about the other suspects?—Jessica, Lida, Barbara, and KC. Are they free to go? Did you hear anything about them?"

"As a matter of fact, I did. Do not quote me. I overheard a phone call from the front office to a Deputy Vincent. Whoever phoned him from the jail, told him the case was pending and to inform the other suspects they needed to remain in the area until further notice."

"Could they do that?"

"Apparently, they did."

"Maybe it's good news. Maybe they know their case is weak. Dad, Aunt Regina is innocent. She's being framed. Too bad once they tie her to Richard Bellmore's murder, they'll link it to his fiancée."

"Her lawyer is aware of that. I'll keep you posted, honey. Meanwhile, keep your ears to the ground. You're running a restaurant, and people have been known to talk."

And to lie.

"Do you mind putting Aunt Regina on the phone for a minute?"

"Of course. But try not to talk about murder."

Seriously?

"Aunt Regina?"

"Hi Katie."

"I wanted to see how you were doing and to let you know that I'm trying to do everything I can in order to—"

"Get me out of this mess? I know. And I've been so obtuse about it. Well, maybe *obtuse* isn't exactly the right word. More like self-absorbed and in denial. I do that, you know. Denial. I've found it easier than facing the truth. But this, well, let's just say it has me rattled more than I'd like to think."

"Try not to worry. You've got a solid crew of my friends and of course, the family, to make sure you don't wind up behind bars for a crime you didn't commit."

"Thanks, Katie. It means a lot."

It was the first time since I'd known my aunt to see that behind that all-business, all-me-me-me, was someone just as insecure as the rest of us. Now all I needed to do was prove her innocence.

Chapter Forty-One

Sunday

The next afternoon couldn't come fast enough. It was the only time Ian and I would have to pull our information together and zero in on the likely killer. I kept my fingers crossed he'd uncover something incriminating on Wilsetta's files, but so far, all he could find were anomalies regarding her electric bills.

But all of that was about to change when he got here a little past three and shared a discovery that left me speechless. We were seated on the couch, laptops and iPhones in front of us. Speedbump at Ian's knees.

"I don't know why this bugged me so much," he said, "but I thought something was off, so I called Arizona Public Service, pretending to be her grandson. Since all of her profile information was on those files for the electric company, including her Social Security number, they didn't question it."

"And? What?"

"When Wilsetta's house was built in the late seventies, it was part of a homestead that included another house and a few barns. The barns were destroyed during a monsoon and never rebuilt."

"I take it, that's the property next door where Dorrie's body was discovered."

"Yep. Now here's where it gets interesting. There's an electrical line that runs from Wilsetta's house to that property. It was disconnected when the original homestead was broken up and sold separately. That was before Wilsetta bought her house. So, no one really knew about it, but somehow Wilsetta found out."

"I think I see where this is going."

Ian smiled. "Hang on. It remained disconnected until the current owners vacated the property and put it up for sale. Once that happened, Wilsetta contacted Arizona Public Service and had them reconnect the line since it originated on her property. The work order was signed by Frank Riley, from their operations office. Anyway, Wilsetta was then responsible for the additional cost."

"But wouldn't that line cover the entire property next door?"

Ian shook his head. "Nope. According to the rep on the phone, it was only connected to a few electrical outlets on the south side of the house."

"Enough to make lights flicker if someone turned the breakers on and off?"

Ian's face erupted into a huge grin. "You betcha. Now the question remains—Why? Why would she do that? If she wanted to purchase the property, why not do so? According to Allison, Wilsetta was financially solid."

"Good question. But it still doesn't help us as far as those murders go."

"I know. And we really can't prove anything without incriminating ourselves. So that means telling Maddie is out of the question for now."

"I'm glad you said 'for now.' That means it remains a good possibility."

"Don't tell me you minored in English?"

I jabbed him on his side, and he leaned over to plant a kiss on my shoulder. Then, I opened my murder book and sighed. That's when Edith decided to make an appearance. She plopped herself on an adjacent chair and adjusted a delicate floral dress straight out of the 1930s.

"It's not what I'd call stylish," she muttered, "but it's far better than that horrid shirtwaist. What were those feeble designers thinking in the 1950s?"

I swallowed hard and ignored her before turning to face Ian. Unfortunately, Edith was persistent.

"You need to attack this investigation as if you were building a charcuterie tray!"

"A charcuterie tray?" The words slipped out.

"What?"

"Sorry, my mind is all over the place. I'm trying to think how we should tackle this."

"Place the big chunks first!" Edith put her hands on her hips and huffed. "Instead of Brie and specialty ham, who are your major suspects?"

Without skipping a beat, I repeated what she said. "I think we should treat this as if we were constructing a charcuterie tray, but instead of edible ingredients, we substitute them for suspects. Starting with our two major players in Richard's death. Once we get that far, Dorrie's will follow suit."

"Hmm. That's a unique way of looking at it. Okay, so who do you think we need to pursue? Because we're running out of time. And by *pursue*, I'm speaking literally, not figuratively."

"So, breaking and entering? Snooping and stalking?"

"All of the above. Don't hold back. Tell me who *your* Brie and ham are."

I chuckled. "Arist and KC. Arist for two reasons—why would he pay Korina to lie for such a thin reason? I'm guessing he was still on Dorrie's insurance policy and needed the money. He wasn't exactly pulling in much as a cozy mystery author. And the second reason? The obvious animosity between him and Richard."

"And KC?"

"According to Allison, KC did Dame Judith a favor in Toronto, and as a result, she agreed to come to this book event. Think about it. A book event in Cave Creek, Arizona. Not New York, Chicago, or Los Angeles. Cave Creek. That's akin to Taylor Swift performing a concert at a high school in the backwoods of Maine. It's not out of the realm of possibility that KC did her one heck of a favor and she had no choice but to be complicit in Richard's murder in order to pay her friend back."

"Whoa! Now's who's the mystery writer?"

I shrugged. "The other players may have motives, but they're weak ones."

"Okay. Let's toss the dice and see which one of them we pursue."

"Seriously?"

"Let's begin with the letter A. Arist. That makes it simple."

"What makes it simple is finding out if he's sitting on top of a mega insurance policy."

Edith had now moved to the window and looked outside. I was thankful Ian couldn't see or hear her and was able to speak freely, unlike me. "We need to find out about any insurance policies, and that's far from easy. We can't very well break into Deputy Vincent's office, and neither of us are computer hackers."

I grinned. "There's one possible way, and you already got a head start. What if you were to call Arist to inform him that he was listed as the beneficiary for an insurance policy? You give him a bogus company name. They all sound similar."

"I'm listening."

"And I'm impressed." Edith leaned behind the couch with her elbows out.

I tried to block Edith's words so I didn't wind up repeating them. "It won't be the first time for us, and at least this won't be in person. Besides, you've already earned a gold star for your APS call about Wilsetta's electric bill."

Ian motioned with his hand for me to continue.

"First, we get a pre-paid phone so it cannot be traced. Then, you phone Arist. I can get his cell number from Allison. You tell him you're from Colonial Life Insurance Company and that a death certificate was received from the Maricopa County Sheriff's Office."

"I don't think they do that."

"Trust me. Arist will be so happy to hear the words, 'Life Insurance Company,' he'll gloss over it. Then, you tell him that there's a small $25,000 policy for Dorrie that listed his name as the beneficiary. Tell him you'll need his email and/or physical address to send him some forms that need to be completed with verification of identity. We need to sound credible."

"You sound diabolical. What if he asks how the company got his phone number?"

"Easy. It was listed on her beneficiary information. Then, see if he asks about other policies."

"Must admit—It's better than breaking and entering."

"It's not as much fun."

"Shh!" I glared at Edith.

"Relax." Ian touched my arm. "No one's listening."

That's what you think.

"If we get lucky, we might be able to take the next step and trap him into a confession."

"And if not?"

We move on to KC.

Chapter Forty-Two

Monday

Since insurance companies were closed on Sundays, we waited until the following morning to place the call from the outdoor porch behind The Char-Board. By that time, we had already purchased a burner phone and rehearsed Ian's spiel.

In the interim, my mother phoned to inform me that my aunt's lawyer was building a strong defense. She sounded razzled, but once she mentioned getting her roots touched up, I knew she wasn't as distraught as my father thought.

At a little after nine, Ian and I stepped outside and looked around. I told our crew not to go onto the porch until we gave the "all-clear."

"Ready?" I widened my eyes and waited for his response.

"As I'll ever be."

Ian tapped the number and put it on speaker phone while I played "Look-out," to make sure Mercedes from the Mexican pottery shop next door didn't decide to take out the trash. Thankfully, Edith was nowhere in sight since the last thing I needed was a distraction.

"Mr. Arnet? Arist Arnet?" Ian asked when his call went through.

"Yes. Who's this? How did you get my number?"

"This is Steven Caslinger from Colonial Life Insurance Company out of Boston, with offices in Phoenix, Philadelphia, and Richmond. Your number was on file with profile information on Dorrie Arnet. My condolences."

"Are you saying she left a policy with me on it?"

"Yes. That's the reason for this call. A twenty-five-thousand-dollar policy was taken out five years ago in March, and you were named the sole beneficiary. Now, all we need is—"

"I had no idea. She had other policies with Mutual of Atlanta and The Guardianship Life Insurance Company, but she never mentioned this one. Are you sure I'm the sole beneficiary? I ask this because that was not the case with the other, more extensive, policies."

"Yes. You are the sole beneficiary. We will need you to complete some forms that I can email you or send to your physical address. Whatever your preference is. We'll also need an official death certificate from the county."

"No problem. I'll give you both."

Just then, someone from the beauty shop a few doors down decided to take their small dog outside, and I charged over to ask if they could please avoid walking in this direction. When I got back, the call had ended, and Ian took a deep breath.

"We need to make a recording on this phone in case he calls back. Let's get Javie to do it. That way, Arist won't question the call."

"Were you able to get any more out of him?"

"He told my alter ego that he was relieved he wasn't "left in the dust," and took heart that his late wife still had feelings for him. Boy, sure hate to burst that bubble. Hate to say it, babe, but I don't think he's our killer."

"Boy, am I disappointed. Money usually rises to the top. Well, on to number two, I suppose. Let's hope I'm right, otherwise, it's back to the complimentary charcuterie elements. You know, the ones that surround the larger pieces. But instead of cured meats, dried fruits, spreads, and nuts, we'll be looking at Jessica, Lida, and, much as I hate to say it, Barbara."

"Did we rule Wilsetta out?"

"For those murders, yeah. Plus, she never left her place that night, so she couldn't have been the one who murdered Dorrie. But I think she's the one who's haunting the house next door."

"Put it on the list!"

I laughed as we retreated back to the kitchen, where I informed everyone that our phone call was a success, if only to cross another suspect off the list. Ian then raced to Randolph's in order to prepare the roux they would need later that night. Meanwhile, we agreed to continue our sleuthing, even if it was only on paper at this point. But little did I know, that random notes, and small observations would lead up to a conclusion I never expected.

"Hey, Lilly-Ann," Matt shouted as he carried an armload of dirty dishes into the kitchen. "You're not the only one who likes that Deenie woman's romantic books."

"Not romantic. Romance. There's a difference."

"Whatever. A customer left her book at the table. I put it on the counter with the coffee makers in case she comes back in."

"I've never read a Deenie Alexandria book," I said. "Might as well take a look."

I lifted *Crimson Sunsets* and flipped it open to the publisher—Pennington Books. They were a household word. Then I read the acknowledgement, which was pretty general except for the mention of an agent—Sydney Brittleson. Something about the name *Sydney* stuck in my head and annoyed the heck out of me. But the "Ah-hah" moment came seconds later when Lilly-Ann shouted, "Can anyone twist the lid off of this pickle jar?"

Twist! A new twist! An agent looking for a new twist!

KC referred to his agent as Sid, the night Ian and I went into the Prickly Pear's bar to chit-chat with him and Arist. And, he said the agent was interested in new and different plot twists. Could it be he shared the same agent with Deenie?

It was an easy search. I grabbed my phone and pulled up Pennington Books. Then I scoured through the divisions and located the authors by name and relevant information. Many, like KC, had promo photos, but others didn't. In this case, KC's "screenshot" stood out like a seasoned cowboy, but Deenie didn't have one.

Then, I pulled up KC's website, and the announcement of a major film deal was plastered all over the banner, followed by a zillion promo shots featuring his riding prowess. Too bad Barbara didn't invite him for a hair-raising ride.

I looked up Deenie, but her website focused on her books with all sorts of cutesy romantic scenes. A strange thought crossed my mind, but I dismissed it. It was, after all, a coincidence that they shared the same publisher and agent.

A murky haze filled the room, but no specter. "Giving up so easily? You've got a hunch. Follow it. If I'm going to do everything for you, I need more time pestering Imogen."

"Shh. Not now."

"Fine. Then I'll leave you with one question, Missy. 'What kind of favor did KC do for Dame Judith?'"

Before I could choke out a word, the haze, and Edith along with it, disappeared. Wasting no time, I phoned Allison at the library to ask if she knew more about that mystery conference in Toronto where KC granted Judith that favor.

"Hey, Katie. So sorry to hear about your aunt. Word travels faster than wind around here. What's up?"

"A while back, you mentioned KC doing a favor for Dame Judith in Toronto at a conference. Would you know any more about it?"

"Off hand, no, but Lida would. She was at that conference. I'm not sure about the others. Quite the big deal. Does this have something to do with the murders?"

"It might. It's a long shot."

"Good luck. It's been pretty quiet, rumor-wise, around here."

That may be about to change.

I thanked her and then phoned Lida. Not that I felt like talking to a back-stabbing liar who threw my aunt under the proverbial bus, but I didn't have much choice. I could play nice-nice, too. *And watch my back.*

After a few pleasantries, I cut to the chase. "Lida, would you happen to know what went on with Dame Judith at that Toronto mystery convention two years ago? I heard you attended. It may shed some light on this investigation."

"Hmm, I don't know how. That's an odd question for sure. Hey, what the heck. I want to get out of here like mad, so yeah. Here's what I know—Dame Judith borrowed a necklace from someone in the Royal Palace to wear at that event. And not just any necklace, if you can imagine."

"I can't, but I don't know anyone in the Royal Palace." *Or any palace.*

"Anyway, it was valued at way beyond the quadruple digits and was supposed to be under lock and key in the hotel safe at the conference."

"Uh-oh."

"Uh-oh is right. Someone must have known about it because the carrying case she had it in got inadvertently switched with another one, and Dame Judith was beside herself. Next thing I knew, the switcheroo had been rectified. Not sure of the details, but that's as much as I know. Maybe Jessica knows more. She was at that conference, too. Seriously, I don't see how this relates to Richard and Dorrie's murders."

"Like I said, it was a long shot."

"Yeah, I suppose I'd be reaching for straws, too, if that was my aunt."

I was about to mention the Silent Witness thing, but held off, and instead thanked her for her time. Then I texted Ian: *Either I've got a terrific plot for a screenplay, or I've figured out who the killer is. Only I'm not sure of the motive.*

He texted back: *Tell me the means and opportunity. That's two-thirds of it.*

I told him I'd email it since it was way too long to text. Then, I ran it by Lilly-Ann, Javie, and Matt when we caught a lull and held my breath they'd find it credible.

Chapter Forty-Three

Monday

"Let me get this straight," Javie said. He consolidated the two large bowls of tuna salad and put them in the fridge. "You think Richard and Dorrie's murders were planned two years ago in Toronto?"

"I know it sounds off the rails, but yeah. I've got part of the *how* and the *who,* and snippets of the *why.* Ian and I have exhausted all of the suspects, and we're left with one—KC Camplin. But the motive eludes me. Barbara said bribery, blackmail, or ruining someone's reputation, but none of those seem to fit a scenario. More like general reasons to commit murder."

"Okay." Javie turned to Lilly-Ann and Matt, then back to me. "Spill out the how and the who, and maybe we can come up with the *why.*"

"And then?"

Javie smiled. "You plant a trap."

"Hold on." Lilly-Ann put her hands out front as if she was stopping traffic. "I still don't get the deal about Toronto."

"All right. Here goes. If my deductions are correct, KC was the one who committed those murders and Dame Judith was his accomplice."

"Wow! That's a cool screenplay," Matt laughed, but it was short-lived when Lilly-Ann smacked his arm.

I backtracked and told them what Lida had told me about the Royal Palace necklace and how close Dame Judith was to losing it. Then I took the Grand Canyon leap and said, "I think KC was behind that switcheroo, and when he righted things, Dame Judith was so elated, so ecstatic, that she told him she owed him a major favor. So, how could she say no when he asked her to help him out when the time came. That's why she flew all the way to Cave Creek for the event."

"I'm still confused." Lilly-Ann shrugged.

"Let's go back to the scene of the crime. The banquet area in front of the waterfall at the library. When Deputy Vincent told me that Richard's hairs were found wrapped around my aunt's bracelet, I wondered how on earth that was possible. Then, I realized something. Aunt Regina had a not-so-pleasant conversation with Dame Judith at one of the tables at the banquet. Then, when my aunt got up to leave, Dame Judith stopped her by grabbing her wrist. What if Dame Judith loosened the clasp so that it would fall off?"

"Oh my gosh!" Lilly-Ann put her palm to her mouth. "Dame Judith would find it later and give it to KC who somehow managed to get a few hairs that belonged to Richard and wrapped them on the bracelet before tossing it into the water. Am I right? Is that your scenario? Is that how she repaid him? An accomplice to murder?"

Matt scratched the back of his neck. "Maybe she didn't know what he planned. And how would KC get Richard's hair?"

"Easy. He was in close proximity and could have pretended to brush something off of Richard's shoulder. Hair always falls out."

"I suppose it's as good a scenario as any," Javie said. "But it's still a scenario. And even if you're right, you'd still need to prove it. Or get a confession. Pulling off a 'Big Reveal' only works in movies and books. That's where a trap comes in. A well-thought-out, conceivable trap."

"Go on."

Javie shook his head. "That's as far as I got."

"A trap, huh? That's going to require a lot of planning, and there's not much time. The other suspects are still being detained, but I doubt they can keep them for long."

And then, just what I needed—Edith's input. "A trap! A sticky, cobweb of a trap that the killer would never be able to extricate himself from. I love that idea! It's splendid!"

"It's not splendid." I tried not to look, but Edith made it impossible.

"I know," Javie said, "I can see the look on your face, but it's the best I could come up with."

"It's a start. Okay, guys. Think of killer-catching traps as we continue to prepare foods and serve the customers. If anyone gets a major brainstorm, clue me in."

Unfortunately, no one did, and I ended the work day on a frustrating note. That is, until I got home and changed into comfy jeans and a sweatshirt. As soon as the soft denim touched my legs, I had an epiphany like no other.

True, I vowed never to do this again, but my aunt was on a slow march to the gallows, and all the other players would be dismissed, leaving her to take the blame for a crime she didn't commit.

"Maddie or Ian will take good care of you," I said to Speedbump, "if I don't survive this."

"Good evening, Sarah Bernhardt."

I turned to face a barrage of cluster flies. "Who?"

"A French actress and the queen of melodrama in the late 1800s."

"How am I supposed to know that, Edith? And get rid of those horrid cluster flies, will you?"

"I'm trying something new. Like I mentioned before, my talents are expanding. Who am I to question it? Or try them out, for that matter."

"Try them out elsewhere. Tell me, what brings you here? I thought you were otherwise occupied."

"I was, but you definitely need my expertise if you're going to pull off what I think you are."

"How did you know what I was up to?"

"The minute you touched those denim jeans, you gave it away. Go on. Call her."

"I vowed I'd never do this again."

"Only to yourself. That doesn't count. I'm waiting. Make the call."

I rolled my eyes and phoned Barbara before I lost the courage.

"Katie!" Her voice was sharp and chipper. "Been thinking about you. We really need to saddle up soon. Terrific winter weather for it. Nothing like a spunky horse in the cold, crisp air."

Or a javelin to the heart.

"Actually, I was thinking the same thing, but with the other authors joining us, if you'd be willing. With my aunt under house arrest until her arraignment, they'll be free to leave the area pretty soon."

Barbara burst out laughing. "And you want to give them the proper send-off?'

"I, uh…"

"Say no more. I got you covered. So, Jessica, Lida, and KC, I presume? Pretty hard to ship Dame Judith across the pond."

"Uh-huh. I need to be upfront about this. It's not exactly a send-off in the classic sense. It's more of a—"

"Confession brought about by fear for one's own life?"

"Well, I—"

"Hey, I write this stuff, too, you know. Not sure how you intend to pull it off, but I'll leave that piece of the puzzle for you. Got to admit. You've got some moxie. Meanwhile, let's set a date and get saddled up. Call me an old-fashioned gal, but I believe in cowboy justice. Waiting for karma to kick in is too darn frustrating."

"I knew I liked that woman," Edith announced as soon as I thanked Barbara and ended the call. "Sensible and no nonsense."

"You don't think I've gotten way over my head, do you?"

Look who I'm asking.

"Nah. All you need is a plan to expose the real killer. Or killers. Or accomplices. Or responsible parties if you want to be politically correct."

"This needs to be a two-person job. Well, *two,* in the broad sense of the word."

"Only if we have a signed agreement."

"A signed agreement?"

"I help you catch the killer, and in exchange, you take me to Imogen's once a week."

"How about once a year?"

"Once every two weeks."

We gave new meaning to the words *collective bargaining,* but an hour later, Edith and I reached an agreement. I'd take her to Imogen's six times a year, and one major holiday. I wrote down the terms and conditions, and Edith whirled the paper around in a frenzy that resulted in me spilling coffee on the paper. Then, a whooshing sound and the droplets of coffee formed the letters EE.

"Are you satisfied, Missy?"

I stared at the paper and smiled. "Only if you hold up your end of the deal."

Chapter Forty-Four

Tuesday, Thursday

The plan was well underway by noon the following day. Barbara and I agreed that Thursday afternoon would be a good choice since the weather would be perfect and it would give "the players" time to acquire the appropriate garb. I was positive Lida and Jessica would be on board because both of them were getting restless and bored at the hotel, and both of them mentioned horseback riding in their author information on their book jacket covers.

To sweeten the deal, and add credibility for my participation in the ride, Barbara told them I would provide a charcuterie tray for the crew to enjoy after the ride. As for KC, it was all about his cowboy ego, and Barbara managed to "stoke that like a pro." She told me he couldn't very well turn down the offer when she informed him that Lida and Jessica were both seasoned riders and were anxious to get on the trail.

"Be careful," Ian said when I spoke with him shortly after my conversation with Barbara. "It was harrowing last time, and that was without a potential killer or killers on the trail. If it wasn't for the fact that two of our sous chefs are out with the flu and Sterling is pulling out what little hair he has left, I'd want to be there with you."

"I'd swap places with you if I could, but I don't know a thing about making a roux. At least you know how to ride a horse."

"Don't take chances. Okay?"

"Tell that to the horse. By the way, I asked Barbara straight out why she was going all out for me and she said, 'I attend many of these events with the same authors and frankly, I don't want to be looking over my shoulder for fear I'll be the next target. Face it, people with those tendencies are more than unhinged. They're unstable as hell.'"

"She's right about that. Watch your back."

When the call ended, I returned to the lunch bustle at The Char-Board and craved for an epiphany before Thursday. It was only two days away, if I counted the nights.

A trap. Easy for Javie to say.

Unbeknownst to me, Barbara was one step ahead, but lamentably, she never shared it with me. Then again, it was probably for the best. Had I known, I might not have agreed.

I woke up at three fifteen on Thursday with so many knots in my stomach that an entire troop of Boy Scouts wouldn't have been able to unravel them. I googled more tips about riding and left an email for Maddie to check in on Speedbump if she didn't hear from me by nightfall.

Three and a half hours later, she sent a text: *What's with the drama?*

Rather than texting back, I phoned and gave her the rundown.

"Are you insane?" Her voice was at least three decibels louder than usual. "It wasn't enough to take one wild ride? And that's going to seem like a pleasure jaunt compared to what's coming."

"Maddie, the real killer or killers are going to get a free pass out of here any day now. It's not as if I have a lot of time on my hands. I need to speed things up."

"With a trail ride?"

"It was the best I could come up with at short notice. Um, any new interest on that property?"

"It's got two strikes against it. The ridiculous rumors of a haunting, followed by a dead body in the yard. Yeah, every homebuyer's dream. I'm so frustrated."

"I know you had an inspector out there, but what if you contacted the utilities company and had *them* assess the electrical situation?" *I'm all but handing this to you on a platter.* "Something could be going on with the wiring at their end. That could cause all sorts of glitches. You've got nothing to lose."

"Good point. But Frank Riley should have picked up on it."

"Frank Riley?"

"The building inspector. He works part-time. Only two days a week. The guy is in high demand by realtors for their clients."

"Do you know where he works the other days of the week?"

"Paper pushing for some business. I'm not sure. Why? Do you need anything inspected?"

Nope. I already know what's causing the disturbances in my house.

"No, just curious."

Maddie laughed. "I thought you'd be more curious about my love life."

"The molecular chemist."

"He goes by Kip, and we really hit it off. He's bright, funny, and endearing."

"That's a change from your usual."

"Uh-huh. Listen, I've got to get moving. Text me this evening or call. If I don't hear from you, I'll check on Speedbump. Better yet, get an Apple AirTag and put it in your pocket. Easier to find the body."

"Very funny. Catch you later."

The name, Frank Riley, stuck in my head, so I texted Ian and asked if it rang a bell. He texted back: *The person who signed the work order for Wilsetta's connection.*

There are coincidences and then there are coincidences that aren't those at all, and this was one of them. Too bad I had a murderer, or possibly two, to catch or I would have pursued it further. I hoped Maddie took my advice and called the electric company.

Knowing what to expect on one of Barbara's trail rides, I dressed with extra padding in the form of thermal underwear and donned lots of layers from long-sleeved shirts to hoodies. Lida and Jessica came prepared as well, only with fleece jackets and small backpacks that looked as if they were recently bought. Most likely filled with trail mix or other goodies. KC arrived in worn jeans and a heavy canvas jacket. No fancy belt buckle like the one he wore at the author event, but then again, this was a trail ride, not a celebrity event.

We met at the barn, and like my last visit, we were greeted by Cory and his assistant, who helped us mount.

"Barbara should be here in a jiff," he said. "She's warming up first."

I looked around and noticed that all six horses were saddled. "Are more people joining us?" I asked.

Cory shook his head. "Nah. We saddled all of them in case there was an issue with one or two of them."

I'd be riding Pansey again since I figured "the devil you know is better than the one you don't." That left Snickers, Ruby, Dusty, Blaze, and Maisy. All of them chestnut with one exception—Dusty was pale grey and KC's choice. Lida mounted Maisy, and Jessica mounted Snickers. Then Cory walked over to KC and said, "Dusty's a good horse and follows commands, but he's bat poop crazy anywhere near water. A few raindrops will turn him into a bucking bronco. No worries today. No rain in sight, but figured you should know."

"Thanks for the heads-up," KC replied. "I'll be fine."

I looked around, hoping Edith would keep her word and appear, but no sign of her. Then again, she'd probably start yammering the second we got on the trail. Just then, the sound of whinnying announced Barbara's arrival. She rode toward us on a dark horse with a long, flowing mane and announced, "We're splitting up so we don't get cramped on the same trail. Just stay off the Lemon Squeeze path. It's got a warning on it. The rocks and brush made it too tight for comfort, and it's steeper than the Matterhorn. The horses don't know the difference, but you do. Stay off."

You don't have to tell me twice.

Then she pulled her horse towards Cory and whispered something to him while Lida, Jessica, and KC chatted among themselves. As for me, I kept looking around for Edith.

"Lida and Jessica, you two take the trail to the right. It'll skirt around a large field before getting narrow as it winds through some trees and brush. Piece of cake. KC and Katie, you two hit the path on the left. Starts out narrow but widens out. Don't let Pansey graze, or she'll refuse to stop. And all of you—watch out for low limbs that might fall. After the summer monsoons, some of the branches weakened."

"What about you?" KC asked.

"I'm meeting the guy from Katie's charcuterie place. He's bringing over a large tray. French-themed. Then I'll take a stab at the trails and catch up to you folks. See you in about an hour. Have fun!"

I opened my mouth to speak and then thought better of it. Javie had already delivered the tray. So what was she up to? Clearly, it wasn't the time to ask. In a split second, Barbara clapped her hands, and the horses started walking. Lida and Jessica on the right, and me, right behind KC to the path on the left.

He turned and shouted, "Better view when you're in the lead."

Not for long.

Chapter Forty-Five

Thursday

Barbara was right about the narrow path, and Pansey trotted along behind Dusty without any shenanigans. A few minutes later, we'd reached a wider area that could easily accommodate three abreast. I pressed my knees into the horse and made a clicking sound. Pansey perked up and charged ahead until she was side by side with Dusty. Then I leaned over and said to KC, "No sense for single file when we can talk and ride at the same time."

"We got word we're free to leave Cave Creek. I'll be heading out in the morning. Too bad about Regina."

"If she were a character in one of your novels, what would you call her? Oh yeah—a red herring. Well, for your information, things may change." *Edith, where the heck are you? Things may get dicey.*

"What are you saying?"

"Before we mounted, I got a text from my mother. It seems the lab in Phoenix sent some of their findings from Dorrie's body to the Chandler Police Department for another look-see. Their forensic services section was deemed a top-performing forensic lab by the American Society of Crime Laboratory Directors, or the ASCLD, as they're known." *At least from what I read when I looked this up and memorized it last night.*

KC slowed his horse and turned to face me. Without missing a beat, I went on. "They were able to match trace DNA on the clothing around her neck. Oh, did I mention the cause of death was strangulation? Anyway, the DNA didn't match my aunt's. I wouldn't be packing my bags all that soon if I were you. Right now, it hasn't made the news, but trust me, it will."

KC shrugged. "Not my concern. I'll be sleeping in my own bed in Wyoming tomorrow night."

"Extradition laws are federal. But search warrants are local."

"What are you saying?"

"The MCSO isn't done yet, so whatever you were told just flew out the window with this new finding. Oh, goodness! I forgot to mention the most important thing my mother told me. Since Richard's clothing was still in an evidence locker, they were able to extract trace DNA as well. Seems the Chandler office had a more exacting process. Imagine that."

"Why don't you go on ahead? I need to take a whiz, and I'm headed to those trees on the left."

"No problem." I made sure Pansey ambled slowly so I could turn my head and see what he was really up to. No surprise. He dismounted and bent down to tap something into his phone. Too bad there was no way I could find out who he was most likely texting.

I continued along so as not to let him know that I had watched him. Still no sign of Edith, and I was positive she got caught up in other, not-of-this-world, business. *No surprise there.* Within minutes, I heard the sound of Dusty's hooves making their way toward us. Not wanting to turn this into a race, or worse yet, a chase, I slowed down and waited for KC's approach.

I saw a sign that read, "Stay On The Trail," and muttered, "You don't have to tell me twice."

The sound of hooves grew closer, but something was off. KC should have slowed his pace as the distance between us grew shorter. Instead, the click-clack of hooves on rocky ground picked up speed, like a metronome in quarter beats.

Pansey reacted by snorting first and then racing ahead but before I could pull the reins to the left, she bolted toward the one trail we were warned to stay away from—the Lemon Squeezer. It was too late to force a turn, and the narrow toe-path that was considered a trail grew tighter and rockier as it went upward.

Behind me, horse hooves hit the ground like a hammer. I guessed Dusty and her rider were only a few yards behind me, and I knew the speed was KC's doing and not the horse's. Clearly, I had exposed him, and the risk was too great for him to let me leave here alive.

"Now would be a good time, Edith!" I shouted as a breeze picked up and distorted my words.

Dusty's whiny set a shockwave through Pansey, and she charged uphill with abandon. My right hand was a death grip on the reins, and had it not been for the horn that became an anchor for my free hand, I was certain I'd be thrown off.

Too scared of losing balance, I didn't turn around. Instead, I held on, forcing myself to stay on the seat rise and not fall back onto the raised curve on the back of the saddle, or cantle, where I'd lose what little control I had.

The path grew tighter with every yard, and I felt the sting of brush and branches as Pansey continued to make her way up the trail. Behind me, Dusty snorted, and given the sound, closed the distance between us.

The trail steepened, and my head flung back. That's when I looked up and saw the peak of the trail. *Please let it level out on top. Please let it level out on top.* I reasoned it was only a few more feet and I'd be safe. Lamentably, I reasoned wrong.

No sooner did we reach the top when a rock or stick came out of nowhere, hitting Pansey on the right side underneath the saddle. She reared up for less than a second or two before the path went straight downhill. In that nanosecond, I glanced to the right and saw Dusty's head peering out from thick brush, and as I flew past, I locked eyes with KC, who was seated in the saddle, and froze. Who was behind me?

No time to find out. I flew downhill at a speed most Olympic skiers coveted. Behind me, the horse's hooves were relentless. As the bottom leveled out into a wide path through a field, I turned to see who my tormentor was and caught a quick glimpse of Jessica as she sped off on a side path. Jessica. None of it made sense. But I didn't have time to mull it over.

KC emerged across the field when I heard a familiar female voice. "Move to the small path on the edge by the trees. Don't be a sitting duck."

It wasn't Edith, but the voice was recognizable—Rosaline.

"What are you doing here? Where's Edith?"

"You have to ask? Snatching up the latest acquisitions. I owed her one, so here I am. And I don't know anything about riding a horse."

"That's a big help."

"I do know to get out of the way when trouble approaches, and here it comes!"

By now, I was under thick branches when KC pulled alongside me and cleared his throat. "You're a better rider than I thought."

"You need me out of the way, don't you?"

A beige haze settled over KC. "Don't antagonize him."

"I'm not antagonizing anyone."

KC furrowed his brow. "I didn't say you were. Seems you know too much for your own good." He pulled the bottle of Geyser Spring Water from the leather holder on the horn and took a slug. Then, he tossed the bottle on the ground and grabbed something from his pocket. In a flash, he reached across his horse and thrust the object toward my chest.

I lurched back, but Rosaline had other plans. The beige haze morphed into a dust storm that stung my eyes and blurred everything. Droplets of rain fell over us even though I hadn't seen a cloud anywhere. Suddenly, Dusty went berserk just as Cory predicted he would if he got wet. *Thanks, Rosaline, for unleashing this maelstrom.* The horse bucked, reared up, and kicked his legs at Pansey.

Not willing to sit still, Pansey retaliated. She pinned her ears against her head to display her anger and kicked her feet. I glanced back and noticed she swished her tail as well. But that wasn't the worst—Dusty got too close to her and she bit his mane. Enough to catch KC off guard. I took full advantage, dug my thighs into Pansey, and raced across the field toward the barn in the distance.

Unfortunately, there was one thing I hadn't counted on—Jessica's return.

Chapter Forty-Six

I was midway through the field when Jessica came out of nowhere and blocked the trail by straddling across it on her horse. At that instant, KC came up from behind and blocked me from the rear.

"We're going for the overland route," I shouted to Pansey. With a sharp left-hand turn, I yanked her neck, pressed in on her thighs, and leaned forward. The horse responded with an immediate gallop, but that only lasted a second or two before she slowed down to sniff something in the dried field grass.

By that time, I was surrounded again. Or *locked in,* as I prefer to call it. Jessica's horse was nose to nose with mine, and Dusty was right at my side with KC so close I could smell his aftershave.

"Maybe I do know too much," I said.

"Yep. Barbara already gave me the heads-up."

Oh my gosh. I am such a bad judge of character.

KC nodded to Jessica, and she pulled Snickers alongside Pansey. Talk about too close for comfort.

"What do you want?" *As if I didn't know.*

KC's voice was slow and deep. "The three of us are going to take a nice, slow walk back to the Lemon Squeeze. You're going to lose your balance and fall from the horse before taking the plunge down the gully. And don't think you won't be missed. Those charcuteries were darn good." He chuckled as the three of us moved forward.

This is always the scene in the movies where someone comes to the rescue or the victim pulls an amazing stunt to save his or her life. Unfortunately, I didn't expect any of those scenarios to come to fruition. Instead, I relied on the one thing I had gotten fairly proficient at—lying through my teeth.

"For your information," I said, "I surmised something like this would happen, so I left word with Deputy Vincent to get a warrant and search your room at the Prickly Pear. I'll bet they find your other belt, complete with DNA evidence that links you to Dorrie's murder."

KC didn't say a word, so I went on. "There's still enough time for you and Jessica to turn and head back. That way, you'd be able to phone or text whoever you contacted earlier when you had to excuse yourself for a nature call."

"She's lying," Jessica shouted. "She wants to save her own butt."

KC nodded once and glared at me. "I'll take my chances." Then he pulled out what I thought was the same menacing object from his pocket, only it wasn't a knife or anything of the kind. It was a pistol."

"Start moving."

"No one will believe this was an accident."

He laughed and pointed the gun.

We started for the tree and brush line when a blackish cloud whirled around us, only it wasn't a cloud. It was a dense swarm of mosquitoes, gnats, no-see-ums, and miscellaneous flying pests. Hallelujah! Edith arrived at last!

Only it wasn't Edith. It was Rosaline. And apparently, she was just as surprised as I was. Her voice was high-pitched and frantic. "I'm new at this. Oh good grief—Now what?"

The black cloud engulfed the three of us, making it impossible to take a breath without inhaling insects. *This is your fault, Edith!*

Then, the strangest thing happened, as if whirling bugs weren't enough. Larger insects appeared—a whirl of locusts and grasshoppers that circled around the horses' legs. Pansey went totally off her rocker, preceded only by Dusty, who bucked so hard that KC lost his balance and fell to the ground, the pistol rolling a few yards away from him.

Then, the raspy voice I thought I'd never hear. "Rosaline! Tone it down! Tone it down!"

Before she could respond, a wave of horse flies descended on us. I felt the first pinch on the nape of my neck and tried to swat the dastardly thing. That's when I heard Jessica scream, "Get them off of me!"

She yanked Snickers away from me and bolted across the field. Presumably, to find another trail that led to the barn. Meanwhile, KC's face was blinded by a cluster of flying ants. I identified them without hesitation since they were quite common on hikes in the southwest and called out, "Those are red ants. Their bite is toxic. Best bet is stay still."

"What are you waiting for, Missy?" Edith blared. "Get off your horse and grab that gun."

"I might not be able to get back on."

"Stop whining. Move it!" Then to Rosaline, "On second thought, crank it up! Crank it up!"

I flung myself off of Pansey but held tight to the reins that I had loosened. A runaway horse was not something I wanted to contend with, even if she'd make her way to the barn.

In one of my fastest moves ever, I scooped down and grabbed the gun while KC was still consumed with the ants. Then I got out my phone and texted Deputy Vincent: *Barbara is mastermind. Am holding KC's gun. Get to her ranch!*

In an instant, everything changed. A billowy haze descended, unlike the kind that announced Edith or Rosaline's arrivals. In its midst, I could make out a semi-lucent figure of a man. Medium height, average build, thin mustache, white shirt, and tie. He held a small notebook and a pen and shouted, "Edith! Rosaline! I distinctly told both of you to remain where you were. Now you are getting demerits." With that, he took out his notebook and proceeded to write something.

I kept one eye on the "pencil pusher," whom I assumed to be Larken, and the other on KC. The ants still kept him at bay, and the nuisance flying bugs did their job as well. With the gun in my hand, and no idea if it was loaded,

I pointed it down but tightened on the grip.

Then, the translucent man spoke again. "Did both of you conjure up these annoying insects? Never mind. I'll take care of it myself." With that, the insects vanished in a nanosecond, and the man along with them.

"Obnoxious fussbudget!" Edith exclaimed.

Before I realized what happened, Larken materialized again and broke the sound barrier with his yelling. "That does it, Edith. Ten more demerits! Ponder that!"

For the second time in less than thirty seconds, Larken disappeared. I opened my mouth to say something to Edith and Rosaline, but before I could utter a syllable, both of them had evaporated into the white haze.

In that very instant, KC rose from the ground, no longer fighting off annoying predators. Instead, he walked calmly toward me and cleared his throat. "The gun's not loaded." Then, he reached down to the cuff of his jeans and pulled out a small revolver. Laughing, he said, "But this one is."

Not sure of whether or not to believe him, I kept a steady grip on the one in my hand. "What do you plan to do? Shoot me with the one in your hand?"

He shook his head. "Nope. Same plan as before. Get back on your horse and move to the Lemon Squeeze."

"Uh, yeah. But there's a slight flaw in your plan—I can't hoist myself up without a mounting block." *Great. Now he'll force me to walk.*

Even if Deputy Vincent got my text and hightailed it over here, he'd have to get on a horse to reach me. And if that wasn't feasible, he'd have to walk, and that would take hours. No way could vehicles make it here. Not even the all-terrain ones.

Then I thought about a helicopter landing in the field, but realized I'd have better luck summoning a spaceship.

"If you want me to ride over there, you'll have to cup your hands so I can mount."

"Your feet will do just fine. And when you plummet to the bottom, it will look as if you fell from your horse. Now move it!"

I took a few steps and as I brushed past Dusty, I remembered something I'd seen on a zillion cowboy shows. Someone slaps the horse on the rear, and it takes off or rears up. Praying for the latter, I gave a whooping slap to Dusty. So hard and strong that the sting burned the palm of my hand.

He neighed and rose up for a split second. Long enough for me to take a dead run toward Pansey, but no quite long enough for me to mount her. KC was at my side before I knew it. He grabbed me by my jacket collar and yanked me back.

"Guess I'll have to walk you there myself."

"Or you could forget the whole thing."

"I plan to. Once you're at the bottom of the gully."

Chapter Forty-Seven

Thursday

The sky became more colorful as dusk approached. It would be another forty to fifty minutes before sunset, making the prospects of anyone rescuing me impossible. If I wasn't positive before, I was more than positive now—Barbara was at the helm of this.

If I was wrong, she would have been here by now. Especially with an early return from Jessica. No, I was certain Barbara was comfy at home, waiting for KC to tell her the deed was done.

I walked slowly, but KC shoved me along. The only sound were our shoes on the dry grass and dusty trail. Even the horses were quiet a few yards back. But the crunching noise got louder, and I realized it wasn't a crunch at all. It was the sound of hooves. Hooves moving at breakneck speed.

Barbara! She'd come to make sure KC didn't mess up. I listened intently, trying to ascertain how far off she was. That's when I heard two distinct hoof sounds.

Terrific. She brought Jessica along.

For a fleeting second, I wondered what Barbara and Jessica's involvement was, but my reverie was cut short when a man's voice sliced through the stillness of the early evening air. At first, I thought it was my imagination.

"Hold it right there, KC. Don't make another move!"

I started to turn, but KC shoved me forward. "Keep walking."

The clip-clip of hooves grew stronger, and the man called out again, "Give it up while you can."

Certainly not Deputy Vincent's voice. Unless he could appear like Edith. The voice I heard didn't belong to anyone I recognized. Not at first. Then, the speaker said something that I'd heard before—a verb without a noun. "Suppose you think you'll get away with a third murder. Got news for you. You won't."

Cory! It was Cory! Next thing I knew, he and his ranch assistant shot through the field and charged toward us. Suddenly, it became clear to me why he had the other two horses saddled. He knew there was going to be trouble.

Maybe Barbara isn't at the helm of this nightmare after all.

KC was unfazed, and by now we stood at the peak of the Lemon Squeeze. His hand gripped my shoulder, and he pressed tight. I heard Cory's footsteps, but he was too far away to stop KC from giving me a shove.

Bracing for it, I threw myself down, causing him to lose his balance and fall forward. He grazed my neck, and his gun dropped. I reached for it, but he was quicker. We were inches from the steep drop-down trail, and I was no match for his boulder or his weight. But I was agile. Agile enough to roll in the opposite direction and do the only thing I could think of—grab a handful of dirt and throw it in his face. I'd seen it done a hundred times on TV and it always worked. Too bad there was an exception to everything.

His hand caught me by the wrist, and I was immobilized on the ground. That's when I felt the barrel pressed into my side. I was out of options. But I wasn't out of friends. At least not the unworldly kind.

I didn't notice the pink and blue haze as the sun lowered into the horizon, but I caught the pungently sweet scent of honeysuckle that was followed by an orange and yellow luminance that was quickly overshadowed by a murky grey vapor and the noxious odor of automotive grease and cigar smoke.

Yep, Edith and Rosaline made landfall! And not a moment too soon. KC started coughing and wheezing. A result, no doubt, of Edith's cigar stench. And then, the unexpected—a cluster of lightning bugs swarmed his face, some of them getting caught in my hair.

"Over there!" Corey shouted. Next thing I knew, he and his assistant ran toward us, and one of them jerked the gun from KC's hand.

"You okay?" Cory asked.

"I think so."

He nudged KC, who got up from the ground and looked around. "This isn't what it looks like."

"Murder never is," I said. Then I set my eyes on Cory. "How did you know?"

"I didn't. Barbara did. She told me to saddle up two horses and be ready to move on out. MCSO deputies are at the house."

"How did they know? I barely had time to send a text."

Cory had a sheepish look on his face. "She placed the call before you even left for the ride."

"Huh?"

"She said you wouldn't be happy about this but it was the only way she could trap KC into a confession—by catching him in the act again. She told him that you had absolute proof who the killer was. She knew he'd want to get you out of way."

"She nearly got me killed!"

"We were 'at the ready.' Had you in our sights all along."

"Um, don't look now, but so does someone else." I pointed to Jessica, who rode out of the bushy area and aimed a gun right at us. Her voice was cold and loud. "Drop your guns and let KC mount up and leave with me. No sudden moves or I'll blast this thing like no tomorrow."

"I think she means business," I said.

Cory and his assistant did as she said and stood silently as Jessica snatched the guns and put them in her small backpack. All this while KC walked over to Dusty and mounted up without saying a word.

The two of them bolted for the only semi-wooded area off of the field, and I asked Cory where it led.

"Backside of Lake Pleasant. They'll be able to ditch the horses and get in a car if they planned this far ahead. I'm texting Barbara. Come on, we're on the chase."

"What? They've got your guns!"

He laughed. "That's what you think. He reached down to his saddlebag and took out a pistol while his assistant did the same thing. "Let's move!" Then he added, "I wouldn't stay out here alone with darkness creeping in. Just stay behind us. You'll be all right. Pansey knows what she's doing."

Sure. Pansey. What about me?

The sky darkened with deep red and yellow colors. Another fifteen or twenty minutes, and it would all turn dark. The only saving grace we had were the flashlights on our cell phones. Unless Cory managed to stash a real flashlight in one in his saddlebags.

I reasoned KC and Jessica would be in same predicament, unless they too, thought ahead about the shorter November days. No matter.

In a feat deserving a Congressional Medal of Honor, I reached over Pansey's saddle and used every last bit of strength I had in my arms to hoist myself up. My adrenaline pumped so hard that I never felt the burn in my arm muscles until we were halfway across the field.

Unlike the other trails, this one was rockier with fallen tree limbs everywhere. I expected one of them to cause Pansey to stumble, but we went too fast for me to worry about it. Up ahead, we saw flickering lights that moved in a steady rhythm. Uh-huh. KC and Jessica had flashlights and the foresight to turn them on before the colors left the sky in darkness. Talk about strategic planning.

I wanted to text Ian, but I had all I could do to remain upright on the horse and follow the riders ahead of me. Especially since we were losing more and more light every few minutes. The trail was endless, but I supposed it was because I moved in darkness now with no visible vantage points.

When we finally exited the trail, we were only yards away from one of the entrances to Lake Pleasant Regional Park. I could see a sign on my left for RV parking as well as one that led to the lake. Fortunately, Cory saw KC and Jessica move in that direction and angled a wide turn.

"Stay here and don't let them pass," he shouted to me.

Then, at a decent clip, he skirted around and blocked them. Just as they had done to me earlier in the day. Only this time in dim moonlight. I held steady as he aimed his gun directly at Jessica. "You don't need to do this. Drop your gun."

But instead of dropping it, Jessica lifted the pistol over her head and blasted it in the air. A felony offense in Arizona. The noise wreaked havoc on Dusty and Snickers, causing them to buck and lose their riders. Maybe that's what she wanted after all, because next thing I knew, she darted off to the RV area, leaving KC to take the fall. Figuratively and literally.

Corey dismounted and secured Snickers to the guard rail on the side of the road, while his assistant got hold of Dusty and did the same before finding Maisy grazing on some grass near the edge of the trail we had exited.

KC must have hit the ground hard because he struggled to stand. Still, I didn't trust him. I, too, dismounted but wasn't sure what possible help I could be, or, if KC had another weapon on him.

"Keep him in your sight," Cory yelled to me as he raced over. "I've got you covered."

Next thing I knew, blue and red flashers were everywhere as three or four sheriff cars approached.

"How'd they know we were here?" I asked. "Barbara had no idea."

"GPS trackers on the horses."

"And they couldn't come sooner?" My voice cracked.

Cory's assistant shook his head. "Not on Barbara's trails. Impassable with a vehicle. This is a regional park. You could take a stroller or wheelchair on the paths."

"I'd like to take a long shower and eat a gigantic dinner."

"Not right now, you won't!" It was Deputy Vincent's voice, and I knew my evening couldn't possibly get any worse.

Chapter Forty-Eight

Thursday

In a flurry of activity, KC was handcuffed and read his rights. Cory was given a ride back to Barbara's by one of the deputies in order for him to return with the horse trailer for Dusty, Pansey, and Maisy, as well as the two horses Cory and his ranch hand rode. As for Jessica, it was anyone's guess. She was on foot now.

Deputy Vincent pulled me aside and questioned me regarding my "foolish choice to take matters into my own hands."

No matter how strongly I objected, I had to credit the guy. He had gotten that part right. For what seemed like an inordinate amount of time, although it was probably less than fifteen or twenty minutes, he grilled me about the events of the day, beginning with my arrival at Barbara's place. Satisfied with my responses, he asked a deputy drive me back to her house where I'd be free to jump in my car and make a beeline for Cave Creek before anyone changed their mind.

I agreed to provide a detailed written statement the following day, and thankfully, he didn't specify the time.

"Jessica's still on the run," I said. "Although I'm not sure where she actually fits into this scenario. Then again—"

"Miss Aubrey! Didn't you listen to what I said? The case belongs to the Maricopa County Sheriff's Office in conjunction with the state marshals. I implore you. Leave it at that!"

The deputy motioned to his vehicle, and I got in the back seat. Conversation wasn't exactly this guy's strong point, so I took out my phone and texted Ian: *Harrowing ride. KC arrested for murder. Am headed to Barbara's. Then home.* I closed with the gritted teeth emoji.

He texted back: *Will be at your house when we close.* It was followed by a hug and kiss emojis.

The porch lights on Barbara's house illuminated the driveway and the surrounding mesquite trees. When the deputy dropped me off in front, Barbara stood with the door open and motioned for me to come inside.

"Thanks for the ride," I said as I closed the door behind me and hurried to the door. The evening air had turned cold, and even though I had plenty of layering, I knew the chill I felt didn't come from the weather.

"You should have told me your plan," I announced, the second I stepped through the threshold. "I could have been a third victim. Plus, I thought you were the mastermind behind both murders."

Barbara chuckled. "Not likely on both counts. But then again, I had the advantage of knowing a bit about the situation that led to all of this."

"What situation?"

"Come on in and make yourself comfortable in the dining room. Lida and I can't finish that wonderful charcuterie by ourselves. There's a carafe of coffee as well."

"Hey, Katie." Lida gave me a wave and handed me a coffee. "I heard about what happened to you. I wish I had known sooner that Jessica was involved. It was only when she split on us during the ride that I knew something wasn't right. She's been pretty guarded this entire time."

"Do you know about 'the situation' too?"

Barbara cut in before Lida could answer. "I haven't told her yet. Guess both of you will hear it now. Like Lida, Jessica, and KC, I was at that Toronto conference too. Did I mention it was an international conference that brought in all of the mega players in the literary world? And world-renowned culinary chefs for the banquet?"

"Does this have anything to do with Dame Judith and the borrowed necklace? Lida told me as much."

Barbara smiled at Lida before returning her gaze to me. "Lida told you what she knew, but that was only the synopsis. It's time you heard the full recount. And mind you, I didn't piece all of this together until recently. And that was after a few long-distance phone calls with Dame Judith. I don't relish seeing my cellular bill."

I took a small piece of the triple cream Brie and a few seasoned crackers. Hours ago, I was ravenous, but now all I craved was information. "Did she tell you KC was the murderer?"

"Not exactly. I surmised it, but had to be sure. That's why I told him you snooped around and had undeniable proof of who the killer was. And that you knew both murders were connected. I knew he'd want you out of the way."

"Cory said as much, but it didn't sink in. Um, up until now."

"Yes, it's difficult to grasp, but trust me, you were always being tracked by Cory, even at a distance. But first," she went on, "let's go back to the conference and the royal necklace, shall we?"

Like one of those bobbleheads, all I could do was nod as Barbara spoke.

"Jessica was going through a horrible divorce, and due to a pre-nuptial agreement, she would have to pay an inordinate amount of alimony to her ex-husband. Meanwhile, KC's publisher was negotiating movie deals."

"What does any of that have to do with murder?"

"It's all about motive, honey."

Oh my gosh, she's sounding like Edith.

I sipped my coffee and ate more crackers as Barbara went on.

"Dame Judith was supposed to put that priceless necklace in the hotel safe following the banquet, but stopped at the bar for a nightcap on her way to the front desk. Like all hotel bars during conferences, the place was standing room only, and someone managed to switch her carrying case with one that looked similar. Clever, huh?"

"Clever and diabolical. That's awful."

"KC, who sat in a corner and appeared to be three sheets to the wind, caught the action and put his own plan in motion when he saw Jessica make the switch. Mind you, she did her homework, including the kinds of carrying cases used to transport the royal jewels. After all, it wasn't unusual to loan them out to movie stars or other celebrities."

"Why did he hatch a plan and not just report it to the police?" I asked.

"KC needed a favor. And he needed to know that it wouldn't be reneged."

"But I thought Dame Judith granted that favor, not Jessica. After all, that's why she agreed to come to little old Cave Creek for the author's event, right?"

"Oh, Dame Judith owed him a favor, all right, but not *that* favor. Jessica owed him *that* favor, or she would have been serving a long sentence for grand theft." Barbara stood and refilled the coffee carafe.

I bit my lip. "The alimony money?"

"Not that it's an excuse, mind you, but it explained a lot."

"I'll tell you one thing," Lida said. "It doesn't explain the favor KC needed. And if it was to have an accomplice in murder, then what was the motive?"

Barbara shrugged. "It may be one of those things none of us will ever know until he's arrested and tried."

"Speaking of things no one will ever know," I said to Lida, "tell me, why did you make one of those Silent Witness calls that implicated my aunt?"

Lida looked at me as if I'd emerged from a spaceship. "What Silent Witness call? I never made one. Although I wouldn't put it past Jessica. She had so much to lose."

"Did she happen to mention anyone else she might have been in cahoots with?"

Lida shook her head. "No. She was a solo player."

I snickered. "Probably a good thing."

A few hours later, when I finally set foot in my house, Ian was there to greet me, along with Speedbump. He swept me into a huge bear hug, and that's when I totally broke down.

"Hey, it's okay," he said. "You were nearly killed. And I wasn't there to protect you."

"You can't always be there. Life doesn't work that way."

"I know, but I still feel horrible. I want to be there whenever you need me. I know now's not exactly the best time to delve into our relationship, but

Katie, we need to talk." He hugged me again and pressed his lips against my neck.

"I know. It's okay." I squeezed his shoulder and planted a kiss on it. "I'm just glad the real killer is behind bars and my aunt will be free to return to New Jersey."

"Who do we call to give the Garden State fair warning?"

I laughed for the first time in what seemed like ages.

Ian wiped my cheek with his hand and motioned to the kitchen. "I brought us leftover shrimp diablo with Mexican rice and bollos. You must be hungry by now."

"I had some of our charcuterie Brie at Barbara's and thought I couldn't eat another crumb, but now my appetite has returned with a vengeance."

"Good. Let's dig in!"

It really wasn't that late, it only seemed that way. When Maddie called shortly after we had eaten, it dawned on me that I had asked her to check in.

"Yay! You picked up," she said. "I don't have to drive to Cave Creek. At least not tonight. You're not going to believe this in a million years, but our office got word late this afternoon that someone filed with the zoning board to rezone the property where the dead-body-haunted-house is. Ugh, I suppose I should find a new descriptor, huh? I take it all went well with your horseback ride sleuthing."

"If you call 'attempted murder' as going well, then yeah. All went well."

"Huh? What?"

"Oh, you heard me. KC tried to kill me, and he almost succeeded."

"My gosh. I can be at your house in less than an hour. Hang on."

"I'm fine. Ian's here. This may make it to the ten o'clock news, but I'm not sure."

"Listen, I have a showing in Carefree tomorrow afternoon. How about if I pop over to The Char-Board and we can fill each other in? One-ish?"

"I'll have the coffee hot and ready."

And then, two simultaneous voices, making it virtually impossible to separate Maddie's from Edith's.

"Splendid! Larken detained us so long that I have—egg and cheese on a bagel with— no idea what catastrophe you escaped—rezoning from rural to— Merrilee and Faye offered to assist but those two always muck things up so I said—we'll check with the zoning board so—in retrospect, I should have agreed."

It was as if I got off a tilt-a-whirl. Not wanting to make things worse, I ended the call with three words—*See you tomorrow.* Then I moved my eyes to the left, where I spotted Edith admiring her nails as she sat across from where Ian and I were seated on the couch. I gave her the stink eye and hoped she'd take the hint. Unfortunately, once a buttinsky, always a buttinsky.

"Oh goodness," I said to Ian. "I really need Deputy Vincent to search KC's room at the Prickly Pear. I'm positive he'll find tangible evidence that KC committed those murders. I'm afraid the only thing KC will admit to is *attempted murder.* Remember when you told me he mentioned forgetting his belt? He didn't forget it. The DNA on that belt will match Dorrie's. I guarantee it."

"How can you be sure?"

"I saw it on his face when I said the deputies had a warrant to search his room."

"Make the call."

The deputy on duty assured me he'd get the message to Deputy Vincent, but informed me it would be the next afternoon before they could acquire a warrant. I figured it didn't matter since KC was already in custody, and if need be, I'd press charges when I got to their office tomorrow. What I didn't expect was the person who arrived there a few minutes before I did.

Chapter Forty-Nine

Friday

It was a little past eleven, and everything was running smoothly at The Char-Board. I told the crew I'd be less than an hour with Deputy Vincent, but they didn't believe me.

"You caught last night's news, didn't you?" Matt asked. "Jessica is still at large, and KC lawyered up. Deputy Vincent's going to squeeze every last bit of information from you."

I threw my palms in the air. "Great. Like lowering a bucket into a dry well. There's nothing more I can tell him."

"Good Luck!" Javie called out as I walked to the door.

"Call us if you need anything," Lilly-Ann added.

"I'll be a block away, not a continent. But thanks, guys."

When I walked into the sheriff's office, I did a double-take. Korina Kashian, the library assistant, had just left the deputy's office, blowing her nose and wiping her face. She rushed past me, but I spoke up.

"Korina? Is that you? What happened?" I looked directly at her, and she couldn't ignore me.

"I turned myself in, if you must know."

"For what?" I tried to make light of it. "Misfiling a library book?"

"I wish. I made an awful mistake because I needed money. Old story, huh?"

"It happens."

Korina looked around and then spoke. "It shouldn't have. Arist paid me to lie for him. To tell the deputies that he was nowhere near Richard during that man's death. Not that it matters now, I suppose. Those news anchors are saying KC Camplin is under arrest and is believed to have committed those murders. Still, what if it isn't him? I couldn't take a chance, so I turned myself in."

"That was a smart move, but I don't think you have reason to worry."

"I hope you're right. I can't afford to lose my job."

Just then, a deputy called my name and directed me to Deputy Vincent's office.

"Did you get my message from last night?" I asked Deputy Vincent the second I stepped through the threshold.

"Good morning to you as well, Miss Aubrey. Have a seat."

"Have all charges against my aunt been dismissed?"

"I believe *I* was the one who summoned *you* here for questioning."

"He sounds like Larken. They make a great pair. Obnoxious and noxious."

"Shh, not now, Edith."

"Beg your pardon?"

"Um, nothing." *Only an annoying apparition dressed like the ragpicker's daughter. She must have really pushed Larken's buttons.*

"Good. Then let us proceed."

"Fine."

As per the deputy's directive, I told him everything that ensued from the moment I arrived at Barbara's to the minute my ordeal with KC ended. Well, everything except the interference from Edith and Rosaline.

"Don't be too upset with Barbara," I said. "All she wanted to do was speed the investigation up by setting a trap for KC."

"Oh, I'm not upset with her. I'm furious with you. Time and time again, I tell you not to interfere, and yet, well, here we are."

"Uh, yeah. Here we are. But face it, if I didn't insert myself into this process, it would have taken longer."

"Don't justify your actions."

"Okay. You should know that I have reason to believe that KC's belt was the murder weapon used to strangle Dorrie. Actually, it's deduction on my part."

"It's called substantiating the evidence in mine. And as a matter of fact, our crew secured a search warrant to his hotel room days before you called and they found his belt in the closet. Sans the prong and keeper loop. Those were found a few yards from Dorrie's body and sent to the lab the Sunday morning after that vigil party for Richard."

"And the parts matched KC's belt?"

"Indeed. When we showed him the solid evidence, he fessed up to having argued with her and ultimately strangling her."

"What about Richard's demise? Did he admit to that murder as well?"

"At that point, he lawyered up."

"Did he say what the motive was?"

"No. Let me ask you something. How did you reach the conclusion that the belt was a murder weapon?"

"I looked at his book jacket photos as well as the ones on the internet. In every picture, he wore that belt with the large silver buckle. Impossible to miss. Then, after Dorrie's body was found, he had a new belt."

Deputy Vincent rubbed his chin and tried to suppress a smile, but I knew it was hiding on his face somewhere. An hour and a half later, a deputy drove to my mother's house to let my aunt know she was no longer under arrest. He also removed her ankle bracelet and apologized for the inconvenience. From what my mother said, Aunt Regina displayed a tremendous amount of restraint.

"We're going to celebrate tomorrow night at Veggie Village in Scottsdale," she said. "Join us. Your aunt has a flight home the following morning."

"Really? They had ironclad evidence with Richard's hair on her bracelet."

"Not that ironclad. The deputy informed us that there was a breach in the lab, and the hair they tested was a random sample from the debris in that decorative pool, not the one found on the bracelet. When they tested *that* one, it belonged to your aunt."

"Wow. Lucky for her." *And how does such a thing happen?*

"So, will you be joining us for dinner?"

"So sorry. I've got catering engagements." *Or I'll create a few.* "But I want to say goodbye to Aunt Regina. Can you get her on the phone?"

"Sure. Hold on."

"I'm so sorry, Katie. You should have been the first person I called the minute they removed that awful ankle bracelet. My mind was in a whirlwind."

"No worries. I understand."

"Actually, I'm not sure you do." Her voice was now barely a whisper. "Katie, I'm not one to cry. Never have been. But this ordeal was more than I could take, so I chose to demonstrate a tough exterior, all the while I was one step away from a three-day-drunk's crying spree."

"I had no idea."

"Of course not. Word of advice—don't be afraid to show your emotions. It's better in the long run."

"Have a safe flight, Aunt Regina. And maybe we'll see you next year."

Oddly enough, I meant it.

The lunch crush had ended at The Char-Board when Maddie walked in. It was a little past one but many of the tables were still occupied. I motioned Maddie to a corner table and retrieved a cup of coffee for her. "Want anything to eat?"

"Bacon and egg on a bagel. I've been looking forward to it all day."

I let Lilly-Ann know and returned to our table, where I went into excruciating detail about yesterday's experience on the trail ride. By the time I finished, all Maddie could do was mutter, "I'm glad you're still alive."

"Alive and itching to know what KC's motive was. Meanwhile, tell me what's going on with that rezoning thing."

"I did a bit of research, and it's the next-door neighbor, Wilsetta Frum. The one with all those cats. She filed an application to change the rural status in order to allow for animal sanctuaries to be built on the land."

"Holy cow!"

"I know. Right? Naturally, there's a process involved. There'll be a review, followed by a public hearing, and then a decision from the county. It could take months."

"Maddie, did you contact Arizona Public Service to check the electrical lines?"

"As a matter of face, yes. They put it on their schedule for next week. Why are you so insistent?"

"Because Wilsetta may be behind all of this. She gives new meaning to kook-and-nut-case, but she's loaded with money and a major benefactor of the library; that's why they put up with her. The minute you said 'cat sanctuary', everything clicked. She wants that property, but only if it could be zoned to allow for an animal shelter. That's why she didn't put in an offer. But, I'm pretty sure she's behind the so-called 'haunting.'"

"Of all things…"

"There's more. She had to pay off someone to monkey with the electricity and that someone has got to be your building inspector—Frank Riley. That's why he gave you that nonsense about the place being haunted."

"Katie, if what you're saying is true, that kind of manipulation has to be a misdemeanor or maybe even a felony."

I wanted to tell Maddie the truth about Ian impersonating the grandson, but only if there was no other way to get to the truth. Last thing I wanted was to get him in trouble.

"Look, start with Arizona Public Service and ask them to check out the premises."

"I will. And if you're right, I owe you big time."

"Tell her to celebrate by taking you to The Chanterelle."

Oh no. It's Edith again. Doesn't that woman ever quit?

Then Maddie went on about Kip and how well they were getting on and how she never expected to date a scientist.

"Doesn't all that Star Wars stuff turn you off?"

"Heck no! It's kind of refreshing, actually. No different than sports memorabilia when you think about it."

"I suppose."

Maddie and I agreed to meet up the following week and stay in touch. I sent her home with a "to-go" bag with fresh croissants and mushroom Brie.

Then, I texted Ian an update and helped the crew clean and close up for the day.

"Any plans for tonight?" Lilly-Ann asked as we exited the restaurant.

"Armchair sleuthing. It's driving me batty not knowing KC's motive. Plus, I'm curious as anything to find out where Jessica wound up. Last anyone saw her, she darted into the RV section at Lake Pleasant Regional Park. If she was located, it would have been on the news."

"You said she was a planner. Maybe she had an accomplice. I wish I could remember any extended conversations she had at that event, but the only one I saw her speaking with at any length was Korina from the library. Oh well. Let the sheriff's office worry about it. We need to start planning for Danica Patrick's party."

And not another disaster.

Chapter Fifty

Friday

That evening, when I took Speedbump out for his walk, I ran into Colleen, who couldn't wait to tell me what she'd heard on the early evening news. Too bad it was everything I knew, or lived through. "Can you believe it?" she said. "Our library has been on the national news all day. I went over there a little while ago, and they were short-staffed. Korina called in sick, and Allison was pulled in a zillion directions."

Korina. Oh my gosh—Lilly-Ann said she saw her talking at length with Jessica. What if it wasn't about writing mysteries? Sick, my foot. If Korina didn't mind lying for Arist for a payoff, would she have done the same to cover up for Jessica? Or worse yet, be complicit in helping Jessica to get out of Arizona?

I did the only thing I could—I phoned Deputy Vincent the second I got home.

"Not again, Miss Aubrey." His voice was gruffer than usual.

"You'll thank me."

"Dubious, but do go on."

I spouted off my theory about Korina, and he didn't dismiss it. "It's a really long story about a borrowed necklace from the royal palace in London, and Barbara could tell you more," I said, "but Jessica was involved, and she had to do a favor for KC or get blackmailed."

"Is this a fact?"

"Uh, more like speculation, but with talons."

"I see."

"And?"

"I'll take it under advisement. I'm on my way home now. Please don't call back tonight unless it's a dire emergency. Understood?"

"Yes. Perfectly."

I didn't expect Deputy Vincent to do anything except write down my information in a report or, worse yet, on a piece of scrap paper, but he didn't do either of those things. Instead, a BOLO was issued for Korina's car in addition to the one issued earlier for Jessica's rental vehicle. The seven o'clock news announced it and posted it on a ribbon. That meant he must have sent deputies to her house, but didn't have any luck, or the news would have reported it. That was the minute a plan jelled in my head, and I had to go through with it.

Allison was reluctant to give me Korina's address, but when I explained the situation, she relented. Ten minutes later, I was in my car and on my way to a boutique apartment complex on North Ootam Road, directly behind North Cave Creek Road and in close proximity to the sheriff's office.

With the apartment number written on a scrap paper, I parked my car in the small lot and headed straight to Korina's ground-floor dwelling. Dim lights were visible through venetian blinds, but I didn't hear any obvious signs of it being occupied. Still, I rang the bell and waited. With no one in sight, I shouted, "Korina! It's me, Katie! Let me in before the next knock is the sheriff!"

I heard the sound of the door knob turning and through a narrow opening, saw her standing adjacent to the door.

"Are you alone?" she asked me.

"Yes."

"Come in."

She closed the door, locked it, and motioned me into the kitchen. Jessica was seated at the table, and I froze. No one knew I was here. Not even Ian. I opened my mouth to speak, but Jessica beat me to it.

"I wouldn't have shot you, Katie," she said. "Heck, the gun was loaded with blanks. I bought it a while back for protection, but was too scared to use real bullets even though I took gun safety lessons."

"Yeah, well, you could have fooled me. Were you part of those murders along with KC?"

"Heavens no! I wish I never laid eyes on that man, but my own circumstances led to some awful decisions on my part. Now I'll be facing murder charges, or accomplice charges. It's all the same. A life behind bars instead of in front of a computer."

"Maybe not. But you'll have to confess and cooperate with the sheriff's office, or it will be worse. Tell me, does this have something to do with the Toronto conference and Dame Judith's necklace?"

"Everything." Jessica put her head in her palms and bent over the table. Meanwhile, Korina took the seat next to mine and didn't say a word. Then Jessica held back tears as she explained her miserable divorce, the pre-nuptial agreement, and her reckless attempt at grand theft.

Just as Barbara had explained, Jessica admitted to switching the carrying cases when KC saw her. He was being blackmailed by Richard and Dorrie, and their demand for money escalated at every turn. With no way out, KC planned to rid himself of "those two leeches," according to Jessica.

Her voice was low and deliberate. "They must have discovered something horrendous about Richard's past or something heinous that he and Dorrie did, in order for him to sketch out a plan for double murder." Then she wiped her eyes and took a breath. "KC didn't do anything heinous or illegal at that point. He needed to prevent some information from getting out to the public. It would have ruined him."

"But murder?"

Jessica shrugged. "Like most people in those positions, they always think they can get away with it. And I'm no better. I was a fool for sure."

I lowered my voice even though we were the only ones in the apartment. "Do you know what that was? What he didn't want leaked out to the public?"

She nodded. "Only an inkling on my part."

Just then, I heard a rustling noise and looked up to see Edith and Rosaline tugging over something. *This I don't need.*

"Larken said I could have it." Rosaline pressed the Chanel 2.55 bag against her chest."

"That Audrey Hepburn bag was mine," Edith said. "I was supposed to get it. He knew how much I liked *Breakfast at Tiffany's*."

"That was before your latest incident with him. Larken was not amused."

"Will the two of you please leave!" The words escaped me before I knew it.

"What?" Jessica and Korina recoiled.

I gulped. "What I started to say was, 'Will the two of you please leave this up to me. I should call Deputy Vincent."

"Is there any other way out?" Korina asked. "If you must know, once I agreed to cover for KC, he told me that if I didn't help him and Jessica, he would implicate me. I couldn't take that chance."

"Good grief," I pressed my fingers into my forehead. "It was triple blackmail—Richard and Dorrie held something over KC's head and KC held something over your head and Jessica's. Barbara was right when she told me that the motive had to be bribery, blackmail, or reputation sullying."

"Now what?" Jessica asked.

"I think you already know."

Both women nodded, and I tapped Deputy Vincent's number on my cell. Seconds later, the deputy on duty answered.

"I need to speak with Deputy Vincent immediately," I said. "Not anyone else."

"Is this an emergency?"

"Not exactly, but it's pressing. Really pressing. And urgent. Really urgent."

"What is your name and number?"

I gave him the information and he told me to hold. When he got back on the line, he connected the call to Deputy Vincent, who was at his home.

"It's been what?' His voice was gruffer than usual. "An hour and forty minutes since I explicitly told you *not* to phone me unless it was a dire emergency. Unless there are dead bodies strewn all over the place, or you are being held hostage, we can resume this conversation in the morning."

"I'm sitting across a table from Jessica and Korina. Now can we speak?"

Less than thirty minutes later, two deputy cars pulled up in front of Korina's apartment. No flashing lights, and no sirens at my request. That was part of the deal I made with the deputy. Both women were read their rights and I promised to put them in touch with a good legal counsel.

"You astonish me, Miss Aubrey," Deputy Vincent said as I walked toward my car.

"You're welcome," I shouted before he could continue.

Once home, I sank into the couch and called Ian, who couldn't disguise the concern in his voice.

"And all this time, I thought you were safe and sound at home. Talk about taking chances. Anyway, it's a relief to hear your voice. Whatever led you to Korina?"

"The clues were all there, all I had to do was put them together. But KC's motive is still is mystery and most likely remain that way until his trial."

"I doubt that. You're like a bloodhound. You won't stop sniffing until you find the answer."

"Right now, all I want to find is a giant box of cookies and my warm, soft bed."

"That's all?"

"Not all," I chuckled, "but some things may have to wait."

Chapter Fifty-One

Saturday

"You're bouncing all over the place like a ten-year-old on his or her birthday," Lilly-Ann said to me as I wiped down the counter for the third time in ten minutes.

"KC's lawyer convinced him to confess, and my aunt should be on a flight to Newark, New Jersey."

"You've got one of those cat and mouse grins," she laughed. "What's the real reason?"

"I'll tell you the real reason. Her hunk of eye-candy has the night off and will be spending it with her. I'll be forced to listen to all sorts of romantic dribble from the two of them while they snuggle on the couch and wake up there." Edith materialized out of nowhere like she usually does. This time in a thick pinkish vapor. Petrified to take her outfit in all in at once, I lowed my eyelids. It didn't help.

Dressed like Scheherazade, complete with golden veil and peacock feather, I had all I could do to keep from doubling over. I turned the other way and addressed Lilly-Ann. "Ian's coming over, and he doesn't have to be at work until Sunday afternoon. That means we can—"

"I know what you can do," Edith muttered under her breath. "Or in your case, what you don't."

Again, I ignored her and focused on Lilly-Ann. "KC refuses to provide a motive for those murders, and it's driving me nuts. Like preparing a charcuterie tray without settling on a theme."

"Shouldn't that be MCSO's concern?"

"Technically, yes, but seeing as KC confessed, it really doesn't matter to them. It would, however, matter to the prosecuting attorney."

"Well, good luck with that. By the way, according to social media, KC's movie deal is still going through. They already started casting for *Don't Ride Alone*. Can you believe it?"

"That was fast. He must have known all along. Too bad he'll miss the preview."

"Have you read it?" she asked. I got a copy last week and finished it last night. I think it will surprise you."

"Why?"

"Because it's kind of like an outline for happened to you on Barbara's trail. Funny, but there was something so familiar about his writing even though that was the first book of his I read. Hey, my copy is in my car. I'll get it for you when I catch a break. Let me know what you think, okay?"

"Sure. Maybe it'll even give me a clue about what Richard held over his head, but right now we'd better finalize those charcuteries for Danica's party this Sunday. I'm glad Matt and Javie will be doing the set-up. All you and I have to do is help with serving."

"Think any good-looking racecar drivers will be there?" Lilly-Ann widened her eyes.

"It's a family affair, but hey, who knows?"

In spite of my concern that Edith would be a nuisance when Ian arrived later, she either behaved herself or decided to bother the other spirits in the netherworld. In either case, he and I couldn't have asked for a better weekend. Then Monday rolled around, and we were back to the proverbial treadmill for the remainder of the week.

No new news on KC, but Jessica and Korina had posted bail and were released, pending trials. I picked up *Don't Ride Alone* for my night reading and Lilly-Ann was right. There was something awfully familiar about it. Almost as if I had read another one of KC's thrillers, only I hadn't. In fact, up until that point, all I read were cozy mysteries and romance novels.

Then, at a little past ten on Thursday night, I read a sentence that I was positive I had read before. But that happens sometimes. Books get so muddled up in our minds. Still, it nagged at me.

The next morning, Maddie texted and asked if I could go with her to Wilsetta's house that afternoon. Arizona Public Service did, indeed, check on the electricity for Wilsetta's place and the house that Maddie was trying to sell. And, although I knew what their finding would be, I acted as surprised as could be.

"Can you believe it, Katie? There was an old electrical line that ran from Wilsetta's house to the one next door. It was part of the original homestead. She *has* to be the one who's manipulating the lighting and who knows what else in order to scare clients away."

I voiced my astonishment, and she continued to speak.

"I believe Wilsetta wants to buy that property for an animal sanctuary, but needs approval from zoning to change the status. That's why she's scaring everyone else off."

"What are you going to do?" I asked.

"I'm going to speak with her. That's why I want you to come with me. If she's as whack-a-doodle as I hear, I don't want to go alone. Will you come?"

"What time?"

"How about I pick you up at The Char-Board at three-thirty and after our visit, we can grab a bite to eat."

"Sure. I'm curious as well."

Chapter Fifty-Two

Saturday

At a few minutes before four, Maddie pulled into Wilsetta's driveway and sighed. "I probably should have phoned, but didn't want to take the chance she'd refuse to see me. It's harder to turn someone away in person."

"Tell that to Larken! He's always refusing to see me."

Oh no. I should have figured as much.

When Maddie wasn't looking, I mouthed, "Keep quiet, Edith," even though I knew it was useless.

Wilsetta opened the door on the second knock, and a large orange tabby skirted past us and down the steps.

"Hi!" I said. "This is my friend, Maddie, and she's the real estate agent for the property next door. We wondered if we could have a few minutes of your time."

Wilsetta looked around as if she was expecting a throng of people. "Don't tell me they've taken the property off the market. Vacant properties bring down the values in the area."

"No," Maddie said. "It's still listed." She pulled her jacket tighter, and Wilsetta took the hint.

"Why don't you come in for a few minutes. And don't mind the cats. They're everywhere." She directed us to her kitchen table but didn't offer us coffee or anything. Not that I expected it.

"I'll try to be succinct," Maddie said. "My agency has been trying to sell the property next door for a long time. Too long, considering it's in wonderful condition and in a prime location. Clients make offers and then back down. When pressed for a reason, they believe the place is haunted. Even the building inspector concurred."

Wilsetta sat perfectly still and didn't utter a word as Maddie leaned closer to her.

"Naturally, I did my homework and had the utility company conduct a complete inspection of the underground electrical lines in the hope of explaining the flickering lights and other unexplainable phenomena."

Wilsetta clasped her hands and held them close to her chest. "Go on."

"I think you already know what they found. There's an old connecting line to your house, and you can turn the power on and off. Isn't that so?"

"Wilsetta," I cut in, "Tampering like that is a punishable offense." *I think...* "Just tell us what this is all about."

Then Maddie spoke, "I believe I know. You want to buy that property, but don't want to invest your money if it doesn't get zoned for an animal shelter. A very noble cause." She emphasized the word *noble* and smiled.

"I didn't think I was operating outside of the law," Wilsetta said. "After all, I did pay all those bills."

"What about the building inspector? Was bribery involved?"

"Frank is an old family friend and a cat lover, too. No bribery. Just loyalty."

I don't know how Maddie managed to negotiate the sale of the house with Wilsetta, but she did, beginning with adding a clause that the sale would be null and void if the zoning changes did not pass the county.

As we started to leave, Wilsetta sighed and muttered Richard's name. "He and Dorrie knew something all right, and that's what put them six feet under. But of course, any studious reader would have been able to figure it out. I know I did."

"You know KC's motive?"

Wilsetta tilted her head at me. "What's the one thing that would send a movie deal and future book sales crashing down?'

I shrugged. "I have no idea."

"If the author isn't who he or she appears to be."

Maddie brushed the hair across her face. "I don't understand."

"Richard had an image to uphold. Same as KC. Big, tough men who wrangle their way through life. Now suppose word got out that in KC's case, it was a lie."

"A lie?" My pulse quickened as I waited for Wilsetta to respond.

"I've been reading since before both of you were born, and let me tell you, KC had another side that he needed to keep under wraps if his macho image was to survive. Especially with that motion picture. If his readers found out that he was also a famed romantic romance writer, it would change everything."

Suddenly, the little observations from Lilly-Ann and the ones I encountered, made sense. I glanced at Maddie, then back to Wilsetta before I spoke. "Is KC Camplin also Deenie Alexander?"

The grin on Wilsetta's face couldn't have been any bigger. "According to my comparisons of text and style, he is. Right down to the same expressions, sentence structure, and language usage. If you have the time, we can dissect some of his writing."

"Um, sounds fascinating, but I need to get home."

"This stays between us," she said.

"Out of loyalty?" I gauged the look on her face.

"Yes. Loyalty. But not to KC. To his romance readers. Why ruin it for them? They have a somewhat fantasy delusion as to who Deenie Alexander is, and that adds to their enjoyment. It would be like telling a five-year-old that Santa Claus wasn't real."

I gulped. "I get it. Don't worry. My lips are sealed."

Maddie thanked her and assured her that no action would be taken on the part of the real estate company, no matter the outcome of the purchase offer and subsequent sale. Once outside, she said, "Let's celebrate—We killed two birds with one stone. Yahoo!"

True to my word, I never said a word to Deputy Vincent, but I did tell Ian, and he agreed with Wilsetta. The week passed quickly, and before I knew it, it was Danica's party. Matt and Javie did an amazing job with the setup, and since Matt was hell-bent-for-leather to meet the guests, he remained at the party with Lilly-Ann and me.

"Can you believe it?" I said to them. "We've gotten five requests for Super Bowl parties for February. This is terrific!"

"Make it six," Matt said. "The woman I just spoke with gave me her name and information."

"We may need to hire some temporary help that week," I mumbled.

"No need," came a raspy voice. "I'll do the layout designs."

I looked around, and thankfully, Matt had moved to another spot. Unfortunately, Edith hadn't.

Her voice got deeper and louder. "Remember, our sixth-month visitations with Imogen are still on. Plus the major holiday."

"Oh no, they're not! You ditched me at the trail, and if it wasn't for Rosaline, who knows how things would have worked out."

And so it began…another negotiation. But at least it wasn't another dead body. Not yet, anyway.

Epilogue

The media hashed and rehashed the double murders and subsequent arrests of KC, Jessica, and Korina until there were no surprises left. Only KC remained behind bars until his trial, and there was reason to believe the women would get much lighter sentences for their roles in those homicides.

The county approved the zoning change, and Wilsetta purchased the property next door, converting it to a goat sanctuary of all things. "Bucks, Nannys and Kids Rescue" opened to the public with great fanfare and press.

Then, of all things, Colleen stopped by to inform me that the tiny screwdriver she found on the windowsill was part of a stash of silvery things, including paper clips, broken necklace chains, and a cuff link. So she did her own sleuthing. *Heaven help the neighborhood.* And it turned out they were *gifts* from a crow she had been feeding and not a stalker or peeping Tom. Go figure!

But the real surprise came months later when Ian and I ran into Maddie in Old Town, Scottsdale. It was a Sunday afternoon, and as we exited The Rusty Spur Saloon on Main Street, Maddie was on her way in with a tall guy who I presumed was Kip, the chemist she'd been seeing.

Ian immediately said, "Hey, Warren, fancy running into you here! Hi Maddie, good to see you, too."

Warren? Sterling's nephew?

Talk about not picking up on clues. My jaw hit my knees, and I don't even remember closing my mouth. Maddie made the introductions, and I somehow managed to reach out my hand and shake his.

"This is Warren, but he goes by Kip."

"And you call yourself an amateur sleuth." Edith materialized for a split second, shook her head, and disintegrated into fragments of light before I could respond.

Amateur sleuth..., charcuterie chef..., and co-inhabitant with a ghost!

Dessert Charcuterie Tray

Ingredients

- 8 – 10 black and white pastry cookies
- 8 – 10 small shortbread cookies * feel free to substitute with any butter cookie
- 8 – 10 small thumbnail cookies or similar cookie
- 8 – 10 thin pretzel rods dipped in chocolate and covered with sprinkles
- One small dish of white chocolate or yogurt covered pretzels
- Assorted white and dark chocolate bonbons or similar small chocolates
- One small dish of strawberries
- One small dish of assorted nuts
- One small dish of raspberries, blueberries or a mixture
- One small dish of dried apricots
- Pie shaped slices of soft cheese (Brie or similar)
- Plain bite size crackers

Design

- Place the pretzel rods in a clear plastic cup and center them in the middle of the tray
- Surround the pretzel rods with the thumbnail and shortbread cookies
- On one side, place half the amount of the black and white cookies. Do the same with the other side.
- In between the black and white cookies, place the small dishes of strawberries and raspberries/blueberries
- Surround that layer with the small crackers and sliced soft cheese

- Add a new layer of assorted chocolate candies and in between them, place the small dishes of nuts, chocolate or yogurt covered pretzels, and dried apricots
- Please keep in mind, you can use an oval tray, a round tray, or a rectangle tray, but adjust the design to fit the tray
- Amounts can vary depending on how many people you wish to serve. This recipe should serve a dozen people. Hint: Keep some extra ingredients on hand if you need to add more!
- Remember – Have fun! This is meant to be entertaining, not to be judged by Edith Ellroy!

About the Series

The Charcuterie Shop Mysteries are humorous cozies that feature an enterprising charcuterie chef, a laidback beagle, and a feisty food critic who just found out she's a ghost. Together they forge a wacky relationship as they tackle one whodunit after another so the ghost can get enough "brownie points" to leave the earthly world for good.

Acknowledgments

So many accolades for the amazing scrutiny and attention given to our manuscript by Regina Kotkowski from the U.S. and Susan Schwartz from Australia! How we ever managed to find these incredibly savvy and discerning "first round" beta readers/editors is beyond anyone's imagination!

To Gale Leach and Larry Finkelstein, whose technical support has been unwavering!

And talk about editors – Thank you, Shawn Simmons from Level Best Books. You are incomparable. No one can pull a rabbit out of a hat like you! And those eagle editing eyes – Wow!

Dar Albert, from Wicked Smart Designs, you dazzle us no end and we are so fortunate to have found you!

About the Author

Ann I. Goldfarb and James E. Clapp, writing as J.C. Eaton

New York native Ann I. Goldfarb spent most of her life in education, first as a classroom teacher and later as a middle school principal and professional staff developer. Writing as J. C. Eaton, along with her late husband, James Clapp, they have authored the Sophie Kimball Mysteries (Kensington, Beyond the Page), The Wine Trail Mysteries (Kensington Lyrical Underground and Beyond the Page Publishing), The Charcuterie Shop Mysteries (Level Best Books) and the Marcie Rayner Mysteries (Camel). This current novel was authored by both writers. Ann is continuing the Sophie Kimball series as well as the Charcuterie Shop Mysteries with Jim's notes, plotlines and spirit. In addition, she has nine published YA time travel mysteries under her own name and three award-winning screenplays. When she's not catering to two demanding Chihuahuas and two annoying felines, she's swimming to escape the Arizona heat, frequenting coffee shops, or finding herself tethered to her desk, writing!

When James E. Clapp retired as the tasting room manager for a large upstate

New York winery, he never imagined he would co-author cozy mysteries with his wife, Ann I. Goldfarb. Non-fiction in the form of informational brochures and workshop materials treating the winery industry were his forte, along with an extensive background and experience in construction that started with his service in the U.S. Navy and included vocational school classroom teaching. Writing became a genuine passion for him, and he will be missed. His murder notebook, along with numerous plotlines, are now fodder for Ann.

Special Endnote:

With sadness, Jim passed away in January 2025. We were married for forty-two years and co-authored for twelve of them. I miss him every day. But there is a bright side. We always "stockpiled" our writing, and the next two books in this series were written by both of us. In addition, Jim left a detailed "Murder Notebook," with plotlines, notes, ideas, and his "must-haves." So, essentially, he is still writing with me! Keep laughing and guessing whodunit!
　Ann

AUTHOR WEBSITE:
　https://www.jceatonmysteries.com
　www.timetravelmysteries.com

BLOG:
　https://www.jceatonauthor.com

SOCIAL MEDIA HANDLES:
　https://www.facebook.com/JCEatonauthor/
　https://www.bookbub.com/authors/j-c-eaton
　https://twitter.com/JCEatonauthor
　https://www.instagram.com/j.c.eaton/
　https://www.goodreads.com/author/show/15931568.J_C_Eaton

Also by J.C. Eaton

Kensington Publishing: The Sophie Kimball Mysteries
Booked 4 Murder
Ditched 4 Murder
Staged 4 Murder
Botched 4 Murder
Molded 4 Murder
Dressed Up 4 Murder
Broadcast 4 Murder
Railroaded 4 Murder

Beyond the Page Publishing: The Sophie Kimball Mysteries
Saddled Up 4 Murder
Grilled 4 Murder
Strike Out 4 Murder
Revved Up 4 Murder
Pinned 4 Murder
Puzzled 4 Murder

Kensington Lyrical Underground: The Wine Trail Mysteries
A Riesling to Die
Chardonnayed to Rest
Pinot Red or Dead?
Sauvigone for Good

Beyond the Page Publishing: The Wine Trail Mysteries
Divide and Concord
Death, Dismay and Rose'
From Port to Rigor Morte
Mischief, Murder and Merlot

Camel/Epicenter Press:

Murder in the Crooked Eye Brewery
Murder at the Mystery Castle
Murder at Classy Kitchens

www.ingramcontent.com/pod-product-compliance
Lightning Source LLC
Chambersburg PA
CBHW030126010826
48973CB00002B/436